THE
SECRET

THE
SECRET

&

CYNTHIA
VICTOR

A DUTTON BOOK

DUTTON
Published by the Penguin Group
Penguin Books USA Inc., 375 Hudson Street,
New York, New York 10014, U.S.A.
Penguin Books Ltd, 27 Wrights Lane,
London W8 5TZ, England
Penguin Books Australia Ltd, Ringwood,
Victoria, Australia
Penguin Books Canada Ltd, 10 Alcorn Avenue,
Toronto, Ontario, Canada M4V 3B2
Penguin Books (N.Z.) Ltd, 182-190 Wairau Road,
Auckland 10, New Zealand
Penguin Books Ltd, Registered Offices:
Harmondsworth, Middlesex, England

First published by Dutton, an imprint of Dutton Signet,
a division of Penguin Books USA Inc.
Distributed in Canada by McClelland & Stewart Inc.

 REGISTERED TRADEMARK—MARCA REGISTRADA

ISBN: 0-525-94034-0

Printed in the United States of America

For
Susan Ginsburg
and
Jenna Steckel
With all the love in the world

ACKNOWLEDGMENTS

Grateful thanks to the following people for their generous help, support and advice:

Harriet Astor, Betsy Carter, Carolyn Clarke, Jean Griffin, Jean Katz, Mark Kress, Susanna Margolis, Susan Moldow, Harriet Rattner, Richard Reinstein, Diana Revson, David Skurnick, Joan Skurnick, Mark Stark, Mark Steckel, John Thornton, Lane Tobias and Sandra Zwick.

Very special thanks go to Meg Ruley and Audrey LaFehr.

THE SECRET

Chapter 1

It was *him*.

Miranda almost tripped as she walked into Wendy Lattimore's messy dorm room. Three people were seated around a portable aluminum table that had two decks of cards stacked neatly in the middle. And right there, in a blue shirt and a pair of jeans, there he was, Stephen Shaeffer, in the flesh, one-fourth of the bridge game for which Miranda was fifteen minutes late. She'd had no idea he would be one of the people playing today.

Pushing her reading glasses up to the top of her head, Wendy stood and shoved a pile of her T-shirts off the end of one of the twin beds.

"Sit here, Ran," Wendy instructed, indicating the newly emptied space. "Only three chairs," she added, as she lowered her glasses back into place. "Don't mind the mess."

"Makes it homey," Miranda answered, trying not to stare at Stephen.

Clearly, she was unsuccessful, and Wendy picked up on it immediately. "So, you two know each other?" she asked.

"Yes," Miranda answered, humiliated as she heard Stephen's "No" an instant later.

She looked at him shyly, wishing she could suppress the blush that was traveling up her cheeks. "We were introduced on Parents' Day a couple of years ago. Your parents did a seminar, and my mom and dad took part in it."

"Sure," Stephen answered casually, reaching across to pick up one of the decks of cards and beginning to shuffle them.

Miranda couldn't tell if he really remembered, but it was a day she would never forget. Dr. and Dr. Shaeffer, whose psychology lectures she loved, were demonstrating team teaching, a form they'd pioneered. It was of little surprise to Miranda that the team exercise turned into a shouting match when her parents, Esther and Louis Greenfield, were chosen as participants.

They were divorced by then, but both had turned up for Parents' Day. Asked to assess the single trait from each of their personalities manifest in their daughter, the dialogue that began with words like "risk-averse" and "intelligent" quickly elevated to "you should burn in hell for what you did." They had managed to stay on the subject of Miranda for mere seconds; their diatribes against each other went on for a good ten minutes, during which over twenty-five sets of parents got to witness what Miranda had experienced all her life. The Drs. Shaeffer tried to intervene politely several times, but finally they had to threaten Esther and Louis with ejection, and it was only after they actually advanced toward the two that the Greenfields quieted down and resumed their seats, both completely unashamed, while Miranda prayed for oblivion in any form to get her out of there.

Miranda watched Stephen as he dealt the cards. His touch was deft as he gave each of the four players thirteen cards. Everything about him was just right, she thought, feeling again the almost physical pleasure the sight of him gave her. Tall, with dark hair and light eyes, Stephen Shaeffer seemed perfect, one of those people who were totally comfortable with themselves, who always knew what to say and how to say it. Well, she thought sadly, who wouldn't be perfect when they were part of the happiest family on earth. Eric and Alida Shaeffer were well known in scholarly circles, and the University of Florida was lucky to have them on staff. And to be the only adored child within that golden circle . . . Miranda could only imagine the pleasure of such a background.

"One heart," Wendy declared, beginning the bidding.

Miranda's turn was next, but she could hardly make sense of her hand. Out of panic, she thought of simply passing, but she was at least clearheaded enough to know what a mistake that would be. "One spade," she finally uttered, hoping the five spades in her hand, two of them the king and queen, merited the bid.

Ordinarily, Miranda was an excellent player, but being so near Stephen made her dizzy. It was only when her partner, Andy Fallowell, made the final bid of four clubs, and Miranda got to lay her cards down as dummy, that she began to relax. She listened as Wendy teased Andy about his playing out of the game, then answered Wendy's phone when it rang.

"It's your mother," Miranda said, handing the receiver to Wendy.

"Say I'm busy," Wendy responded.

When Miranda hesitated, Wendy yelled, "Call back later!" so loudly, Miranda didn't have to add a thing.

"You're lucky your parents are divorced," Wendy said cavalierly to Miranda. "My parents are such a mess, whenever I hear of a couple splitting up, I'm jealous."

Miranda looked at her as if she were crazy. Her parents' divorce had caused nothing but pain, as far as she was concerned. At least once every week, Esther Greenfield would tell her daughters exactly how unsatisfying Louis Greenfield had been as a husband. And certainly, in Miranda's memories of before Esther left him, the two had done little but fight in the tiny living room of their Pittsburgh apartment. When her mother took Miranda and her older sister Lydia out for ice cream one night, not stopping until they reached Miami Beach two days later, it did little to improve parental relations.

It took Louis four days to locate his wife and children at Esther's aunt Sissie's house.

"How could you take my children from me?" her father had screamed so loudly, Miranda heard it from across the room, even though the receiver was firmly pressed against her mother's ear.

"How would you know we were gone, you're home so little!" her mother had shrieked back.

That fight had gone on for hours, although Miranda had crawled into the linen closet upstairs to try and avoid the sounds. But it wasn't the first fight she'd been unable to escape from, and certainly not the last.

God knows, they must have been a crazy match right from the beginning, her mother full of dreams, always wanting more, ready to take risks like the one she took when she moved the girls to Florida. Esther saw a rainbow in every storm. She was going to move to the sunshine state, where she'd start with a job at the Eden Roc or the Fontainebleu, then go on from hotel management right through to ownership. It hadn't worked out exactly that way, but, to this day, Esther never lost faith.

Her one mistake, she realized too late, was imagining that Louis Greenfield shared her dream. When she met him, he was so much more worldly than other boys she'd dated. Louis thought about intellectual and political issues, worried about racial integration and matters of foreign policy. When he joined marches on Washington rebelling against American involvement in Vietnam, Esther had been proud of him. But when his political activities began taking up all of his spare time, Esther grew annoyed. Still, for a while at least, she admired his courage and dedication.

It was only when she realized that politics was *all* that mattered to him that she became completely disenchanted. She'd always thought he would rise up through the ranks of American business, using his keen mind to make a better and better living. But Louis was content with the job he held, admitting patients to Mercy Hospital in Pittsburgh. As far as he was concerned, making money was secondary, a necessary evil that required little attention and was worth little energy.

She soon realized how blind she'd been to their basic differences, that nothing would ever change. Even if Nixon ended the war, even if complete racial harmony was achieved countrywide, Louis Greenfield was never going to be the man she'd thought she'd married. That was when she decamped for Florida.

Esther was much happier there, even when she was stuck cleaning rooms in cheap inland motels that were nothing like the oceanside palaces of her dreams. For Miranda, though, it never stopped being sad.

At night, her father would call to argue with her mother; during the day, her uncle David would yell at her aunt Sissie about the fact that they were all stuck together in the minuscule house. Miranda never got used to the constant screaming. As a little child, she would try to explain her parents to each other, to make them a family again. By the time she was nine or ten though, all she could do was try to avoid the unpleasantness, shutting out the sounds of confrontation.

In contrast to Miranda, her sister Lydia seemed energized by the move. With what proved to be characteristic resourcefulness, she traded three afternoons a week of telephone answering, filing, and envelope stuffing at a ballet school four blocks away for free lessons. Her natural talent was immediately obvious, and with Esther's blessing, she focused almost all her attention on ballet, treating school as a secondary concern. Her efforts were rewarded with acceptance into Miami's professional ballet company when she was sixteen.

Miranda admired her sister's incredible determination and perfectionism, although it was those same traits that made the sisters' relationship so prickly. Lydia never hesitated to tell Miranda what was wrong with her and how to fix it. The combination of Lydia's loyalty and sharp tongue seemed to ensure that Miranda would be eternally compelled to feel close to her, but hurt and angry at the same time.

Miranda's scholarship to the University of Florida provided the final escape from the battleground of her childhood, and she was ecstatic. Other students complained of the swampy grounds, the constant humid heat, while she reveled in the pleasure of the days she spent on campus, taking challenging courses, relaxing over bridge with friends. *Not* being at the center of an impending storm was sheer joy.

"Anything to eat around here?" Stephen's voice brought Miranda's attention back to the game.

"Only what's fattening and dangerous," Wendy answered, as she lay down a seven of hearts. "Not that I'm dying to live so long. I was so depressed in high school that every time I heard about some kid being killed in a car accident I used to think, 'Why her? Why not me?'"

The three others in the room looked at Wendy and began to laugh. Miranda finally felt relaxed enough to talk directly to Stephen.

"I'll get you something from the machines if you want," she said, standing up and going for her purse.

He looked at her, pleased surprise on his face. "Anything salty or sweet, thanks."

"Yeah," Wendy added sarcastically, "if the machine dispenses olives or a hot fudge sundae, bring 'em on back."

Stephen grimaced slightly, then turned to Miranda and winked.

When she walked back into the room with two Snickers bars and a large bag of potato chips, he smiled broadly. Grinning in return, she sat back down on the bed.

"Well done," he said, patting her on the head, then leaving his hand there for a few extra precious seconds before reaching for the candy. "This must have set you back three or four bucks," he said thoughtfully, looking deep into her eyes. "Just about the price of a ticket to the Orpheum. Maybe you'll let me pay you back tonight."

"Sure," Miranda answered quietly. *I have died and gone to heaven*, she added, only to herself.

"No, Alida, I'm sure Princeton is the better choice. Their History of Science is much stronger than Harvard's. After all, they've got Kuhn." Having said his final words on the subject, Eric Shaeffer turned away from his wife, to whom his remarks had been addressed, and once more poked at the three large hamburger patties that were browning on the grill.

His father's assured voice had sailed out over the backyard, but Stephen, seated on a chaise right next to him, hardly took in the words. It was fine for his parents to debate the relative merits of various Ivy League graduate schools, but he hated to imagine what they'd be saying once they found out the truth. The scores from his graduate record exams had come in the day before, and they'd confirmed his deepest fears. When you were alone with a number-two pencil and a question booklet, who your parents were and how high their expectations went didn't matter a damn.

Stephen Shaeffer had ranked in the fiftieth percentile. Nothing for the average person to sneeze at, but Eric and Alida Shaeffer didn't expect their son to be average. The fiftieth percentile might get you into Delaware or Wayne State. It did not get you into Princeton.

Stephen had always known he was going to disappoint them. Elementary school had been fine, especially in Gainesville, where the schools weren't exactly world-class. High school had been tougher. He had worked dutifully, always secretly suspecting that he wasn't nearly as smart as he was supposed to be. Over dinner, his parents would be discussing Kant and Freud, while Stephen would be mulling over the secret words in "Louie, Louie." Maybe he had been switched with another baby in the hospital. That's what he used to fantasize when he'd wonder how leading intellectual lights like his parents had ended up with a son like him.

When his sophomore year average was only a B, his parents began to take notice, hiring tutors and carefully overseeing his homework. *Fear of success*, he'd overhear them saying late into the night, as they tried psychological explanations for his lack of genius. But he'd always suspected the truth. He simply wasn't smart enough. Smarter than most maybe, but in his heart he knew he'd never measure up. It would have been such a relief to have them accept that in him, to hear them say, "Stephen, it's *you* we love, not your brain." But, of course, that never happened.

When he began to excel in English, always his best subject, they'd brag to their friends about how he'd *found* himself. And sometimes, even he thought it was true. That there was some lurking genius aching to get out. But yesterday's scores made it plain. He wasn't Princeton material. Shit, he wasn't Shaeffer material.

He picked up the glass of iced tea from the tray table beside him and took a long sip, wishing it were something stronger. But the Shaeffers were confirmed teetotalers. "Alcohol makes you stupid," they'd say anytime the subject came up. *Well, guess what Mom and*

Dad, he thought, *I don't need alcohol to make me stupid. I'm stupid perfectly sober.*

"So, what do you think?" his father asked, turning to look at Stephen with a big grin. "Harvard or Princeton? After all, it's your future we're mapping out here."

Stephen took in his father's rumpled check shirt, the stray whiskers he hadn't quite reached with his razor that morning, the glasses perched haphazardly on top of his balding head. Ordinarily his father seemed a pleasant-looking man. Professorial, nice looking even. But to Stephen right then, he appeared almost menacing. Like some character out of a Stephen King novel about to change form.

"I don't know," Stephen replied hesitantly.

"Well, you've got to know. It's your job to know," his father responded impatiently. "What you decide has impact on everything that comes later." With that, he lifted the burgers off the grill and placed them on a large white platter. Then he sat down opposite his son.

"From here on in, where you go has real consequences. It was fine to do your undergraduate work here. It certainly saved your mother and me thousands of dollars. But those applications have to be in within a couple of weeks."

"Pop," Stephen swung his legs off the chaise and sat up straight, looking his father in the eye. "What if I'm not quite ready for graduate school? You know, I'm not even sure about History of Science. I mean, English has always been my stronger suit."

A look of disgust passed briefly over his father's face. "English!" he said as if it were a four-letter word. "That was fine for undergraduate work. But for a career . . . let's be serious."

Alida Shaeffer nodded approvingly at her husband's words, as Stephen stared miserably into his glass of iced tea, wishing suddenly that it were filled with arsenic. Would he feed it to himself, he wondered, or would he feed it to his parents. *Let's be serious*, indeed. Like he was a mentally retarded five year old or something. Maybe it was time to tell the truth, he thought angrily. Time to get his parents to face facts. Why wait anymore? After all, what would he achieve by putting off the inevitable except more hours of private torture. *Screw you both*, he thought as he worked up the courage to speak.

He heard the phone ringing, and watched his mother go back into the house to answer it. Maybe telling one parent at a time would be less terrible. Then his father could tell his mother, and Stephen could go back to his dormitory and drink himself into a Budweiser stupor.

"Dad," he began, "there's something—"

His speech was interrupted by the sound of his mother calling him from inside. Her voice was the cool one she used when something slightly unpleasant was happening.

"It's Miranda Greenfield for you," she said.

He noticed the downturn of his mother's mouth when he entered the kitchen and reached for the phone. Well, she might not approve of Miranda, but Stephen certainly did. Her pure adoration was about the only thing that made him feel alive these days. She was pretty and smart, and she thought everything Stephen did, every word he said, was absolutely brilliant.

"Hey, you," he said tenderly, as his mother pretended not to listen.

He watched as his mother grabbed a jar of marinated artichokes and walked back out to the yard. Go to hell, he thought, observing her as she made her way to the chair next to his father's.

"I got you a new work shirt," Miranda was whispering into his ear. "I hope you'll like it."

"You know I will," he said sincerely. That was another thing about Miranda. She thought about him all the time. Never evaluated him or compared him to guys who were smarter or taller or better looking. And the stuff she did for him was stuff he liked. She'd bring him things that were cool to wear, or fun to play with, or delicious to eat. Just the week before, she'd brought him ten old Rex Stout mysteries he'd been unable to find in the library. Miranda understood his love for mysteries. His parents hadn't even allowed such popular fiction in the house.

He thought about what it would be like not to have her around the next year. After all, even though there wasn't a prayer he was going to get into Harvard or Princeton, he undoubtedly would land somewhere, probably due more to his parents' pull than to his actual record. He imagined Detroit or Cleveland, stuck in some graduate program, away from the one thing in his life that brought him any pleasure at all—his relationship with Miranda.

His attention came back to the phone when he realized Miranda had been talking.

". . . and I think they thought I was okay, I really do," she was saying.

Stephen forced himself to concentrate. "I'm sorry, I dropped the phone. What were you saying, who thought you were okay?"

"The guy from Midfield Bank who interviewed me this morning." Her voice was perfectly patient. "Remember?"

"Sure I do," he answered, more tactful than truthful. He thought about the announcements on the board in the student union, where she must have signed up for the interview. Stephen had noticed one of them just that morning.

"You know," he said, certain that Miranda's response would be genuine interest, "there are people coming down to interview from a big advertising agency in New York next Thursday. Doesn't that sound like a fun job?"

"Sure it does," she answered immediately. "And you'd be great at it."

God, she was terrific. Stephen could imagine his parents' reaction to his applying for a job in advertising. They would just about die of shame. He looked out the back door. His father was already chomping down a huge burger, while his mother kept glancing toward the house, obviously impatient for him to return. He knew he should hang up the phone and join them. But an idea was nagging at him. Maybe he didn't have to tell them about his test scores. Maybe they never had to know. After all, he reasoned, twirling the phone cord nervously around his fingers, lack of scholarly achievement was abject humiliation to his parents, worse even than death; romantic passion was merely stupid.

"Hey, Ran," he said softly. "How about if we went to New York together next year?"

Her easy laugh came right away. "You know you're going to graduate school. Although," she added hopefully, "Columbia is a wonderful place."

Stephen held the phone even closer to his mouth. "What if I didn't go to graduate school right away? What if we got married and I earned some money first?"

"Oh, Stephen!"

Her pleasure was palpable, even over the phone, and for the first time in months, he felt the tension in his chest relax.

Chapter 2

Miranda Shaeffer trudged up the last few steps to the cottage's front door, relieved that she would finally be able to drop the canvas bags she was holding, their contents of sandy toys, towels, and other odds and ends threatening to spill over at any second.

"Come on, Sophie, let's go inside," she called cheerfully over her shoulder to the three year old several feet behind her. The little girl had stopped to peer intently at some of the pink impatiens lining the walk, paying no attention to her mother's words.

Gratefully releasing two of her bags onto the ground, Miranda opened the screen door and held it ajar with one hip while she pushed open the inner wooden door. As she deposited her remaining bag inside, she winced at a sudden sharp pain. She paused to give her five-months'-pregnant belly a gentle rub. Over the past few weeks, she had been experiencing all sorts of aches and pains, something that hadn't occurred during her other two pregnancies.

In her head, she compared this vacation to all their others. In the years before they'd had children, they'd gone away to a number of vacation spots, but they had never found one they liked enough to return to. The Hamptons were too expensive and the Jersey shore too crowded. They had celebrated their fifth anniversary in a bed and breakfast in Savannah, a place they both loved, but that was too far away to go back to on a regular basis.

It was only after she became pregnant with their son, Jack, that

Stephen started talking about renting a house in Camden, Maine, the town in which he had spent his summers as a child. They'd been spending these same two weeks in August in this house every summer since. That first time, Miranda recalled, she had spent much of the two weeks throwing up in the tiny bathroom, the ubiquitous sand crunching beneath her knees, the mildew smell that never seemed to go away despite her best efforts making her nausea even worse. It had been pretty gruesome, she reflected, but of course the end result was more than worth it.

Every summer here was different, as they came back with an infant, then a toddler, then two children. She had come to love it, but the truth was, it was more and more work for her each time, and less of a vacation. The laundry and cooking and cleaning consumed most of her days. That also meant she had less time to give to Stephen during what was supposed to be his period of relaxation and creative rejuvenation.

This year in particular she felt useless to him, slow and waddling. He didn't actually like the beach that much, but he had always enjoyed his daily tennis game and their get-togethers with the couples that they knew from previous summers. This trip, though, even those activities seemed to bore him. It was probably time to start looking into another sort of summer getaway for next year.

Miranda was eager to put up her swollen feet. I'm getting too damn old for this pregnancy business, she thought, not really meaning it, but superstitiously half-believing she could drive away bad luck if she didn't act too confident about the impending birth. She waited for her eyes to become accustomed to the darkness of the living room after the bright glare of the sunshine outside. Her secret fear was that having a third child might be pushing her luck, and she prayed it would all work out okay.

Of course, she and Stephen hadn't even planned on having a third. They were both perfectly satisfied to stop after Jack and Sophie. Miranda was reasonably careful about birth control, yet she had nonetheless become pregnant again. The most surprising thing about it was how secretly thrilled she was. This one was like a special gift.

She pushed her bangs, sticky with sunscreen and perspiration, back off her forehead as she turned to watch Sophie, who was engrossed in tearing off flower petals and tossing them into a pile beside her. I suppose I should stop her, Miranda thought idly.

"Sweetie, come on in. Let's go see Daddy."

At the mention of her father, Sophie looked over, her eyes lighting up. She tossed away the petals in her hand and came bounding up the walk as fast as her little legs could carry her.

"Where's Daddy?" she demanded as Miranda stopped to brush off some of the sand from her daughter's hands and feet. Sophie broke away and ran into the living room, calling for her father.

"In here, Sophie."

Stephen Shaeffer's voice had always been one of Miranda's favorite things about him. It had this quality she could never quite describe, but it was low and sexy. When they'd dated back in college, the sound of his murmuring to her while they were making love was one of the most exciting sensations she had ever experienced. Even now, after all these years together, just hearing his voice on the other end of the phone still produced a slight sexual jolt in her stomach. She used to tease him about having been born a few decades too late for what could have been a huge career in radio back in the thirties.

Her husband emerged from their bedroom wearing navy shorts and a white tennis shirt, looking fresh and clean despite the heat. His thick, dark hair, combed so neatly into place when he went to the office, was boyishly tousled. His face was slightly tanned, the expression on it now somewhat preoccupied.

"Hey, Soph, Miranda," he said absentmindedly, gazing off into the distance as if trying to figure something out.

"Daddy! Come to the beach!" Sophie ran over to hug his legs. Miranda plopped down on the faded flowered sofa, feeling even more bedraggled in contrast to her husband. "Honey, we're kind of done with the beach for today," she explained gently to her daughter.

She looked over at Stephen. "What's up? You look like you're working. But you didn't bring any, did you? You swore you wouldn't do that to yourself this year."

"No, no, nothing from the office." Stephen brought his attention back to Sophie, who was attempting to stand on his feet, one of hers on each one of his. He responded, leaning over to take hold of her arms and moving around the room with big steps, carrying her along as if they were dancing. She laughed happily at the familiar game. "Artie canceled our tennis date, so I was just kind of hanging around. I started noodling with something."

"Is Jack still at Graham's house?" Miranda asked, her attention diverted as she realized how quiet the house was.

"Yeah," Stephen replied. "Carol said she'd feed them both, and bring him by later."

The subject of their son's whereabouts resolved, Miranda nodded. "Okay. Sorry. You were saying . . . ?"

"It's not important. I just started playing with something." He picked up Sophie and, to the child's screaming delight, quickly swung her around in a large circle.

"Does it have to do with your job?"

"No, not really."

"Ah." Miranda wanted to ask more, but she was suddenly seized with a desperate need for a cold drink. Awkwardly, she raised herself up off the sofa and headed to the small kitchen area. "Want something?"

Stephen set Sophie down. "No, thanks. I want to get back to this. Let me know when dinner's ready."

He turned and walked back into the bedroom, shutting the door behind him.

Sophie looked at her mother expectantly. "Play with puzzles, Mommy."

Miranda pulled a pitcher of water from the refrigerator and poured herself a large glass, gulping it down gratefully. It would have been nice if Stephen could have spent a little time with Sophie after she'd spent all morning watching her at the beach. With Jack out of the house, Miranda would have been free to lie down for a half hour. Well, it wouldn't have been quiet enough for much of a rest anyway, she reflected, all of them in such small quarters. And this wasn't the time to ask Stephen. He was clearly busy with something he considered important, so he might get annoyed. There was no point in causing trouble at the end of a perfectly pleasant day. God knows, she'd seen enough trouble between spouses as a child. She had vowed she would have none of it in her marriage.

Miranda smiled at her daughter. Besides, she reminded herself, Stephen worked so hard at the agency, it wasn't fair to expect him to take on additional jobs at home during his time off. Her own job at the bank didn't require quite as many hours.

"Puzzles it is, cutie," she said brightly, setting down her glass and going over to the closet where she stored the toys and games.

The next morning, Miranda woke up to the sight of Stephen already dressed and seated at the small writing table in the corner of their bedroom. He was making notes on a yellow legal pad. She glanced at the clock. Seven-twenty. What was he doing up so early, and why had she been permitted to sleep so late? Normally one or both of the children would have awakened her by six-thirty. She waited, listening. There was the sound of the children's voices in the other bedroom. How great, she thought. They were playing together, a fairly rare occurrence, given that Jack normally had little to do with his baby sister.

She turned her attention to her husband, who was deeply engaged in whatever it was he was doing.

"Good morning," she said softly. "What are you up to?"

He glanced over at her. "Hi. Looks like you caught up on your beauty rest."

"Yeah." She smiled and stretched languidly. "I can't believe I got away with it. What are you doing up, all dressed and efficient?"

He gave her a satisfied smile. "If you must know, I'm writing a novel."

Her eyes opened wide in surprise. "You're what? I didn't know you had any interest in writing."

He gave a shrug, his demeanor suddenly changing to indicate he didn't really care about it. "Well, it's not a real novel. It's a silly Ninja sort of thing. You know, I've read some of them, and most of them are pretty terrible. Yesterday, I started thinking that I could probably do one myself. It can't be any worse than the garbage that's out there."

"Well, well, well." She sat up in bed. "Good for you."

He tapped his pen on the table. "The guys in Creative are always writing books and screenplays on the side, so why not me? It would actually be a hoot if an account executive could get something published. They always act like being creative is a goddamned calling or something. Like somebody outside of their exclusive little fraternity shouldn't even dare try it. What do these guys really do for a living? They write stupid jingles and cliché ad copy." He looked over at her apologetically, realizing his gaffe. "No offense."

"None taken." Miranda had been happily ensconced in her copywriting job since just after college, first with Midfield Bank and now with Unity.

"But imagine if one of us suits produced a book." He smiled at the thought.

"I didn't have a clue you were doing this." Miranda threw back the sheet and got up. "How far along are you?"

He started drawing stars in the pad's margins, something Miranda had seen him do countless times while he was working out ideas. "Not far at all. There's a formula for these novels, and right now I'm kind of analyzing it all. Once I've got that, I'll come up with the plot."

For the first time, Miranda noticed a stack of six paperback books at his elbow. "Is that what those are? Research?"

He nodded. "I got them Tuesday when I went to the drugstore."

"I'm impressed by your intrepid pursuit of this project," she teased. "Do you have a company in mind to publish it?"

"No, not at all." He shook his head. "I'll have to take whatever I can get. Being somebody in an ad agency doesn't make you somebody in publishing, Ran. I'll be just some schlub with a manuscript. That's going to be the tricky part, getting somebody to take notice of me."

Miranda headed for the bathroom to brush her teeth. "I'm sure you'll think of something. You're great at that."

"You are, too," he responded. "Maybe you can think of some angle, or write me some publicity copy."

"If it'll help," she called back.

That would be nice, she thought, doing something to advance a book Stephen had written.

"How would you feel about your husband being known for writing a trashy novel?" he yelled out to her.

She paused, toothbrush in hand. "I'd feel swell. Who wouldn't?"

He lowered his voice, but she could still hear the words. "My parents."

She shook her head sympathetically. It never failed to amaze her that Stephen still courted his parents' approval after all these years. It was so obviously a fruitless endeavor, doomed to failure. She had never seen them show more than the most minimal acceptance despite his best efforts. They certainly made no secret of the fact that they regarded his career in advertising as a complete waste of his talents in a contemptible field. She could just imagine their reaction to their son's writing this type of novel. A great work of art, born of suffering, was one thing. This wouldn't even be worth dignifying with their notice. They would die of shame to be associated with such a thing, however remotely.

"Don't worry about it, Stephen," she called out reassuringly. "Besides, it's not as if they frequent bookstores picking up the latest fun read. Maybe they'll never find out. We can just keep it a secret."

There was no answer. She waited a moment, then decided to change the subject.

"You taking Jack for a tennis lesson today?" She stuck her head out of the bathroom.

He gave her a contrite look. "Jeez, I really want to work on this. Do you mind if we put it off until tomorrow?"

"Okay. But can we keep our bridge game with the Browns tonight?"

"Sure."

Miranda went back to stand over the sink, and regarded herself in the mirror. No point in counting on Stephen today.

Next year, maybe Club Med.

Chapter 3

Lydia Greenfield looked at the reflection of her six a.m. class in the mirrored studio wall approvingly. The combination of ballet techniques and aerobics she'd developed had proven very popular, and the taut bodies and well-muscled legs of her students reflected how well her ideas were working. Of course, she had to hand it to the twelve women and two men following her instructions so diligently. Like herself, they were disciplined and focused. She still exercised a minimum of three to four hours a day and hadn't gained a pound since her days as a ballerina.

Not that she didn't have moments where she'd have given just about anything to eat the biscotti a waiter set in front of her, or to lie around until ten in the morning, then gobble down some French toast and a rasher of bacon. But in her experience, when a person let down a little, they were likely to let down a lot. One shortcut led to another. One bite of chocolate cake, then one more, and before you knew it you weighed two hundred pounds.

She had no patience for that kind of laziness. She had taken control of her destiny early on, had refused to become a victim of her parents' brawling or their relative poverty. She had made a career as a ballerina in Florida, and if it killed her, she was going to make it as a gym owner here in New York.

She'd learned a lot from watching her mother's attempts to make a life for herself. Maybe she hadn't accomplished everything she set out to do, but she never stopped trying. Even when Lydia and Miranda had been little girls, and the whole family was living together in Pittsburgh, her memories of Esther Greenfield were of constant movement. She was always trying to get somewhere.

So different from her father. When she thought about him, which she did as rarely as possible, she mostly remembered his inattention. "I'll see you later, cupcake," he'd say every night after dinner when she would ask him to play with her or to read to her. But "later" would usually mean the next morning or the five or ten minutes before he left for his job at the hospital.

Only vaguely did she comprehend that her father's outings were for, as he would call it, "a higher purpose." All she knew was that he was gone all the time. She supposed she missed him when her mother had taken them to Florida, but the truth was she had already learned not to expect much. And when he'd call and beg to talk to her and Miranda for "a little longer, please, pumpkin," she'd usually hand the phone to her sister. It made her angry somehow. When they'd been right there, he hadn't had a minute for them. Why should she be late for her ballet class or unprepared for an English test just because suddenly he had time for them?

With a start, she realized the music had stopped. She'd been so caught up in her memories she'd been teaching on automatic. She forced herself back to the present and led the class in a cool-down exercise, finally curtsying to them as she did at the end of every session. It was a sign of respect from her to them, a way of thanking them for their best efforts.

Wrapping a towel around her neck, she walked gracefully out of the studio, smiling warmly at two young women who held the door open for her, then taking the steps up to the second floor two at a time. As she approached her office, she noticed a delivery man knocking on the door. In his arms he held a large package.

"I'm right here," she called out as she stepped to his side, unlocking the door to the medium-sized room and letting him in behind her.

The man placed the delivery on the glass coffee table that sat low in front of a brown leather couch. "Sign, please," he said, holding a pad out to her and offering her a pen with his other hand.

She wrote her name quickly, then walked around to the cherry-wood desk on the other side of the room. As she reached into the top drawer for her purse and extracted a couple of dollars, she grinned. "Double or nothing, bet you I can name who they're from."

"I'd be a fool to bet against that," he answered, smiling back at her and accepting the money she offered.

Of course, she thought with satisfaction, she knew exactly who they were from. And the nice delivery man from Lexington Florists knew perfectly well that she knew. Nicky Simon had been sending her flowers every week for the past four months. To the man in the gray uniform, bringing Lydia Greenfield two dozen roses had become routine.

Idly, she wondered if she would ever have let Nicky get so close to her without the flowers. In fact, the first few times he'd asked her out, she'd turned him down flat. He was too good-looking, too sure of himself. A lot of women would have loved all that, she knew, but not her. She'd always believed the message she'd once found in a fortune cookie. "Beware of the shiny red apple," it had read. "Inside, may be worm."

But Nicky had sent her those beautiful roses each and every week, called her every few days, just to remind her he was still there. She had successfully pushed thoughts of him aside. After all, she knew danger when she saw it. But then he'd stopped calling, stopped sending the roses. She noticed right away and even felt relieved for a couple of weeks. Then she started to miss the phone calls and the flowers, started to wonder what had made him turn away.

After six weeks of silence, he called her once more. This time, she agreed to have lunch. Lunch had led to dinner, and within a couple of weeks, dinner had led to the most intimate relationship she'd ever allowed.

"What magic wand did he wave?" Miranda had asked playfully, after she and Stephen had had dinner with the new couple for the first time. Lydia hadn't taken offense. She knew she could be tough on men. And if she hadn't known it, her sister's gentle urging over the years would have forced her to recognize it. "Let someone within three feet of you," Miranda would say in exasperation as Lydia would dismiss some man as too fat or too bossy or too rich or too poor. Well, she had finally let someone get close, and she had to admit it felt terrific.

A lawyer by training, Nicky was associate director of the Children's Defense League. One week, he'd be conducting a fund-raising drive to pass legislation in Georgia or Alabama, the next he'd be helping out with a parental custody case in front of the Supreme Court. She didn't mind all his traveling; in fact, she preferred it. She needed time alone; time to organize her work and her life. Time just to be. Besides, it made her hours with Nicky all the sweeter.

Luxuriously, she eased herself onto the couch. Right now, she was looking forward to an entire weekend with Nicky. Just the two of them, nothing they had to do, no place they had to go. It sounds like heaven, she thought, as she leaned back against the seat cushion and closed her eyes.

"If I were a cat, I'd be purring," Lydia murmured, as she felt Nicky's hand trailing up her spine.

They'd met at his apartment at six, made love immediately, ordered a pizza—all of which he'd eaten by himself as she chewed on a carrot stick—and then made love once more. In the background, Lydia could hear the final measures of a Bach prelude.

Moving his hand around to encircle her breast, Nicky whispered softly in her ear, "I wish we could stay like this for the rest of our lives."

"Mmm . . ." was Lydia's only response.

Without warning, he released her and leaned across her to open the drawer of the night table.

"I mean it," he said, as he extracted something and came back to his side of the bed. He spoke more loudly now. "I want us to be together forever. Maybe not in bed twenty-four hours a day," he laughed as his arms came around her once again. "But eight hours a day at least."

Lydia snuggled into his chest, appreciating as she always did the musculature of his upper body. That he had been an athlete as a boy was obvious. "Eight hours would be nice." Lazily she rubbed her cheek against the inside of his arm. "One hour is nice."

Abruptly he sat up and held out his hand, revealing the small gift-wrapped package he'd taken out of the drawer. "No, honey. One hour is not enough." He pulled the wrapping off what proved to be a small velvet box.

Lydia watched in amazement as he pushed back the lid to reveal a square-cut diamond ring, adorned on each side by a crush of tiny rubies.

"Marry me. Let's do this right," he urged, removing the ring from its container and lifting her left hand.

Lydia closed her hand into a fist without even realizing she had done so. She suddenly felt as if she were choking.

"Why . . . now?" she stammered, staring at the ring as if it were a live electrical wire.

Had she been looking at his face, she would have seen the disappointment clouding his eyes, followed by the resolution that enabled him to go on speaking.

"Now," he stated, "because I love you. And," he admitted hesitantly, "because my office wants me to move to Philadelphia."

He paused, then forged on ahead hurriedly, refusing to acknowledge the panic he saw in her eyes. "It's only about an hour and a half away from here, and we can get a house smack in the middle. The commute will be under an hour for each of us. Metuchen would be only forty-five minutes or so, right into Penn Station," he went on earnestly, "or Princeton, that's under an hour." The words were practically tumbling out. "Or, if you prefer, you could drive."

Lydia watched him in horror. She could barely take in what he was saying. He couldn't be serious.

"Nicky, I could never leave New York. My whole life is here. My students are here. The ballet is here."

Nicky slipped his arm back around her, attempting to hold her close once again, but her body was stiff.

"I'm not asking you to leave New York. Just to commute for a couple of years. You'd still have your life. You might even want to keep your apartment, sleep in the city a night or two a week."

Lydia pulled away from him. She said nothing as she got out of bed, pulling his flannel robe off the back of a chair and wrapping it around her. Nicky was still talking, but she had ceased to even hear the words. She stood in front of him, trembling.

Finally he stopped speaking, but his eyes were filled with pleading. She stared back, but she didn't really see him. Men, she thought bitterly. Nicky. Her father. All of them. The same protestations of love, the same victimized expression in their eyes. The same damned selfishness underneath.

In a small part of her mind, she knew she was being unfair. It was as if a distant voice was telling her how crazy she was being. *You're standing in the way of your own happiness.* But Lydia ignored the admonition. She knew better. Nicky had been holding out the shiny red apple. But there it was inside, just where she'd always known it would be—the worm.

Frantic suddenly, she rushed out of the room and looked around for her coat. She didn't even stop to change into her clothes. Her life depended on her getting out of here as quickly as humanly possible. That was the only thing she cared about right now.

Chapter 4

Miranda looked at her watch for what seemed like the hundredth time, wishing that Stephen would show up. He was already thirty-five minutes late. Despite the din of a crowded Saturday afternoon at Fairway, Miranda was certain everyone in the store was cursing her as they listened to the wailing of her ten-month-old son. Even her six year old was casting a malevolent glance at his little brother. She considered taking Ethan out of the backpack and comforting him in her arms, but actually accomplishing that transfer amid the line of thirty or forty people squeezed together waiting for the register seemed too daunting. Instead, she gently jogged in place, attempting to lull the baby with her body's rhythm. After a few moments, he quieted down, but as soon as she stopped moving, he started right up again.

She glanced at her watch once more. Come on, Stephen, she pleaded silently, resuming her bouncing up and down in an effort to quiet the baby. Out of the corner of her eye she watched four-year-old Sophie, who was standing near the packaged soups, talking to everyone who passed by. Miranda assessed her spot on the line. There were at least fifteen people in front of her, with twenty or more behind. Can I leave Jack here alone to save my place while I retrieve Sophie, she wondered, automatically reaching down to brush back the light brown hair that was falling over his green eyes. Her son didn't even bother to acknowledge her, continuing to scowl into his Gameboy.

She thought briefly about asking the man in front of her to keep an eye on Jack while she went to get her daughter but decided against it. *Mom invites child molester to watch over son.* The man turned toward her suddenly, as if he knew what she was thinking. Embarrassed, she looked down at the floor, noticing the contents of the red plastic basket at his feet. Half a pound of nova, five bagels, and a large container of scallion cream cheese. Oh yeah, she laughed to herself, definitely the groceries of a deviant.

"Lose something?"

Startled, Miranda turned toward the familiar voice. Her sister, Lydia, had somehow appeared right behind Miranda and the two boys. She stood there with Sophie in her arms and an accusatory look on her face.

"Lydia, what are you doing here?"

Lydia ignored the question. "She's going to get kidnapped one of these days," she said sharply, easing her niece down to a standing position. The little girl immediately poked the man in front, asking him what the funny green things were in his cream cheese. Lydia put one arm protectively around her shoulder.

Miranda scratched her forehead. "Actually, I was thinking more about molestation today."

Lydia looked horrified. "That is not a joking matter."

"I know, Sis. Pay no attention."

With one eyebrow raised, Lydia eyed what was in her sister's shopping cart. As if using X-ray vision, she pulled out two of the most fattening items.

"An entire wheel of brie plus a couple of pounds of gruyère," she said sharply, dropping them back into the cart and continuing to examine the rest of its contents. Her tone had assumed the critical edge that Miranda had been sidestepping since earliest childhood. "Are you sure the fat and cholesterol content of all this is high enough? Perhaps some lard would pretty up dinner even more."

Miranda smiled. "I did consider foie gras and Crisco, but I thought the colors would come off as too drab." She laughed out loud as she watched the distaste on Lydia's face. Miranda sometimes forgot how seriously her sister took such things.

"Stephen's parents changed their minds, and they're joining us tonight." Miranda sighed. "I figure if I stuff them with cheese, they might get too sleepy to test the children's knowledge of eighteenth-century poetry, or to make sure that the movie in the VCR was made in Europe.''

She was gratified to get even the fleeting look of understanding that crossed Lydia's face.

"True, true," Lydia said sympathetically.

"Promise you'll distract them if they start up."

Just then, the baby resumed crying.

"Listen, how about pulling Ethan out? Stephen's going to be here in a minute, and he'll take him."

"What time is he due?" Lydia asked as she extricated the baby from the backpack. "I can't stay—I have twenty things to do in the next half hour."

Miranda bit her lip. "Actually, he was supposed to be here about forty minutes ago."

"He should be helping you with this. You let him get away with murder."

"Ease up, Lydia. He's been working like crazy."

"And you're lying in bed watching the soaps?" Lydia asked sarcastically.

Miranda laughed. "My job is a heck of a lot easier than Stephen's."

"Which job? Writing promotional copy for the bank or raising three kids?" Lydia wasn't about to let it go. "I'm telling you, Ran, between doing your own work, trying to get these three in line, and eating all that crap you keep in the house, you're going to look fifty before you turn forty." She pinched the area around her sister's waist. "No kidding, you should come to the studio for Saturday classes, and let the king watch the tykes for a couple of hours. It won't kill him."

Miranda just smiled. Lydia's exercise studio was known to give the toughest workout in Manhattan, catering to former dancers like herself and serious athletes. "I don't think the sedentary mother of three would be an asset to your client list," she answered lightly. "My husband is just going to have to love me for myself."

"What self," Lydia snorted derisively. "The doormat who lets her husband walk all over her, the junk food queen who's paying no attention to her body—" She paused, her gaze shifting to the right. "—or the mother whose daughter seems to be offering herself to the highest bidder."

With that, Lydia pulled Sophie back to the family, jarring her from her conversation with an Indian couple waiting on the adjacent line.

Miranda wished she could stop her sister's assault, but this just wasn't the place to tangle with her, not with the kids standing there. Having heard so much arguing during her childhood, she loathed the idea of arguing in front of her own children.

Although, she chided herself, that wasn't the whole truth. In fact, she'd *never* chosen to answer back to her sister at all. By now, she wasn't even sure she could.

She settled on addressing one small point at a time, keeping her tone pleasant. "Sophie is not offering herself to any bidders," Miranda said. "She's outgoing and friendly, and she's going to be a happy, well-adjusted adult." She lovingly stroked her daughter's cheek.

Without taking his eyes off the electronic game in his hand, Jack snorted loudly at his mother's comment. Miranda was surprised that he had been listening; he rarely showed much interest in what she was saying, regardless of whether it was directed to someone else or to him. His air of indifference was something that had pained Miranda greatly ever since she was forced to admit that it wasn't just a passing phase. He might be only six, but he still hurt her feelings when he so pointedly ignored her. She reminded herself that he was the same way with everybody. And she knew his jaded facade was just his way of hiding his feelings; she was certain that inside he was boiling with emotions he had no intention of showing. Still, there didn't seem to be much she could do about it, other than to give him all the love she had.

She spotted her husband making his way to her through the crowd. Stephen kissed her lightly on the cheek and nodded warily at his sister-in-law.

"In the better-late-than-never sweepstakes, I guess you just came in number one," Lydia said, handing the baby to his father.

Stephen was holding a Barnes & Noble bag, which he handed to Miranda as he lifted the baby up on his shoulder with one hand and grabbed Sophie with the other. "Come on, Jack," he called out to his other son. "I'll wait outside," he said to his wife, nodding to Lydia and walking away.

"You could use a little more Esther, and he could use a little less Louis," Lydia remarked caustically as she watched him go.

"That's ridiculous," Miranda replied. "I don't know that I want to be anything like Mom, and Stephen is nothing like Dad."

"It wouldn't hurt you," Lydia responded, pecking her sister on the cheek. "See you guys later."

As Lydia walked away, Miranda thought about what her sister had said, grimacing. More Esther? Of course, Lydia had always sympathized with Esther's view of the Greenfield marriage, agreeing with their mother about what a terrible husband and father Louis had been. Even at Louis's funeral seven years before, Lydia didn't weep, refusing to alter her view of him in any way.

Maybe it was because she was older than Miranda and had clearer memories of the years their parents lived together. Or maybe it was because Lydia and Esther were so similar underneath, both pursuing dreams, both possessed by a boundless will that pushed them forward no matter what. Even when Lydia decided she was too old to dance professionally, she hadn't paused to bemoan the loss, but went right on to the next goal. Miranda felt that Lydia's antipathy toward her father had unfortunately translated into a distrust of most men. Although she occasionally deigned to avail herself of their companionship, she seemed unable to connect with them in any real way. Not even Nicky Simon, whom Lydia had proclaimed the love of her life, had been able to break through Lydia's shell.

Surprised, Miranda realized she had finally worked her way up to the front of the line. She took several twenties out of her wallet as the cashier rang up her items. She wished Lydia would temper her criticisms, but she never lost sight of her admiration for her sister's accomplishments. Lydia had used the Esther Greenfield drive to achieve some pretty impressive feats.

So I'm not such a go-getter, Miranda thought, shoving the change she received into her jacket pocket. Is that so terrible? She picked up the two large shopping bags containing her purchases and stuck the small bag Stephen had given her inside one of them. Maybe she wouldn't build tall buildings or get her name in the paper, but she liked her life just the way it was.

She walked outside to join her husband and kids.

"Sorry for Lydia, honey," she said, squeezing Stephen's arm for a moment before relieving him of the baby.

"I wish you wouldn't report me for tardiness," he said.

Miranda sensed the real annoyance in his voice, but she could tell he had something else on his mind and was more excited than angry.

"What was in the bag from the bookstore?" she asked, already knowing what his answer would be.

Stephen just grinned.

Gazing at her reflection in the bathroom mirror, Miranda reviewed everything she had done in the past hour. Dinner was in the oven, hors d'oeuvres were assembled in heavy silver trays, the brie soft and creamy, the vegetable platter lined with ice chips to keep everything crisp. Every available lamp in the West End Avenue apartment was turned on, their beams throwing cheerful light across the plates of cheeses and pâtés scattered on various tables in the large living room. She had gotten all three children to sleep, the two boys in the larger bedroom, Sophie in the room that for another family might have functioned as a maid's room. Now, she thought, evaluating her pale skin and shoulder-length brown hair, all I have to worry about is my face.

As she stroked rose blush along her cheekbone, Miranda heard her in-laws enter the apartment, their voices tired after a day of touring both the Metropolitan Museum and the Whitney. Hurriedly, she applied some mascara, then added some gray shadow above her green eyes. She was dotting her lips with a sheer gloss when she heard her husband mention her name. His footsteps echoed in the long hallway as he came toward the bedroom.

"Honey, the adoring throngs are waiting for the empress to alight," he said only slightly impatiently, bending down to kiss the top of her head.

"I'm practically there." She brushed her hair one last time.

Stephen straightened the stiff white collar of her navy blue dress. "You know, if you organized things a bit more stringently, you might get to your own parties on time."

Miranda stuck her tongue out at him in the mirror. "Why is it you only use words like 'stringently' when your parents are here?"

He put his right hand up in the air, as if in surrender. "Caught. Guilty. If you shoot me right now, I don't have to die a year older." He draped his arm affectionately over her shoulder and turned her toward him. "After all, my birthday's not until tomorrow."

"Such a shame to lose a gifted author at such an early age," she said, placing her arms around his neck.

Stephen pulled her closer, his voice dropping to a whisper. "That is our secret, and only our secret." He held her at a distance suddenly. "You haven't gone and told anyone, have you?"

Miranda looked reproachful at the accusation. "Honey, when I make a promise, I keep it." She rubbed his cheek tenderly, trying to ease a smile out of him.

Stephen looked relieved as they walked out of the bathroom to join the party. Miranda watched him contentedly as he mingled among the party guests. The Belkers and the Lights, their friends from Jack's school, stood in one corner of the room, hovering over the food, drinking wine, and smiling relaxedly. Miranda understood what pleasure uninterrupted adult company and leisurely eating were for parents of small children.

Stephen's parents sat on the couch eagerly discussing the paintings they'd seen that afternoon with the art director of Colby & Cummings, the advertising agency where Stephen worked. Miranda would have marveled more at the depth of erudition displayed by both his parents if she hadn't had to sit through countless such lectures since the Shaeffers had moved to New York to take teaching posts at Columbia University four years before. Miranda was still fond enough of her in-laws, but their pomposity had grown with their professional reputations, and more and more often she found them difficult to take.

No, she realized, more than that. Disemboweling was more like it. Not that their piercing remarks hurt her; it was their effect on Stephen that was the real problem.

Stephen's book was a perfect example. When she had teased him about keeping it a secret from them, back when he first started writing it, she'd only been half kidding. She knew how disapproving they would be of *Stranger from the East*, an adventure story so light, without much deeper meaning. She could only imagine their reaction, their son producing such a novel. And she knew their disapproval was the thing Stephen most dreaded in the world.

But her husband had cleverly skirted the problem with an ingenious idea.

Stephen had decided to submit the manuscript entirely in secret, to keep his identity a mystery to the whole world. He sent the four-hundred-page manuscript through the mail to a selected group of literary agents, using the pen name Forrestor. There was no return address except a post office box in lower Manhattan, miles from their apartment. The mystery piqued the interest of several agents, and the one who wound up taking it on generated enough talk about it to get Highland Press to agree to publish it.

No one—not the agent, not the editor at Highland—no one except Miranda knew who Forrestor actually was. When Stephen's editor at Highland, Paul Harlow, wished to communicate with his author, he sent notes to the post office box. Eventually, the two men began to communicate by E-mail. But from the first draft through galley corrections, page proofs, and the final finished book right off the press, only "Forrestor" responded to everyone involved.

The people at Highland Press had been clever enough to capitalize on this as a publicity angle when the book came out, and several newspapers had included stories about the mysterious new writer on the popular fiction scene. Even *People* had picked up on it, printing a tiny paragraph about Forrestor in the issue that came out the week of the book's publication date.

Stephen had been so tickled by seeing the book in stores, he'd bought half a dozen copies, which he and Miranda had admired lovingly in the privacy of their bedroom. The book had been out for almost a month, but both of them still felt a thrill when they'd see it in their neighborhood bookstore. There it was, with a shiny red jacket, a picture of a man's face half-hidden in shadow, and the title in raised gold-foil lettering.

The extra money was fun, too, not that it amounted to very much. The day Stephen brought home his check, an advance against future sales, he also picked up a bottle of Dom Perignon. He and Miranda had joked that between the agent's taking his fifteen percent, and the cost of the champagne, there was barely anything left. But they had stayed up late that night, drinking the champagne and planning how to spend the remainder of his five thousand dollar advance.

What had amazed them was that, even before his first book came out, the publisher had offered him forty thousand dollars to write another one. It seemed like a small fortune to both of them. Just that afternoon when they had returned from Fairway, the kids retreating exhaustedly to the television set in the living room, Stephen had urged Miranda to consider giving up her job. She'd have more time for the kids, he'd reasoned. Time to play bridge even. She'd smiled when he said that. After all, it was her passion for the game that had brought them together in college.

But giving up her job was such a big step. It wasn't that writing promotional copy for Unity bank was so fascinating. How many ways were there to brag about interest rates and location convenience? Still, she liked being part of the working world, mingling with people whose shoelaces she wasn't expected to tie, whose hair she didn't have to comb.

On the other hand, her life had become so hopelessly complicated. She often felt stretched to the breaking point, and, worse, as if she were cheating everyone—her children, her co-workers, even her employers. And there wasn't a single minute that she couldn't have laid her head down on any available surface and gone straight to sleep. Rest was one indulgence she never got to experience.

She gazed around the living room, making sure her guests were all involved in conversations. What would it be like to have all day to herself, she wondered. Not exactly to herself, she amended, spying one of Sophie's stickers adorning the side of the CD player. But it was an interesting thought. Enough time for each of her three children, enough time for a quiet cup of coffee once in a while. Imagine, she chuckled to herself, how wonderful a man Forrestor must be to afford his wife such luxuries.

The copy of *Stranger from the East* that Stephen had bought that afternoon lay on the coffee table, tossed with seeming casualness between a four-volume Mark Twain set and a pile of *Scientific Americans*. Miranda saw her husband's eyes dart repeatedly toward the bright red jacket as he discussed art and politics with his parents. Every now and then, she caught herself looking at it as well, and their eyes would meet. They laughed silently together, feeling deliciously alone in the crowded room. They were smiling at each other when Stephen's father noticed the volume, picking it up in his hands and tossing it back on the table with disgust.

"This is exactly the kind of trash that is celebrated in America today," he said vociferously, his head bobbing up and down, his narrow-eyed disapproval making his face look almost feral. "Why do you even have it in your house, Stephen?"

Miranda turned to her father-in-law, hiding a smile as she managed to say mildly, "I don't know, Pop. I read it and it's pretty entertaining."

He gave her a look of disdain.

Miranda smiled broadly. "Intelligent, really. You'd be surprised at just how well written it is."

She stifled the urge to wink at Stephen, though she hoped he was finding the exchange as enjoyable as she was.

Stephen, however, stayed silent. In fact, as she turned back to him, she saw that he looked stricken. Moving quickly to his side, she linked her arm through his, although her next remarks were aimed at her father-in-law.

"Pop, I bet if you picked it up, you wouldn't be able to put it down." She smiled sardonically, trying to enlist Stephen in her private pleasure, but he pulled away from her.

"Hello, all." Lydia Greenfield entered the room with her customary grace, despite the bulky Sunday *Times* she carried under one arm. She walked across to Miranda, wincing as she passed the platters of creamy dips and chocolate truffles. Placing most of the news sections down on a wooden chair, she extracted the *Book Review*, holding the front page up for everyone to see.

"May I point to page one," she announced theatrically. "The very bulimic and talentless prima donna who vomited in every backstage bathroom across the forty-eight states has written her story for all the world to enjoy. Or, I should say, has spilled her guts to a ghost writer for all the world to bow down to.'' Disgustedly, she dropped the section on top of the rest of the newspaper. "Not only can she not actually *write*, but she could not actually *dance* when we started together at the Miami Ballet. Of all people to get this kind of attention."

Miranda watched Stephen, still disgruntled from his father's words, pick up the book section, absently turning the pages. Suddenly, she saw his expression change to one of near wonder. Without a word to their visitors, he pulled her from the room, walking to the kitchen and slamming the door behind them.

"My God, look," he said, his eyes alive with excitement.

Miranda took the proferred page and turned it toward her. It was the hardcover best-seller list. And there, nestled in at number five in its first appearance, was *Stranger from the East* by Forrestor.

Chapter 5

Uncertain of what her destination should be, Miranda found herself walking more and more slowly. With Ethan now in preschool, she suddenly had so much time on her hands, she wasn't quite sure what to do with all of it. Not that there weren't a thousand errands to run, squiring Sophie and Jack around, food shopping, taking in the dry cleaning, picking up this or that. But, somehow, it still didn't seem to add up to much.

Turning left at the corner, she wandered down Broadway, smiling briefly at the sight of Stephen's last book in paperback, *Deadly Moonlight*, in a bookstore window. Once again, the cover looked terrific, the art for this, his fourth of five novels, a bright turquoise warrior posed against a stark white background. His fifth book, *After Darkness Falls*, had just been published in hardcover, but this earlier book was still selling like crazy in paperback.

She still enjoyed the success of his books, even if she'd grown more used to it. She didn't imagine she'd ever get used to the enormous amount of money these books were generating. If beginning to write as Forrestor had been a lark, it was now a bonanza. Miranda had been shocked when Stephen had informed her that his third book would earn him an advance of five hundred thousand dollars. After that, he had signed a three-book deal for the unimaginable sum of five million dollars. And there were all sorts of financial perks, like bonuses for every appearance in the top five spots of the *New York*

Times best-seller list. The money hadn't actually changed her life all that much, but she'd never in her wildest dreams thought she'd turn out to be rich. Her childhood had been devoted to watching one parent reach for the brass ring and fail over and over again, and the other simply not caring. That she'd even gone to college had been the result of state scholarships and constant hard work. Whenever she had pondered the question of finances, which was not very often, she figured her own children wouldn't run much risk of getting spoiled. It certainly never occurred to her that they would be sent to private schools, to the combined total of over forty thousand dollars each year, without her and Stephen having to worry about it at all.

Stephen had grown to enjoy the fruits of his newfound success greatly. His closet held Armani suits and handmade Italian shoes. He'd even started talking about buying a house in the Hamptons, one right on the water.

Well, why shouldn't he think about things like that, she said to herself as she stood in front of a new shoe store that had appeared seemingly overnight where a small deli used to be. He worked for it, after all. Each night, after he got home from his office, he'd sit at the computer for a couple of hours, and Saturday and Sunday mornings were also devoted to writing. *Lucky that kids are so self-absorbed*, she often laughed to him when he didn't appear until after noon on a Saturday. Very occasionally, one of them would ask for him, and her explanation of his sleeping late or working on their income taxes immediately satisfied them.

At work, Stephen had been teased a few times about his new wardrobe. He would laugh it off, claiming he was finally growing up. Actually, she'd never imagined her husband would turn into such a fashion plate. In the morning, the dark hair he used to push a comb through, was now gelled and blow-dried to perfection, slicked back on his head, not a wispy trace to be found. His socks now came to the knee, no unsightly leg ever showing, and his cologne was a special brand he imported from Paris by mail twice a year. Miranda knew she should find the new Stephen enticing, but it was downright unnerving to her. As a housewife with three children, she rarely changed out of her pair of jeans and a baggy sweater. After all, why dress up when there was no office to go to?

She thought about her old job as she made her way toward West End Avenue. In retrospect, Unity Bank seemed an almost romantic place. There were all those interesting people to talk to all day long, the deadlines that had kept her frazzled but sharp. Now she talked mostly to her children and her husband, or made a little idle chatter with the doorman or the woman behind the counter at the hardware store. Her only real conversations came about when she'd have dinner with her sister—that is, if "You might think about the Atkins Diet, Miranda," or "Your hair is a mess—why don't you get a decent haircut?" could be considered conversation.

Her duplicate bridge games with her friend Marie Belker gave her pleasure, not that anyone did much talking when they played competitively, but at least she felt good at something. In fact, the two of them had racked up over one hundred masterpoints in the past couple of years.

She walked into her building and pressed the button to summon the elevator. I wonder if I could even *do* my old job anymore, she reflected, as she stared above the doors at the descending floor numbers. Banking procedures must have grown infinitely more complicated in the last couple of years, and all her creative energy was gone. Some creative energy, she chided herself silently. All she did was write idiotic copy about checking accounts. Not exactly a creative whirlwind. Besides, these days she could barely manage to write a shopping list. She didn't even have to balance a checkbook anymore; Stephen took care of all that.

She vaguely remembered herself, dressed in a gray wool suit or a black dress, seated in her small but attractively furnished office on the seventeenth floor, attending weekly meetings, writing clean, strong copy, and making sense of difficult concepts. Who was that woman?

"Surprise!"

Miranda was shocked to hear her husband's voice coming from the kitchen as she walked into the apartment.

"What are you doing home?" she asked.

"I'm going to be home a lot from now on." He lowered his voice mysteriously as he emerged from the kitchen. "As of today, my work is at home."

"What do you mean?" Miranda asked.

"I mean, I quit my job."

"You did what?" She couldn't believe her ears. "Without even telling me?"

"I'm telling you now," he said brightly, striding toward her. "Come with me, my little chickadee, and I'll show you the other wonders that await us."

A slight frown marred his exuberance for a second as he took in her outfit, the worn blue jeans and the red-checked flannel shirt. "But do me a favor and change. Put on the outfit I brought you from Singapore.''

She looked at him as if he had lost his mind. That he had gone to Singapore alone the previous summer for research was still a sore subject with her, and the obviously expensive two-piece shantung number he'd presented to her hadn't made her more sanguine about it. Besides, at the best of times, dressing up made her slightly uneasy. On an average Wednesday, it seemed insane.

"It's ten-thirty in the morning," she said as patiently as she could, hiding the annoyance that she felt. "What would I do in a red silk suit?''

"Humor me, okay?" Stephen walked over and put his arm around her shoulder, then pushed her toward their bedroom. "Just this once.''

Forty minutes later, Miranda found herself in a cab.

"Seventy-fourth and Fifth, please," Stephen instructed the driver.

As the cab sped through the Seventy-ninth Street transverse, Stephen kept up a steady stream of conversation, the fingers of his right hand tapping restlessly on his knee as he once again ran through his oft-repeated litany of complaints about his editor.

"In *Deadly Moonlight*, the bastard had the nerve to change the location of the fight scene in chapter five. He claims that the stadium would be locked up tight during the siesta hour. As if Paul Harlow knows anything about Europe.''

He kept looking at Miranda, waiting for her to agree, but she couldn't bring herself to make much of a response. She just watched the stream of traffic through Central Park, more than a little apprehensive about where this surprise trip would end.

Stephen continued despite her seeming inattention. "The bastard keeps taking out all my good verbs. I mean, the idiot replaces all the four-syllable words with two-syllable words. He was out of control on *After Darkness Falls*. As if America is too stupid to understand an intelligently written sentence. I'm beginning to think Paul is too stupid to get it himself." He shook his head in disgust. "What a jerk. It's like he wants the novel to be his instead of mine.''

As the cab left the park and turned onto Fifth Avenue, Stephen stopped talking. When they slowed to a stop, he began to smile. The building they pulled up to was large and imposing, one of the grand prewar edifices that housed Manhattan's most coddled elite.

"So?" Miranda said as she stepped out of the taxi.

"So welcome to your new home," Stephen said, waving to a gray-suited doorman who instantly recognized him and walked them inside the formal lobby.

Miranda gazed around. Marble floors and long refectory tables, polished to a perfect shine, gave the impression of the kind of old money she had only seen depicted in movies. Wordlessly, she allowed Stephen to move her into the waiting elevator, operated by yet another uniformed man. When the doors parted on the fifteenth floor, she looked around in bewilderment. Rather than opening onto a hallway, they opened directly into an apartment.

"I don't understand," she said breathlessly.

Stephen beamed. "It's ours. The whole floor."

For the next fifteen minutes, while she said nothing, he led her through the enormous apartment, pointing out every detail. She could hardly keep track of how many rooms there were.

"This is perfect for Sophie," he said in the entryway of a large sunny bedroom. "And look here." He walked through a doorway at one end of the room, showing her into a bathroom with almost blindingly bright white porcelain fixtures and views across Central Park.

Miranda stood at the window trying to find her apartment amid the array of West-Side buildings rising on the other side of the park. Her real apartment. The one she'd been living in all the years of her marriage. She looked back toward her husband, a wide grin emblazoned across his face. For a moment, he looked as unfamiliar as the room in which he was standing.

Chapter 6

"Oh, Daddy, look at that! And look over there!"

Sophie was twisting excitedly on her side of the hansom cab's bench seat, as she had been for the past ten minutes. She craned her neck, pointing and pulling on Stephen's sleeve.

"Yes, Soph, I see," Stephen answered dutifully as he glanced at his watch, hoping the ride was almost over. He knew that the clip-clop of the horseshoes along the city streets was generally considered a pleasant sound, but it was giving him a terrible headache. Or maybe it was Sophie's ceaseless chattering that was making his temples throb.

She had been begging to be taken on a horse-drawn carriage ride around Central Park for years, and he was glad he had finally carried out his promise to take her. But he was slightly embarrassed by the whole business; as far as he was concerned, these rides were a rip-off designed for tourists. And as proud of himself as he was for taking his daughter on an impromptu afternoon outing, he fervently wished it were over so he could get back home for a good book and a martini. No, wait, he reminded himself with a sinking feeling, his parents were coming over to see the apartment for the first time before taking the family out to dinner. The martini would have to wait. And he would doubtless need it even more by the time this evening was over.

"The buildings are so amazingly big when you think about it, aren't they?" Sophie asked, gazing up at the skyline looming over Central Park South.

"Um-hmm." Stephen picked a piece of lint off his jacket sleeve.

"Oh, rats," she cried out disappointedly, "we're coming to the end."

The driver steered the horse up alongside the curb to stop behind another carriage, then turned to face his passengers. "All done, folks."

Relieved, Stephen practically leaped onto the sidewalk, then turned to help his daughter down.

Sophie linked her arm through his and leaned in for a hug. "Thank you, Daddy. That was so great."

"Sure thing, princess. Now we'd better head on home. Grandma and Grandpa will probably be there already."

They started up Fifth Avenue, where Stephen paused before a street vendor selling soft pretzels.

"Want one, Soph?" he asked his daughter. "I know it's close to dinnertime, but what the heck. Let's live a little."

Her eyes lit up. "Sure."

He turned to the man behind the silver cart. "Two, please." He glanced over at his daughter. "Should we be big sports, and bring some back for your brothers?" he asked.

She nodded.

"Make it four, my good man," he said grandly.

Sophie laughed. Stephen paid for them, then handed her one. He took the other three, bowed to her, then, with a flourish, began juggling them.

"Daddy," Sophie said in delight, "I didn't know you could do that."

He grinned, pleased. "It's been years since I tried. I wasn't so sure I actually could."

They began walking, Stephen continuing to juggle the pretzels for almost a full block. When he stopped, Sophie rewarded him with a burst of applause.

"Very cool, Dad," she said.

"You mean you didn't know your Dad was cool?" he asked, arching one eyebrow. He put an arm around her, surprisingly pleased by her approval.

The good feeling lasted all the way home. When they entered the living room to see his parents already engaged in conversation with Miranda and the two boys, he greeted them effusively, glad to have his happy mood spill over. His wife was in the process of serving coffee to their guests, and Stephen was relieved to see her reach for the sterling coffeepot he had bought at an antique shop just the week before; he'd told her he didn't want to see that old Fiestaware ever again. Jack and Ethan seized the interruption provided by their father's arrival to disappear into their rooms, and after kissing her grandparents, Sophie did the same.

"Miranda's been showing us around," Alida Shaeffer informed Stephen after the children had gone, reaching out from her seat on the sofa to take the cup and saucer Miranda was extending in her direction.

"Great," Stephen responded pleasantly, waiting for her next remarks, anticipating praise for what he knew was the absolute correctness of his decorator's taste.

His mother took a sip of her coffee, but said nothing else.

"And . . . ?" Stephen said encouragingly.

Alida nodded noncommitally. "Very nice. Interesting."

Stephen's heart sank. If she had been holding her nose, she couldn't have better communicated her distaste.

He knew he was asking for trouble, but he couldn't keep himself from prodding further. "The decorator is one of the best in the city. Of course, we're far from finished. But she's done some great things, don't you think?"

Eric Shaeffer had moved to stand before a painting on the wall, clasping his hands behind his back as he studied it. He turned around to face his son.

"This painting was an odd choice, wasn't it? Must have set you back a pretty penny, even though it's one of his lesser works. You didn't think it was worth spending a bit more to get one of his really good paintings?"

Stephen's blood was rising. He struggled to keep silent.

"I'm not quite clear on why you need quite so much space, and so grandly furnished," his father went on. "It's a bit . . ." He looked at his wife, waiting for her to supply the right word.

"Showy?" she suggested.

Stephen dropped his gaze to the carpet, not wanting his parents to see the murderous rage he knew must be showing in his eyes.

"Hmm, yes." Eric turned back to the painting. "I don't know how much money you have, son, but you're trying to make it clear to the world that you have plenty. A questionable tactic."

Stephen looked up, accidentally catching Miranda's gaze. She said nothing, and she was clearly attempting to keep her expression neutral, but it was obvious to him that she agreed with his parents.

He stared at her. *I hate you too*, he thought.

Alida gave a slight shrug as her husband joined her on the sofa. "To thine own self be true. If you can say that, Stephen, and mean it, the rest is unimportant."

Stephen turned to look at the two of them. He was almost frightened by the storm of rage building inside him. *You sons of bitches*, he told them silently. *How dare you? What are you, two badly paid college professors, for crying out loud. I'm a world-famous writer.* He wanted to scream, to run across the room and shake them both. *You're nobody, goddamn you, nobody. I'm the only one in this room who's really somebody.*

He noticed that his hands were shaking. Get a grip, he told himself, forcing himself to hold them still.

The ringing of the telephone provided a welcome escape.

"I'll get it," he said tersely. "Excuse me."

He went into the kitchen, quickly crossing the room to pick up the receiver on the far wall. "Hello?"

"Stephen?" a male voice asked.

"Yes," he replied sharply. "Who's this?"

"Howard Sharon."

"Howard." Stephen's tone immediately turned friendly. Howard was one of the top senior vice presidents from Colby & Cummings, his old advertising agency. "Howard, how are you? Good to hear from you."

"How are things going?" the other man asked. "Wife, family—everybody okay?"

"Couldn't be better. And yours?"

"Great." Howard Sharon got to the point. "Listen, we just landed the Bad Boy account."

Stephen whistled. "Menswear only? Or women's too?"

"The whole deal. Five million in billings."

"Congratulations."

"Thanks. Here's the part that interests you. I just found out that Hank Florette is leaving Riverton to take over Bad Boy's merchandising next month. So of course I thought about how much Hank loved you when you were on Riverton's account."

Stephen smiled. It seemed so long ago now, but it was still nice to be reminded how valuable he had been as an account executive at C&C. "We got along well."

"Right. So I want you to come in to consult on this. Help us fine-tune the campaign, and get Hank on our side when we go for their okay on the final thing. He trusts you. And you are consulting these days, aren't you?''

Stephen was so taken aback by the offer he didn't answer for a minute. Of course he had told his former employers that he was going off on his own to consult, just as he had told everyone else. But he had never solicited any work from them. It was supremely flattering that they had come looking for him.

"So what do you think?" Howard went on without waiting for an answer. "We're having a meeting Monday at nine-thirty. Come hear the plans. We can take it from there."

Stephen turned over the offer in his mind. It wasn't as if he needed the money. But it would help legitimatize his cover story of being a consultant. If he continued to claim he was one, he should be able to produce a client or two. Besides, he did spend an awful lot of time alone in front of the computer, and it would be a nice change to be around the hubbub of his old office again, especially since they had come asking *him*. Hell, the whole thing would be fun.

"Okay, Howard, you convinced me," he said at last. "See you Monday morning."

When he hung up, his good mood was restored. He headed back to the living room, ready to face his parents once more. Actually, he reflected as he walked, you couldn't really blame them for their response to the apartment. They weren't used to life on this scale. They simply didn't understand it. He just needed to keep reminding himself of that.

When Stephen emerged from the elevator into the reception area of Colby & Cummings on Monday morning, he was already smiling broadly. He had enjoyed setting his alarm clock, getting up early for coffee and a quick perusal of the newspaper before putting on a suit and heading to Madison Avenue. Unlike the days when he lived on the West Side, now he could walk to C&C from his building, and it had been a pleasant stroll, past all his old lunchtime and cocktail-hour haunts.

"Hello, Cary," he said brightly to the receptionist. "Nice to see you again."

"Hi, Mr. Shaeffer," she responded, smiling. "You're back?"

"Just temporarily."

He waved as he went down the hall. It was only nine-twenty-five, and he didn't want to go into the conference room early. He decided he might as well comb his hair and straighten his tie in the restroom.

The heavy door to the men's room led to a sleek, well-appointed bathroom suitable for the agency's top executives, most of whom had offices on this floor. As he pushed it open, he was startled to hear his name being mentioned from within one of the stalls. He stepped inside quietly but went no further, knowing he couldn't be seen by anyone inside the stalls if he stayed off to the side.

". . . yeah, he'll be at the meeting this morning," one of the men was saying.

"You're kidding."

Stephen recognized the voices. One belonged to Brian Tannen, the other to Arnie Haverman. They were the two top men in Creative.

"Didn't Howard tell you?" Brian went on. "I mean, what is that all about? Have you heard of a single client of Shaeffer's since he left? It's such a load of b.s. Yeah, he's consulting—like my dog Eugene's consulting."

Arnie Haverman laughed. "I didn't even know he was supposed to be consulting. Shows you how hot the buzz is on him."

Brian gave a derisive chuckle.

"Same old story, I guess," Arnie continued. "He didn't quit, he got canned. Poor bastard."

"But I hear he moved to this incredible place on Fifth. Enormous. Where's that money coming from?"

"Maybe his wife?" Arnie speculated.

"It's somebody's," Brian said, "because that ain't coming from no severance package. What's probably part of the severance package is this consulting gig. Maybe they agreed to throw him a bone, give him something here and there."

Stephen didn't wait to hear the reply. He yanked open the door and left, striding down the hall back toward the bank of elevators, his cheeks burning. He was damned if he was going to sit opposite those two in a meeting after what he'd just heard.

These little run-of-the-mill corporate cretins could rot in their stupid little jobs, he thought as he stormed out of the building's lobby onto Madison Avenue. No-talent know-it-alls—he was surrounded by them. Looking down their damned noses at him. It made him nuts.

But living well is the best revenge, he reminded himself.

He was going home to write.

Chapter 7

Kyle Nichols lunged across the squash court with a loud grunt, his racquet sending the tiny black ball slamming up against the wall. Stephen made an attempt to get to it, but he knew the point was lost even before the ball went whizzing by him.

Smiling, Kyle straightened up, his stance now relaxed.

"That's eleven to three, Stephen. And that makes the match for me."

Damn. Stephen lowered his eyes so the other man wouldn't see his disappointment. He'd desperately wanted this to be a competitive match to show Kyle he could keep up, but Stephen had lost two games in a row, and the only word for his scores would be *pathetic*. It wasn't as if Kyle were any younger than he was or in better shape, he fumed to himself.

"Another two out of three?" Stephen looked over at him, trying to keep his tone casual.

"Uh . . ." Kyle glanced at his watch. "Can't do it, sorry. I have to be someplace."

Was he telling the truth? Stephen wondered. He resolved to practice a lot harder for the next few months, or at least until he saw some improvement in his game. Kyle would never sponsor him to join the Manhattan Club if he thought Stephen was a weak player.

The two men left the court together, each wiping their brow with a white towel.

"Tell you what, though," Kyle said, slinging the towel around his neck, "I can manage a drink before I have to leave."

Oh, he doesn't have time for a game, but he does for a drink, Stephen thought, feeling even more annoyed and humiliated than before. "Sounds good."

They headed for the bar area where both ordered a gin and tonic, then carried their glasses to a small table in the corner.

Kyle took a long sip of his drink before setting it down and leaning back into his chair.

"So, what have you been up to since the Fields'?"

Stephen and Miranda had initially met Kyle and his wife along with Nina and Daniel Field at a charity dinner for the homeless. A few weeks later, the Fields had invited both the Nicholses and the Shaeffers to a dinner party at their Park Avenue apartment. It had been an extremely pleasant evening that went late into the night. The only glitch, Stephen recalled with irritation, was that Miranda had been so quiet. Not quiet, really, he amended, just . . . not *contributing* anything of value or interest. She was pleasant and polite. But she was obviously unwilling to make the effort to sparkle that the other two wives had made. The other tall, thin, and blond wives he reflected with a mixture of pleasure and envy.

But that was so typical of her, he thought. Here was an opportunity to meet some new people, exactly the kind of successful people he wanted to be around, and what does his wife do but sit there like some frumpy housewife, then announce that they'd better be getting home because she had to be up with the kids the next morning. He could have killed her for that.

Perhaps he should be grateful she hadn't fallen asleep right there on the arm of the Fields' white silk sofa. She just couldn't understand how important it was to befriend people like these. But no, as usual, she left that work to Stephen, who had done his damnedest to make them like him, and luckily had succeeded enough to cover for her dullness.

But, hell, it was just what he had come to expect from her. Instead of wanting to broaden their world, she was determined to stay in her narrow little slot with her tedious friends. She'd completely let herself go, putting on weight at a slow but steady rate—despite his many warnings that she would be as big as a house if she didn't get a grip on it right away. Even assuming she could get rid of the weight, she had done nothing else to improve herself as a person, to *grow*.

She couldn't seem to grasp that his financial success as Forrestor meant a completely different life was opening up for them. At first, it hadn't occurred to him to what extent his bigger income could transform the very fabric of their everyday lives. But as Forrestor's checks grew by leaps and bounds, he realized that these sums could catapult them into a social circle where the air was much rarer.

Thanks to him, they were traveling in totally different circles now. Of course, there hadn't been anything *wrong* with the way they lived before, but those days were dead. Now they had a chance to really see the world, be part of the action.

Well, he was damned if he was going to miss that chance. He'd given her every opportunity to change over the past few years, and she had refused to take them. If she couldn't—or wouldn't—keep up with him, then he was going to have to consider the once-unimaginable. He would have to leave her behind.

He sighed. In his heart, he knew he'd already made the resolution to leave her. The delay was really about how to manage it. There was no way on God's green earth he was going to give her half of what he had earned, or get wiped out by child support payments. A judge could really stick it to him for three children. If he wanted to give his kids money, that should be his choice, made with his own generous heart, not decreed by some third party.

Not that they especially deserved it. His eldest son was so damned moody and full of himself—it was tiresome beyond belief to be with him. And Sophie and Ethan were both spoiled rotten. It was an end-less chorus in his house of *give me, take me, do for me*. Christ, he was sick of it. He had always known three kids were too many, and he'd been right.

As for Miranda, she hadn't done a day's work in God knows how long. Sure, she was entitled to get something in a divorce, but it wasn't anywhere near what he knew a good lawyer would take him for.

There was only one thing to do. He had to find a way to hide his money. Miranda paid no attention whatsoever to their finances, and certainly never kept track of the payments from his publishing com-pany or what he was owed by them. But actually diverting income could be tricky, and he wasn't some dope who was going to get in over his head only to get caught. He knew he couldn't do it alone.

That was why he was particularly happy to be getting to know Kyle Nichols, a broker with Winter and Moore. Of course, he couldn't tell Kyle that he was the famous Forrestor, whose books were now published in over twenty-five countries, whose sales figures were in the millions. Stephen was suddenly struck by the realization that if the other man had known who he really was, he damned well would have let Stephen win at squash, instead of humiliating him that way on the court. I could live with that scenario, Stephen thought, permitting himself an inward grin. But there was no point in going over all that. Stephen was stuck with his usual cover story about being a consultant.

He had observed Kyle carefully, and was feeling fairly sure that this was the guy to help him. There was something about him that made Stephen sense he could test the waters without endangering himself too much.

And now was the time to do it, he decided.

"Well, since the Fields', I've been working hard and playing hard." He assumed a pensive expression. "And I've been trying to decide what to do with a chunk of money. I'm thinking maybe you could be involved somehow."

At that, Kyle instantly became more alert. "Oh? How so?"

Slowly, Stephen took a drink from his glass, making the other man wait.

"You know," he said finally, as if he hadn't spoken before, and was starting a completely new conversation, "I was talking to this guy over lunch at the University Club last week, and he told me something pretty interesting. He says he's got about two million in investments overseas that his wife knows nothing about. I mean, I can imagine why someone might find that necessary, but I'm wondering how you would do that, what with filing joint taxes and so on. Maybe it's not that hard—I guess it's just not the kind of stuff I know about."

He gazed impassively but steadily at his companion. Kyle sat there for a long moment, then began nodding, almost imperceptibly.

"It can be done, yes, it can," he said slowly. "You need someone who knows what they're about. But, yes, I understand the idea." He smiled. "Unfortunately, it *is* necessary sometimes, isn't it?"

"Hmmm." Stephen answered as if his mind were already elsewhere. He rose, picking up the racquet he had deposited next to his chair. "It was a great match. Let's do it again soon."

Kyle nodded, waiting for what was coming next.

"Maybe we can meet at your office next week, and then come by here together. How does that sound?"

Kyle got to his feet and extended his arm for a handshake. "How does Tuesday sound? The end of the day, say six o'clock?"

Stephen put his hand out in return. "Perfect."

He headed toward the locker room, whistling under his breath.

Forty minutes later, showered and dressed, Stephen was walking on Central Park South. He planned to go home and put in a few hours of work, but something in him resisted the idea. Hell, he'd written five books. Wasn't he entitled to a break? When he reached Fifth Avenue, he couldn't resist, and turned right, striding quickly until he arrived at his destination.

It was just such a great display, he thought, stopping in front of the enormous front window of Doubleday. There before him were dozens of copies of his most recent book, stacked in artistically arranged piles, the top book on each pyramid standing up. Suspended in the center of the window was a huge blowup of the glossy black cover. The title, *After Darkness Falls*, gleamed out at him in silver letters below a picture of an antique dagger. Above the picture, larger than the title, was the reason the book had leaped onto the best-seller list in the first week of its release: *Forrestor*.

Stepping back, he folded his arms across his chest, taking it in. Even now, after five books, he still got a charge out of seeing them in store windows. There was something so mesmerizing about those multiple copies all grouped together, practically demanding to be bought. He knew that if he went inside the store, he would find the paperback editions of his first four books displayed together, all of them still in print, all of them still going strong.

Forrestor had become a phenomenon beyond Stephen's wildest dreams. Just last week, he had managed that much-envied feat of having his new book hit number one on the *New York Times*'s hardcover best-seller list, while his last one, *Deadly Moonlight*, was sitting at number one on the paperback list. Highland's marketing director had sent exuberant congratulations via E-mail, saying that if Forrestor should choose to show himself, the publishing company would be delighted to throw a party in his honor, even if it were only with a select few guests, sworn to secrecy.

Stephen chuckled as he started walking uptown. What an idiot he would be to do something like that. Creating the big mystery surrounding his identity was the greatest idea he had ever had. Sure, *Stranger from the East* was a pretty good book of its kind, but even he had to admit that the hype around who he really was had made all the difference. There were all sorts of outlandish rumors going around, one about his being an ex-CIA agent, another having him as an internationally known action-movie star.

It had all come from that offhand remark of Miranda's about keeping his book a secret from his parents. He remembered sitting at that table in Camden, hit by the bolt of lightning that suggested to him he write under some exotic pen name and hide it from the world.

Plenty of people wrote under a pseudonym, but they were known to their agents and editors and a whole slew of people. There weren't too many authors who refused to let anyone at all know their name or face. Miranda never realized that it was her comment that had given him the germ of the idea, but he was the one who had taken it one step further. Now he had it all—success, money, and the blessed absence of further contempt from his parents.

Not that there was any shortage of their contempt. He could still recall how he felt hearing their disdainful reaction back when they first visited the apartment. That disdain for his success had actually gotten worse as they observed his financial status continuing to escalate—the result, they believed, of his doing even more despicable things in the already despicable profession of advertising. He knew for a fact that they told people he was "a corporate executive of some sort," accompanying the description with a laugh that said they really didn't understand what he did—and didn't care to. Finding out that their son was Forrestor would be like having a stake driven through their hearts. He could easily imagine their comments about his lack of dignity and self-respect, no doubt followed by a heated lecture on the end of literacy in America. The bigger his books got, the more they would have despised them.

Of course, he reflected as he started to walk away, the notion would be so devastating to them, they were just as likely to have no outward reaction at all. They might say nothing, act as if they didn't know the books even existed. For all he knew, they might not even speak of it to one another.

Hey, he pleaded with them silently, it's not as if I don't *want* to write something good. Something worthy.

It was a thought that had begun to nag at him more and more often lately. Producing the Forrestor books had shown him that he was a natural at the nuts and bolts of storytelling. But by this point, he was certain he had a good book—maybe even a great book—inside him. *Real* literature. A dark, textured novel, into which he could pour his real self. Not just a superficial action-adventure story with larger-than-life characters and a lightning-fast plot.

Goddamn it, I want to see *Stephen Shaeffer* on the best-seller lists, he fumed, clenching his fists. All his success, and he couldn't tell a soul about it, couldn't use it for the thousand perks that came along with fame. Besides, he wanted to be known for having written something important, not for the shlock he turned out. Make his parents sit up and take notice, treat him with the respect they reserved for the literati, instead of acting like he was a wayward child who was going nowhere with his life. Hell, he'd make everyone sit up and take notice. And he could do it, too, he really could. He had the talent.

It was painful to recall how little he'd thought of his own abilities when he first decided to go into advertising. His view of himself hadn't changed much during his years in the industry. But the birth of Forrestor showed him how wrong he had been. He should have pursued English in graduate school as he'd wanted to so long ago; it truly *was* his calling. And the more he wrote, the more his once-locked-up abilities broke through. There was no knowing how far he could go as a writer.

Not that anyone could actually write a serious book in that madhouse of an apartment, the children constantly underfoot, everyone wanting a piece of him. It was as if that whole part of his life was all wrong now. Miranda was simply the wrong wife for him. The way she wanted to live was all wrong for him. The kids were all wrong, too. They weren't actually bad kids, but they were dragging him down when it was his time to soar. He realized he'd made a mistake early on which was finally catching up to him.

He needed time and space, to be left alone so he could reach inside for what he knew resided there. *I've got to write my book*, he thought fiercely. *I deserve it*.

He stopped at a red light on the corner of Sixty-fourth Street, where his reverie was interrupted by a questioning female voice.

"Stephen?"

An attractive blonde had come up alongside him. He smiled automatically, waiting for some clue as to who she was.

"God, it's been ages! How nice to see you," the woman said animatedly.

Of course, he thought, Jane Connors. He and Miranda used to play bridge with Jane and her husband, Sam, about a hundred years ago, before Jack was even born. Stephen couldn't recollect what had broken up their game, but regarding Jane before him right now, he had only pleasant feelings for her.

He gave her an appraising look. She was slender and well dressed in navy pants, a blazer, and expensive-looking leather flats. He noted the gold jewelry at her throat and wrists. A class act, he said to himself. She had always been attractive, but she was really put together now. Why couldn't *his* wife look like that?

Jane was smiling warmly at him, and he found he liked it.

"Well, hi, stranger." He returned her smile with a genuine one of his own. "What a surprise."

"It's been so long. You two still playing bridge?"

"Gee, no." He shook his head ruefully, although the truth was he didn't miss the game. "What about you and Sam?"

She paused for only a moment. "Sam and I are separated."

The light changed and they both moved forward as Stephen digested this information. So she was available.

"I'm sorry to hear that," he offered.

She shrugged. "It's for the best."

He caught her gaze and held it. "I have to admit, you're looking wonderful. So I suppose it is. I mean, you look fantastic."

He saw by the flicker in her eyes that she was wondering what the flattery was all about.

"Well, thank you," she answered hesitantly. "How are Miranda and the kids?"

He pursed his lips regretfully. "I'm afraid we're splitting up, too." She just doesn't know it yet, he added silently.

"Oh, my," she said in surprise. "Then I can say I'm sorry back to you."

He raised his palms in a resigned gesture. "As you said . . . it's for the best."

She nodded.

"Do you still have the apartment over near Second?" he asked casually. "At Seventy-first Street, right?"

"Yes, I kept it. I'm on my way there."

"Hey, I'm going in that general direction. We can keep each other company."

They continued together, talking about Jane's job as a travel agent. Stephen explained that he had left Colby & Cummings, all the while bemoaning to himself that he couldn't tell her that he was Forrestor. Boy, that would have her cooing all over him. He wouldn't have to work so hard at turning on the charm.

By the time they had turned onto her street, they were laughing about the old times, at how the four of them used to yell at each other over their bridge games, although it was always forgotten immediately afterward. Stephen took her arm and gazed directly into her eyes when he had the chance. They approached her building. He was gratified to realize she had gotten the message when she invited him upstairs for a drink.

If only I could tell you that I was Forrestor, he said silently. *You have no idea what a big fish you're reeling in.*

Holding open the door for her, he realized that this would be the first time he had cheated on Miranda. For a moment, he was flooded with guilt, painfully aware of the violation of a long-standing trust. He conjured up her face in his mind, envisioning the wounded expression in her eyes if she should find out.

Just then, Jane turned to him, brushing back her long hair and giving him a smile that he would have to describe as flat-out dazzling.

Screw it, he said to the image of his wife. You brought it on yourself.

Chapter 8

"Frankly, Abby Morris has been over the hill for years."

Miranda watched her husband's face as he spoke, the slightly cynical expression mirroring the one worn by the tanned middle-aged man across the table. It was an expression she had been seeing more and more of.

"How can you say that," she said earnestly, envisioning the face of the actress to whom he was referring, a woman who couldn't be over thirty-one or thirty-two.

Stephen didn't bother defending his comments, but Anthony Perry, the investment banker her husband had met at his trainer's studio, spoke out vehemently.

"She's doing all the plastic surgery, but she can only put off the inevitable for a few more years."

Stephen reached across the table and picked up the bottle of merlot, refilling his own glass, then Anthony's.

"To women in their twenties," he toasted, holding his wineglass high in the air.

"You'll excuse me if I don't join you," Miranda said in annoyance, looking momentarily at Anthony's date before realizing that Sally Winnick probably *was* in her twenties. Maybe even her early twenties, Miranda realized, looking closely at the young woman's poreless skin.

I'll be damned if I'll let my husband's obnoxiousness ruin a perfectly nice evening, she decided, burying the irritation that was causing her head to start aching. She listened as Anthony Perry continued what had been pretty much of a monologue for the past hour. From aging movie stars, he switched to the stock market, then back to real estate, the subject that had taken up the first part of the evening.

Bored, she found herself staring at the dessert cart being wheeled across the floor by the maître d'. The apple tart looked beautiful, huge chunks of apples under the smooth brown caramelized sugar topping. Turning her head as the cart went right past her, she noticed the chocolate cake, its top and sides powdered with cocoa, which only emphasized the creaminess of the frosting underneath.

"Yum," she said out loud, evidently to the consternation of Stephen, who arched an eyebrow in recrimination.

Across the table, Sally wrinkled her nose in response. "I couldn't possibly touch another bite, not after all I ate."

You mean the tiny green salad and forkful of sea bass, Miranda felt like responding. But seeing the admiration in her husband's eyes, she kept her mouth shut. Standing, she excused herself. She wandered into the ornate ladies' room, and looked in the mirror. I'm not twenty and I'm not anorexic, she admitted, noticing the tightness of her black cocktail dress around her hips and the new tiny line that had appeared as if out of nowhere across her forehead.

But damn it, she thought, taking a brush out of her purse and pulling it through her hair. I don't want to be twenty, and bulimia wouldn't become me at all.

Nor did evenings like this become her, she thought exhaustedly, adding up the number of times she'd found herself lately in situations featuring overpriced food and wine being eaten and drunk by people with too much money and too little interesting conversation. Since Stephen had left his job, he had become part of a circle of men, many of whose fathers had made so much money, there wasn't much left for them to do. And then there were guys like Anthony Perry who started out like everybody else, but by the time they made their way to the top had forgotten what regular people even looked like. Stephen had made friends at the trainer's, and joined a private club that she'd never even heard of, but her sister, Lydia, recognized as one of New York's most exclusive.

Half the time he went to one of his fancy dress functions, he didn't even ask her along. It's just the guys, he'd say, fastening his cummerbund. She didn't really mind. God knows, the kids provided company. But she missed their old life, the spontaneous bridge games with the Lights on a Friday night when she'd run into Emily and Bill in the elevator, the Chinese food orgies with the Belkers every other Sunday. These days, if she wanted to see òne of their old friends, it was by herself, and, with the children's demands, it was hard to find the time for more than an occasional lunch. But most of all she missed the feeling of being a team, she and Stephen both working hard to better their family.

It's lonely at the top, she thought ironically, knowing that the top was never where she'd wanted to be. She checked herself one last time in the mirror. Better get back to the table, she thought, knowing how displeased Stephen would be by her desertion.

I *do* feel lonely, she reflected, walking into the dining room and seeking a clear path to their table. At least I have the kids and Lydia and my friends. Who does Stephen have? she suddenly wondered. A pack of new best friends, not one of whom knows what he really does for a living. She watched him as she neared the table. He had ordered yet another bottle of the merlot, and was pouring it carefully into Anthony's glass, his napkin in his hand. He looks like an overeager headwaiter, she thought unkindly as she pulled out her chair and sat down.

It was one in the morning by the time they got home, three-fifteen when she was awakened by the sounds of Jack, retching in his bedroom across the hall from theirs. So she didn't have to worry that the new apartment was so large she wouldn't hear the kids, she thought as she climbed out of bed, leaving Stephen undisturbed beside her.

Miranda cleaned up her son's bed, throwing his sheets into the washing machine and putting on fresh ones. It wasn't until five that Jack fell asleep again, and she was able to go back to her room. One hour later, Sophie began vomiting, once again rousing Miranda and Jack, and this time Ethan as well, the only one of the children who escaped the unpleasant symptoms of the virus.

For the entire day, Miranda catered to the three of them, forcing Jack to drink ginger ale, providing Sophie with company while the girl decried her misery, playing with Ethan when the older two felt a little better.

By seven that night, all three children had been urged into their beds. "You can do anything you like, just so long as you do it in your own rooms," Miranda had declared, exhausted. "Your father and I are planning to be in bed by eight," she assured Sophie when the girl complained about the early curfew.

But when she closed the last door and turned out the hall light, she was surprised to see Stephen pulling on his new navy blue cashmere topcoat.

"Are you going out for sandwiches?" she asked playfully, knowing how little food there was in the refrigerator. She'd planned to go to the grocery store that afternoon, but hadn't even been able to leave the house all day.

He shook his head and frowned. "I should think you had enough to eat last night. You might think about skipping a meal for once."

Miranda stared at him, openmouthed. "Did I embarrass you?" she asked sarcastically.

He looked at her critically, taking in her house slippers and flannel robe. In the rush of the day's medical activities, she hadn't even had the time to get dressed.

"You can't embarrass me," he said finally, his eyes narrowing, "no matter how hard you may try."

She felt a pang of fear and humiliation in her stomach as he turned to go. "Where are you going?" she asked. "I thought we would have a few hours together."

"I told you I was going to Mario Selacci's tonight." He tossed the name out casually, but Miranda remembered how impressed Stephen had looked when he noticed the architect's latest design featured on the front page of Thursday's *New York Times*.

"Poker," he said with finality, closing the door behind him.

Poker, my ass, she thought angrily. She walked into the huge sparkling kitchen, past the shining copper pots artfully suspended above the marble-topped island in the center of the room, past the expensive appliances and professional-quality six-burner stove. She remembered her wonderful cozy kitchen in their old West-Side apartment. What a stupid place this is, she thought, glaring at her surroundings as she yanked open one of the hand-tooled cabinets and grabbed a bag of Oreos.

Chapter 9

Jack hurried out of the elevator, clutching the paper bag he carried as if it were filled with diamonds. The tiny store on Lexington Avenue had been closing by the time he got there, but he had convinced them to let him in, making the deck of wizard cards, the Disappearance Box, and the magic wand seem even more precious.

Easing himself onto the sofa in the living room, he pulled the wand out of the bag. Its circumference couldn't have been wider than a quarter of an inch, but as he held the gold-flecked object in his hand, it felt powerful enough to change the world.

"Bimini, mimini, debever, tever," he uttered rhythmically, "make my sister disappear forever."

And it was as if she had, he thought, knowing his little sister was not going to show her face all weekend long. He felt absolute contentment as he leaned back against the cushion and enjoyed the rare silence of the apartment. Not only was Sophie all the way out in Connecticut at some dumb weekend-long birthday party, but even Ethan had a sleepover date with a kid from his preschool.

His sister and brother, the prince and princess of popularity. Who cares, he reflected, delighting in the thought of his mom and dad getting ready for a night with him and him only. A night he'd been dreaming about for weeks. His father and his mother were taking him to Central Park to see Captain Whizzo in his onetime gala New York appearance. Jack watched the Captain on television every Saturday morning, when he would turn chickens into bears or get his handcuffs off just in time to save himself from a crashing helicopter. The guy was amazing. Jack closed his eyes, picturing himself sawing his sister in half. Then he imagined her staying that way.

There was no need to think about Sophie right now. Tonight was for thinking about Captain Whizzo. He recalled the last trick the Captain had performed that week. He'd thrown five fresh eggs up to the ceiling, and instead of breaking into yellow mush, they'd become purple flowers, all five of them sailing right into his hand. If I work hard enough, he thought, maybe I can be just as good as the Captain someday.

Well, almost as good, he admitted to himself, lifting the wand in the air and imagining a rabbit appearing out of nowhere. Opening his eyes, he realized how silly he might look, waving a magic wand in the middle of an empty room and conjuring up absolutely nothing. But he didn't really care. The fact that the room was empty was magic, as far as he was concerned. No little sister getting in his way. He knew that when she was born he was too young to actually remember her arrival, but he felt as if he did anyway. One day, he was *the* kid in the house, two people paying attention to him, and the next, there was the monster with the gold ringlets.

Ethan was okay, but a pain in his own way. And it seemed as if everything had changed yet again since he came along. His mom had started staying home, which was pretty nice, but his father was another story. Before Ethan had shown up, Jack had vague memories of him and his father walking down Broadway, stopping in stores to look at stuff, once or twice even going to Central Park together. Nowadays, even with his father quitting that place he used to work at, he was hardly ever around. He'd be shut up in the den for hours at a time, and if any of them wanted to talk to him, it was just too bad. Tell me what you need, his mother would say, running interference.

Like his father really appreciated her protection, he thought sarcastically. Most of the time, he seemed annoyed at her. He was even mean to her. Jack felt embarrassed whenever he overheard them, like it was stuff he shouldn't be allowed to listen to. It made him angry at his dad, and if he were being honest, he had to admit it made him a little mad at his mother, too.

But tonight was going to be different. He'd mentioned the Captain Whizzo appearance at dinner a month before, and his mother had said right then that she would look into it, so he knew that she'd had plenty of time to make the arrangements. When both Sophie and

Ethan were out of the apartment by four that afternoon, he saw it was going to be even better than he could have hoped. They were taking him and him alone. Maybe it was only one night, he thought smiling, but it would be one great night.

"Would it kill you to be ready on time?" Stephen snapped, smoothing his tuxedo shirt and glaring at his watch.

Standing in front of the mirrored wall of her walk-in closet, Miranda tugged at the waistband of her black Chanel suit. Stephen had insisted she buy "something decent for a change" when they'd gone to Paris the previous summer, but it had become impossible to button since she'd worn it last. Looking at her reflection, she felt more self-conscious than usual. There was Lydia, who would be dancing in front of hundreds of people paying a thousand dollars a plate, weighing ninety-eight pounds like practically every other woman in the room, and here she was, unable to button a size fourteen suit.

She finally managed to squeeze the button through the buttonhole, although the tightened waistband caused the flesh around her midriff to paunch out like a small balloon. Shit, she thought, unable to look at herself anymore, the jacket will just have to cover it.

"You look like something created by Goodyear," Stephen commented as she emerged from the closet.

She felt tears springing to her eyes, but vowed to keep herself upbeat. "Luckily, one of us looks terrific," she answered, walking over to him and kissing him briefly on the cheek. She straightened his bow tie and ran her hand down the rich wool of his Armani tux.

The look of distaste on her husband's face surprised her. Stephen had been unusually self-absorbed and critical lately, but now he looked as if he almost hated her. The urge to cry disappeared, replaced by a feeling of cold fear in the pit of her stomach.

"Let's go," she managed. One foot in front of the other, she cautioned herself, feeling suddenly like an actress in a drama for which she'd never even auditioned.

"Well, if you can't be the most accomplished woman in the room, I guess it's almost as good to be the heaviest," Stephen said loudly as he followed her out of the room. "That's a distinction of sorts."

"That's a disgusting thing to say," she found herself answering before she could stop herself. She turned to face him, angrier than she could ever remember being. "What's come over you?"

Stephen offered no response as he passed her and continued down the hallway.

Realizing that the door to their bedroom had been open, Miranda prayed that Jack hadn't heard their exchange. Of course, the boy spent so little time out of his own room, she knew the odds were on her side. But as they emerged into the hallway, there he was, his face lit up in a grin.

"Ready?" he asked, beaming up at them.

It was so seldom the boy smiled, Miranda couldn't help reaching over to give him a warm hug. For once, he didn't immediately pull away.

"As ready as we're gonna be," she said, loosening her grip. "Your dad cleans up pretty good, doesn't he?" She stepped back so the boy could see his father in black tie.

"Why are you so dressed up?" Jack asked. "You know, in the park you can wear jeans and stuff, even for a performance."

Stephen walked right past his son, while Miranda regarded him with surprise.

"Honey," she offered tentatively, "we're not going to the park. You know this is Aunt Lydia's big night."

"And there isn't anything we wouldn't do for Aunt Lydia, is there?" Stephen said sarcastically over his shoulder.

Miranda frowned at him. "Lydia is a wonderful aunt and a wonderful sister."

"Lydia is a bitch, and you're the world's biggest sucker," Stephen responded snidely. He turned to look at himself in the mirror that hung over the Hepplewhite chest.

The downstairs buzzer kept Miranda from responding. She walked to the house phone and listened for a few seconds, finally saying "okay," and hanging up.

"Tamara's here," she said, pursing her lips tightly and striding to the hall closet for her coat.

"What is Tamara doing here?" Jack asked, his voice both scared and angry.

Stephen didn't bother to answer as he joined his wife at the elevator doors, obviously prepared to leave the moment the baby-sitter arrived. But Miranda regarded her son with distress.

"Tamara's here to play with you while we're at Aunt Lydia's benefit, honey," she said tenderly. "You know about the work she does for the Pediatric AIDS Committee. She's even performing tonight." Her voice grew softer still as she took in his face. "We told you about this weeks ago, sweetie."

"But we're going to see Captain Whizzo." The boy's voice was edged with hysteria.

Miranda was puzzled for a moment, searching her memory. Finally, she remembered his mentioning something about it at dinner what seemed like a long time ago. Damn, she thought, why didn't I pay more attention. She walked over to Jack, and put her arms around him, but the boy pulled away angrily.

"You promised!" he screamed, his face contorting in fury.

"Jack, you know it's impossible. You must have heard us talking about the benefit all week long."

Jack burst out in furious tears, running over to the couch and throwing himself into the cushions. When he heard the elevator doors open and the sounds of Tamara Golden saying hello, he grabbed two throw pillows and held them over his ears.

Impatiently, Stephen kept the elevator doors open. "Come on, Miranda, we're late as it is."

She looked at her husband with shock. "You can't imagine I'd leave Jack when he's this upset."

"I can imagine almost anything. I can imagine you forgetting a promise you seem to have made to your firstborn. I can imagine you ruining a designer suit with an extra fifty pounds. And I can imagine you coming with me right now or watching me leave by myself." Stephen entered the elevator and held his finger on the hold button. When Miranda did not join him, he dropped his hand to his side and let the doors close without another word.

Miranda felt as if she'd been struck by a physical blow. She put all her concentration into keeping her composure. Then she turned to the baby-sitter.

"Tamara," she said, reaching into her purse and extracting a twenty-dollar bill, "we won't be needing you tonight. Sorry to make you come all this way."

The baby-sitter took the twenty with a look of surprise. "Okay, Mrs. Shaeffer."

Miranda watched as the girl rang for the elevator. When it arrived and the doors had closed behind her, she walked over to the couch. Sitting on the edge of the cushion, she stroked her son's light brown hair.

"Okay, honey, let's get going."

Jack lifted his head and looked into her eyes, tears still coursing down his face. "Get going where?"

"To the park," she said gently, wiping the tears from his cheeks with her fingertips.

Jack glared at her and tugged her hands away from his face. He stood abruptly, almost pushing her onto the floor, and stormed off toward his room. "I wouldn't go anywhere with you," he yelled. "You're so fat, I don't even want to be seen with you."

Lydia held Roman Kelaquoya's hand tightly as she curtsied, suddenly afraid of falling to the floor in front of eighteen hundred people. Between the utter exhaustion in her legs and the sweat pouring down her back, the chance of ending up in a wet heap didn't seem that unlikely. She smiled broadly despite her discomfort, as she switched legs and curtsied in the other direction.

Damn, she said to herself happily, *I did it*. It had seemed such a pipe dream, setting up the banquet and then performing Tschaikovsky's *Rose Adagio*, which she hadn't done in at least five years. But it had turned out to be worth it.

When the Pediatric AIDS Committee had approached her to be on the board, she'd said yes automatically. Struggling was what her own life had always been about, and watching these kids struggle when the ending was foreordained was inspiring. She knew some of her old dancer friends thought her participation in the charity was about networking, or a wish to be one of those fashionable rich people whose pictures would appear in *W* the following week, but they were dead wrong. Lydia knew she came off as tough as nails, and maybe she was. In fact, maybe she was proud of it. But she had always had a weakness for kids, kids who knew how to work for what they wanted. On Saturday afternoons at her studio, she gave a free ballet class to twenty boys and girls from some of the worst public elementary schools in New York City. What she got from them in energy and appreciation was worth far more than the money she could have collected from wealthier adults or their spoiled children. If she had her way, two or three of her underprivileged kids would go on to professional dancing careers.

The applause seemed as if it were going to continue forever. She curtsied once again, then knelt and reached out for the bouquets of flowers people had thrown to the stage. She knew the yellow roses would be from her sister Miranda. They were her favorites, and whenever she came to one of Lydia's performances, she would have the flowers brought onstage. Lydia was relieved to think that Miranda and Stephen would be waiting for her backstage. Normally, she wouldn't have cared, but tonight had been so overwhelming for her, she needed her sister's help with the hordes of people that would demand her attention. Organizing this event had been exhausting. As one of only three people in charge, she'd taken part in planning the meal, designing the public relations campaign and fund-raising efforts, and, most annoying, arranging the seating plan. Simply remembering who didn't speak to whom took full concentration.

And then, the dancing. She had retired at thirty-five, and although she'd kept in peak physical shape, doing the Tschaikovsky at the age of forty was no picnic. She'd wanted it to be good. After all, there was no honor in dancing like an ox for her own vanity. The honor lay in making it real. And, by God, she'd done it. Okay, forty wasn't twenty. She knew she couldn't reach the level she might have striven for then. But it had been fine. No, more than fine. Great.

The applause died down finally, and Lydia made her way backstage. The hotel had a large area with several dressing rooms. Miranda could greet the people who would show up immediately while Lydia took a quick shower. She was so soaked with perspiration that if she shook someone's hand, it would probably slide right out.

She greeted several other performers on her way to her dressing room. Sylvia Ames, the cabaret singer, and Kenny Atkins, her accompanist, congratulated her. And Mimi Ladd, a Broadway favorite who still performed all over the world, gave a long whistle as she passed her in the corridor. Lydia paused to take a closer look. Something was definitely different about the actress. Lydia remembered meeting her in a revival of *Annie Get Your Gun* when Lydia had first come with her Miami dance troupe to perform at City Center. Mimi Ladd was beautiful, the toast of the town, but even then, in her midtwenties, she had complained relentlessly about getting old. Suddenly it dawned on Lydia that Mimi had had a face-lift. Jesus, she thought, she's not even forty yet.

And she was as thin as a cover girl. The committee had thrown an informal lunch for all the performers the day before, and Ladd had eaten everything on her plate, plus some of Kenny Atkins's french fries. Come to think of it, Lydia realized, Mimi had disappeared right after that and returned a few minutes later looking pale. Bulimia, she decided, not very surprised. It seemed as if half the dancers and actresses she'd known over the years had indulged in binging and purging. What a stupid thing to do, she thought contemptuously. To her, being a dancer—or any kind of performer— was about discipline and iron will. Gluttony was undignified. And as for vomiting, it was disgusting.

Lydia left Mimi with a wave, and moved toward her dressing room. She stopped, one hand on the doorknob, when she saw Stephen.

"Hi," she said perfunctorily, looking past him for her sister. But no one else was there. "Where's the little woman?" she asked.

"Couldn't make it," he said breezily. "By the way, you were great."

Lydia stared at him. "What do you mean she couldn't make it?"

"I mean," he explained slowly, as if she were a child, "she did not come tonight." That he took pleasure from her dismay at the news was clear.

Lydia looked at him. What a worm he was. What did Miranda see in him? "Stephen, go find your wife. I need her help now. The crowds will arrive any minute, and I have to change."

Stephen started to laugh. "Why would I lie to you about this? Miranda couldn't come. My oldest child decided to have a nervous breakdown as we were leaving the house, and the good mother couldn't bear to part from him. Anyway, I'm here," he said, shrugging his shoulders. "Surely I can protect her highness from the hoi polloi while she rinses and repeats."

Lydia wasn't even listening. She was taking in the fact that Stephen was telling the truth: Miranda really hadn't come. Lydia's biggest night in years, and her sister couldn't be bothered.

Furiously, she opened the drawer of the dressing table and grabbed her purse. Then, she strode past Stephen, down the corridor to a small room in the back. As she made her way, she dug around the black Judith Lieber shell until she located a quarter.

There was a gray-haired man with tortoiseshell half-glasses seated on one of the chairs reading a book, but she paid no attention to him. She deposited the quarter in the pay phone and dialed Miranda's number. When her sister answered, she started in right away.

"What kind of sister are you?" she sputtered, not waiting for an answer. "I killed myself for this, and for once I needed your help. What have I ever asked of you? Nothing. Absolutely nothing. But could you come through for me this one time? No. No. No."

She heard Miranda's apologies. Jack. Some misunderstanding. She realized her sister had started to cry, but she didn't care.

"Fine," she interrupted, "I'll never ask you for anything again. You can save yourself for greasylocks and the three bears. When I need a sister, I'll look in the Yellow Pages." With that, she slammed the receiver down.

As angry as she was, she couldn't bear to return to her dressing room. Stephen Shaeffer was the last person she wanted to see. Depressed suddenly, she sank down onto a chair, her hands trembling as she grasped the arms.

For a moment the only sound she was aware of was the furious beating of her own heart, but after a while, she realized the man across from her was saying something.

"What?" she asked breathlessly, not really caring what the answer would be.

"I said, 'Anger's one of the sinews of the soul. He that wants it hath a maimed mind.' " He smiled at her beatifically.

Lydia looked back at him in confusion.

"Thomas Fuller," he supplied helpfully. "A seventeenth-century cleric," he added, as if that would make a difference.

"You're saying I'm 'maimed'?" she finally replied indignantly. "How the hell would you know?"

The man looked surprised. "No, no. It's the other way around. He would have supported you completely." He smiled at her. "Fuller's point was that anger was necessary, part of the muscle of the mind, you might say. He that *lacks* it is maimed, not he that *has* it." He took the tall glass that lay at his right and offered it to her. "Scotch and soda. Good for the body, good for the soul."

He laughed as she demurred. "Don't worry, I haven't touched it yet." He offered it once again. "Here, I'm a doctor, it'll be good for you."

Lydia took the glass from him. He was right. It was just what she needed. "Who are you?" she asked, handing it back to him after a long gulp.

"Henry Adamson," he said, reaching out his hand to shake hers. "Husband of Mimi Ladd, whom I expect you know." He took his own sip from the glass. "By the way, you were terrific."

"I doubt my sister would agree with you," she said bitterly.

His eyes lit humorously as he offered the glass once again. "No, I meant when you were dancing."

Lydia found herself smiling back. He was attractive, this husband of Mimi's, comfortable looking in a somewhat worn tuxedo, beautiful hazel eyes under graying brows.

"Well, thanks," she answered finally, the warmth in her voice surprising her. "Thanks for the compliment." She stood and handed the glass back to him. "And for the Scotch," she added, laughing. "I'd better go face up to my responsibilities."

She waved once more as she left the room. Amazing, she thought, this perfect stranger had actually made her feel much better. But not well enough to let her sister off the hook quite yet, she added to herself, as she approached the mass of well-wishers surrounding the doorway of her dressing room.

Chapter 10

"Hi, Mr. Shaeffer. How are you today?"

Stephen Shaeffer looked through the bulletproof glass at the pretty red-haired teller. Her smile was so open and sincere. He smiled back.

"I'm very well, Mary. How are you?"

She reached out to take the form he had passed through the opening between the glass and the marble counter. "Great, thanks. I'm going on vacation next week, and I can't wait." She read the form, frowning slightly. "Gee, I'm sorry to see you're closing your account. I guess that means we won't be seeing you anymore."

Pleased by the disappointment in her voice, Stephen stood up a little straighter. "No, I'll still have the pleasure of seeing your lovely countenance. It's just one account. I have another one here."

She nodded. He wondered if he should bother getting her phone number. No, he decided, he wasn't going slumming with this girl. It wasn't worth catching something. He'd stick with Jane for his extra-curricular activities.

"I'd like that in a bank check made out to cash, please," he continued.

"Fine. I'll be right back." She slid off her stool and disappeared with his withdrawal slip.

Stephen frowned in annoyance. He supposed she had to clear a hundred thousand dollar withdrawal with her manager or somebody. He wished he could have done this by phone or mail, but closing this particular account required a personal visit. He wanted to be absolutely certain it didn't get screwed up. It would be so easy for someone to send a receipt or confirming letter to his house where Miranda might see it, instead of mailing it to his post-office box. Not that she had anything to do with their finances, of course. But she might accidentally open a letter from Central Bank and Trust. After all, it was where they had their regular joint account.

He drummed his fingers on the counter impatiently. This was the fifth and last time he'd be diverting a large sum of money. He was determined that within the next few months he would leave Miranda and take his money with him.

By this point, with the help of Kyle Nichols, he had accumulated a respectable nest egg for himself. Thank God for Kyle, he thought. He'd made it all so easy. Now Stephen had three separate accounts. The largest one, to which he would add this hundred thousand dollars, was one Miranda would never find out about. Then there was their regular joint account, where he kept just enough money to cover their monthly expenses. In fact, he had recently withdrawn twenty-five thousand dollars from that account, wanting to keep it as lean as possible. The third account was also secret, but he was prepared to reveal its existence should Miranda hire a sharp divorce lawyer; it would seem far too suspicious if he were unable to produce *any* money beyond their checking account. He would hate to have to sacrifice the money in that third account, but he figured it was better to be safe than sorry.

The teller reappeared before him. "Sorry for the delay."

She slid the check through the opening, and he inspected it to be sure it was correct before putting it into his wallet.

"Thanks, hon."

"Anytime. Have a good day."

He locked eyes with her for an instant. I wonder what you'd say if I told you I was Forrestor, he asked her silently. The same question he asked dozens of people each day—but only in his mind.

Sighing, he considered which way to go. It would be more convenient to exit on Third Avenue, he decided, instead of going out the front entrance on Lexington Avenue. He headed to the revolving doors that would take him into the massive lobby of the Central Bank building. Hurriedly, he strode past the elevator banks, his heels clicking on the dark, cool marble floor, anxious to get to his next stop. Once he had turned over this check, he would finally be—

It was the noise of the blast that engulfed him first, a deafening roar that seemed to come from everyplace around him. Time stopped as he was hurled off his feet and through the air by some invisible force, a burst of energy that sent him crashing painfully into the wall. His head hit something hard, and his body came to a stop. Instinctively, he curled up into a ball to protect himself.

The terrifying tidal wave of noise continued to assault him as thick black smoke began filling the air, making him cough and choke, his throat burning. It went on for a seeming eternity, explosions continuing to come, one overlapping another, getting louder and louder. Vibrations beneath him shook his entire body. He felt as if his bones were rattling. Debris rained everywhere.

His eyes and nose stung like crazy as he gulped for air in what was now pitch blackness. Something warm and wet was dripping along his cheek and into his mouth, and his tongue finally registered the metallic taste of his own blood.

He lay there, waiting to die, listening to a series of new sounds, ominous crackings that grew deafening until, with a nightmarish shriek, there was a final break, and something fell to the ground with a harrowing roar. He realized it was the sounds of sections of the building collapsing. He shut his eyes, not knowing how to prepare himself for the sensation of being crushed to death. His body was still shaking. It occurred to him that it was no longer caused by the ground moving, but by fear.

The noises grew fainter and farther apart. Then, finally, there was just a vast silence. Stephen didn't move. He breathed shallowly as he listened to the blood pounding in his ears.

God almighty. What the hell had just happened?

He heard a man's voice coming from somewhere far away calling over and over for help. From several different directions, he could make out the barely audible sounds of sobbing and moans.

He opened his eyes, afraid of what he would see. But there was still only darkness. Slowly, tentatively, he began to lower his arms, and stretch out his legs. Wiping the blood from his cheek with his palm, he followed the wetness until a stabbing pain told him he'd found the source, a gash over his temple. But it wasn't that deep, and, flexing his arms and legs, he realized that, incredibly, nothing seemed to be broken. In fact, he seemed pretty much unhurt. He drew a full breath, which caused him to cough once more.

He tried to focus his thoughts. Judging from what had gone on around him, this had been a massive explosion. A bomb, perhaps. God knows, it was just a matter of luck that he hadn't been killed. But what was going on now? He wondered how many people were lying there, hurt, bleeding. An explosion like that at midday in such a busy building—he couldn't imagine that all of the people he'd just seen hurrying through the lobby hadn't been badly injured. Maybe some of them were trapped in the debris, buried alive, waiting for someone to come for them. He shuddered.

Suddenly it struck him that he might be trapped as well. He was all alone. Very tentatively, he reached out a hand. He touched something warm and smooth. With a gasp, he yanked his hand back from what he knew instinctively was dead flesh. He slid as far away as he could, only to be stopped by the inert form of another body. Repulsed and terrified, he got onto his feet, desperate to get away from the horror surrounding him.

Coughing and choking from all the dust and smoke in the air, he stepped over the body in front of him and carefully reached straight out. Almost immediately, his hand met with a jagged wall. Swallowing, he moved his arm, feeling around. Whatever it was that had fallen here was big. He twisted to reach in another direction. Something there, too. He continued to search for an opening, methodically reaching up higher and higher, hoping he could climb over all the metal and concrete surrounding him.

He couldn't find an opening anywhere. Was it possible that he was blocked in on all sides, he wondered. That was why the voices he could hear were so muffled. Perspiration trickled down the back of his neck. Christ, if only he could see, then he would know if there was any way out.

He sank back down to the floor, trying to stay calm. He could suffocate, he thought, or die of thirst or smoke inhalation if no one came. Did anyone even know he was at the bank today? Yes, he reassured himself, Kyle Nichols knew he was coming to get the money, he had mentioned it on the phone this morning. And lots of people in the bank knew him by name; if they were still alive, they would remember.

But he had survived in this little pocket of the building, and no one would know that there was this tiny open area, or that he was actually in it. So they might know he was here, but not that he was alive. This six-by-six spot was going to be his coffin along with the dead who were at his feet.

Panic threatened to overtake him. He had to get out of there now.

He turned frantically, putting out both hands to go over everything again, wondering if he could push something aside to make an opening large enough to crawl through. Just then, he noticed a faint red glow in the smoke about eight or nine feet above him. It was the first two letters of an exit sign.

Getting up again, he put his hands out directly in front of him at waist level. Bingo. He felt the long metal bar that could be pushed to open the door.

A palpable sense of relief swept over him. Am I not a lucky son of a bitch? he asked himself. There was no need to wait for people to find him. He could just walk right out.

He froze, his hands locked on the bar. For a long moment, he held his breath as he turned the phrase over in his mind again and again.

He could just walk right out. And go anywhere. Without anyone knowing.

Eventually, people would discover that he had been in the building today. But what if they never found him? They would naturally assume he had been killed and his body buried in the rubble. No one would ever know if he left now and disappeared. He could just vanish. Take off for somewhere else. Become *someone* else. Stephen Shaeffer could stop existing as of this minute.

And if Stephen Shaeffer stopped existing, he no longer had to be married to Miranda Shaeffer. He could enjoy all his money, and he could write the novel he had been waiting to write. No more Forrestor garbage.

All his problems would be solved in one fell swoop. He had enough money to live very comfortably for quite a while, and when he was done with his new book, his *real* book, he would be making money hand over fist once again.

Imagine, a whole new life. How many people would give anything, their soul included, to get a second chance at life, he thought. The novelist in him delighted in this sudden twist of fate.

For whatever reason, *he* was being given that chance. And he was going to take it.

He tried to push the bar forward. Nothing. Bracing himself, he pushed harder and harder until, suddenly, the bar moved with a screech. The door swung open to let in a blinding burst of sunlight.

Chapter 11

Miranda pulled open a drawer and hunted through the assortment of gleaming new utensils for her old aluminum carrot peeler; she had refused to let Stephen discard it when he outfitted the kitchen with all the latest in everything. Finally locating the peeler, she took it out and shut the drawer with one hip while glancing over at the TV screen at the far end of the long countertop. Sophie had left it on earlier, and Miranda hadn't bothered to shut it off.

The tired-looking middle-aged woman on the screen was telling the talk show audience how her sixteen-year-old daughter stayed out until all hours of the night and was threatening to drop out of school. Gee, there's something to look forward to with Sophie, she said to herself, yanking open the plastic bag of carrots. She envisioned her daughter with a face full of makeup, in short black leather and lace, sneering at her mother as she announced her intention of joining a motorcycle gang and moving to New Mexico. Miranda smiled at the image.

She began peeling the carrots, her mind half on her daughter and half on whether she had all the necessary ingredients for the meatloaf she was planning to make. At the moment, Sophie was in her room. Miranda glanced at the clock. In another fifteen minutes or so, the girl would come bounding in, looking for a snack. It never failed— she would be fine all afternoon until just before dinner. Then she would insist she was too ravenous to wait, and find something to snack on, ensuring that her appetite for dinner would be ruined.

Jack, on the other hand, would no doubt be late for dinner, as was his habit. He knew the rule was that he had to be home by six-thirty, but he apparently considered it a point of honor never to show up at the table before six-forty-five, even if it meant dawdling in the lobby or in front of the building. It was a battle Miranda didn't feel was worth waging anymore. She simply put out his plate of food and let it get cold. He would come in, dump his stuff in his room, and slide into his chair to join them, eating whatever was there without complaint. Not a perfect system, she supposed, but it worked well enough.

Ethan was, as always, an angel at dinnertime. Five was a particularly adorable age, she reflected, remembering how sweet Sophie had been only three years before. And it turned out Ethan was as smart as she'd always suspected. He'd been accepted to Hunter Elementary, a school for intellectually gifted children, starting in September. She was so proud; thousands of children applied and only a small number got in. And there was no tuition, icing on the cake.

Ethan was in his room now, playing with his trucks. She decided to stick her head in and see how he was doing, but she was stopped on her way out of the kitchen by the ringing of the telephone.

"Miranda, honey, how are you? How are the children?"

Miranda recognized her mother's voice, but before she could respond, Esther went right on.

"We're off to Alaska tomorrow, Irv and me!"

Miranda sighed with resignation at the familiar burst of enthusiasm that always heralded some new plan. "Mother, how nice to hear from you."

"This is it. We've found the perfect place to build a hotel."

"You already have a hotel." Miranda tried to hide her annoyance.

"Sweetheart," Esther replied, "that's just a Florida motel. We're talking about building a palace in Alaska. The new frontier! Think of the opportunities."

For the next twenty minutes, Miranda listened while her mother regaled her with the fanciful details of her latest venture. Miranda made approving noises, but didn't pay much attention. She'd had enough of her mother's grand schemes.

"So, we'll be back in a month. We're really roughing it. No reservations, no set schedule. Just Irv and me and the penguins. Isn't it great?"

"Yes, Mom, it's great. Have a wonderful time." Miranda knew better than to offer any opposing opinions.

"Love you, bunny, bye," her mother chirped. "Call you when we get home."

Miranda hung up and went back to making dinner. Esther in Alaska. What next?

As she opened the refrigerator door, she noticed that the program that had been on the television had been silenced, replaced by a static screen reading SPECIAL NEWS BULLETIN.

Oh, God, what horror had occurred now, she wondered. These bulletins were usually about an earthquake or some madman on a shooting spree. She paused, the refrigerator door still open, and waited to hear what had happened.

The anchorman from the network evening news appeared, his face somber. "Ladies and gentlemen, as we told you earlier, a bombing took place at the Central Bank building in midtown Manhattan at approximately two-thirty this afternoon. As of now, no individual or group has claimed responsibility. But we do have confirmed reports of numerous casualties, and the situation there is grim indeed. We go now to our camera crews who are on the scene at Lexington Avenue and Forty-sixth Street."

"Oh, Lord." Miranda shook her head and let out a weary sigh. Lex and Forty-sixth, across from Grand Central, right in the middle of everything. The world was going completely crazy.

She shut the refrigerator door and moved closer to the television set. She recognized the building, having passed it thousands of times when she worked at Unity Bank's corporate offices only five blocks away. From what she could make out, one side of the facade appeared to be destroyed. Trucks, police cars, and ambulances choked the street, and the sidewalk was swarming with firefighters and EMS rescue workers. Hundreds of people were gathered around, some screaming, some sobbing, others just staring in disbelief. The camera focused on two firemen carrying out a stretcher. The body on it was covered by a bloody blanket, but one arm had slipped down, a woman's arm covered by a pink sleeve, with a gold bracelet dangling at the end of it. Watching the arm bobbing up and down limply as they hurried toward one of the ambulances, Miranda clasped a hand over her mouth.

Those poor people, going about their business. She stood there, continuing to watch the gruesome scene, contemplating the randomness of it, the fact that it only came down to pure and simple bad luck if you were in a place at the moment some lunatic decided to blow it to smithereens. Call in sick that day, you lived; decide to eat lunch at your desk instead of going out the way you usually did, you died. No warning, no logic, not a thing you could do to prevent it.

The anchorman reappeared finally, promising to keep viewers informed as events unfolded, and the talk show resumed. Miranda shut off the television, her thoughts sober as she went back to her dinner preparations.

I'm going to kiss and hug each one of my precious children when I see them, she said to herself as she turned on the oven. Then, thinking of Jack, she added, *whether they want it or not.*

"But, Mommy, Erin and Tracy both have their ears pierced, and we're always walking around together, so I look like a jerk next to them." Sophie's voice was rising higher with every word, underscoring her sense of desperation.

Miranda continued sponging off the place mats, nearing the end of her after-dinner cleanup. "Soph, please put the salt and pepper shakers back where they belong."

"*Mommy*, you're not listening." Sophie was practically red faced with angry indignation. "This is really important."

Miranda stopped what she was doing and turned to her daughter. She believed in taking her children's requests seriously and not talking down to them, but she and Sophie had been over this ground repeatedly in the past few weeks, Sophie trotting out a new argument every couple of days. Miranda admired her daughter's determination in going after what she wanted, but she had had enough of this subject to last her a lifetime.

"Honey," she said as patiently as she could, "we're not going to keep talking about this. You may get your ears pierced when you're thirteen and not a minute before. Now please drop it once and for all. And go get ready for bed."

Screwing up her face in frustration, Sophie stormed off. "I can't believe how unfair you are," she called back over her shoulder as she went. "I'm going to ask Daddy again."

Miranda smiled at her child's last-ditch attempt to keep the subject open, at the same time remembering the mother on the talk show she'd been watching earlier. You and I may have quite a bit in common sooner than I could have dreamed, she told the woman in her head. Boy, who the hell would have thought an eight year old would be carrying on about pierced ears. Miranda recalled that she and her friends didn't get into that particular war with their parents until they were about fourteen. Sophie was certainly wasting her time approaching Stephen again. He had assigned this problem to Miranda and wanted to hear no more about it.

Where was Stephen, Miranda wondered, wringing out the sponge and trading it for a dish towel to dry off the countertop. He had said he would be back for dinner, and it was seven-thirty, well past what he knew to be dinnertime at home. She gave a little shrug. It wasn't as if this was the first time he hadn't appeared when he said he would. In fact, it was becoming distressingly habitual for him to disappear without her knowing where he was going or with whom. When this kind of thing had started, she'd been frantic with worry over his unexplained absences, but by this point, she knew better than to be concerned. Still, it would be nice if he could say goodnight to the kids, she told herself, trying not to acknowledge her mounting anger. It might at least calm Sophie down a little.

Maybe I'm wrong to stop her, Miranda suddenly thought. Maybe the standard of too-young-for-ear-piercing had changed, and she was the only one who didn't know it. She stopped wiping the counter for a moment, contemplating whether she was totally out of step with what kids were about these days.

"Nahhhh . . ." she finally said aloud with a laugh, resuming her task. More likely the whole damned world was just spinning out of control.

She tossed the dish towel over the side of the sink and began singing off-key. Spotting Sophie's hair ribbon on the floor, she stooped to pick it up. "Doo-*doot*, doot, doot, doot, doot, doot, doot."

The buzz of the house phone interrupted her. She lifted the receiver, dropping the ribbon onto the table. "Hello."

"Two men here to see you, Mrs. Shaeffer. They say they're from the police."

"The police? Are you sure, Tom?" Miranda frowned.

"I've already checked their identification, Mrs. S."

In spite of her trepidation, Miranda felt glad for once to be in a fancy building with efficient doormen and good security. "Oh, well, thank you. Send them up."

She hung up, her stomach uneasy. Thank God she knew her children were all here, safe and sound, or this would be the longest wait in the world. Could it possibly be Stephen? After so many nights of suspecting the worst and being mistaken, somehow she felt certain that couldn't be it.

Still, she hurried over to stand in front of the elevator doors, waiting there until they finally opened. Two men in raincoats stepped out into her foyer, looking slightly startled to find themselves already inside an apartment, as did many of their first-time visitors.

"Mrs. Stephen Shaeffer?" the taller one asked.

"Yes, yes," she answered quickly. "What can I do for you?"

The second man, short with thinning red hair, took a step closer to her. "We're from the New York City Police Department. I'm Detective Michaelson." He paused. "Your husband isn't home by any chance, is he?"

"No." Miranda shook her head.

"Has he called you or anyone else you know of this afternoon?"

Miranda's stomach was clenching. "No, no, not that I know of. Why? Is he okay?"

"Are you expecting him at any time?"

She nodded. "Actually, I expected him a while ago, but he hasn't come home yet." Her words started tumbling out more quickly. "He's just late, though. I'm sure he has a good reason."

The man spoke very gently. "Are you aware that there was a bombing today, Mrs. Shaeffer? At an office building on Lexington Avenue?"

She looked from one man to the other. "Yes I am. What about it?"

"There's a bank in that building, ma'am," the detective continued. "A branch of Central."

"Yes?" she prodded uneasily, not permitting herself to consider what might be coming next.

"The bomb went off at the opposite end of the building, so some of the people inside the bank were ..." he faltered, "... less injured."

The taller man picked up the story. "There was a teller who worked at the bank, a Mary Lubrow. She's over at Lenox Hill Hospital, and she's among the people helping the police and the F.B.I. piece together what happened today."

"Mary Lubrow," Miranda repeated uncomprehendingly. Fear was settling into her bones now. Something was terribly, terribly wrong. For a split second she contemplated turning and running into her bedroom, locking the door behind her, knowing how ridiculous an idea it was even as it came into her mind. She struggled to keep her composure. "I don't know who she is."

"Well, she informed us that your husband was at the bank today and had just left when the bomb went off."

"Stephen? Stephen was there?" Miranda's heart seemed to rise right up into her throat. "But he left, that's what you said, right? So he wasn't there in the building."

Detective Michaelson shook his head sadly. "No, ma'am, we didn't mean that he left the building. Ms. Lubrow said he went out through the revolving doors into the lobby, not out onto the street."

Miranda felt hysteria building inside her. "She could be wrong. How would she know where my husband went?"

The man softened his voice further. "She said she was actually watching and saw him go into the lobby. She was certain. And a second employee who was there confirmed that he also saw a man matching your husband's description leave through those doors at the time."

"No, no, they could easily be mistaken. It was someone else."

"The teller said he was wearing a navy blazer and a red striped tie."

Miranda saw her husband standing in front of her that morning, contemplating the black shoes he wanted to put it with, a frown on his face, asking if she could please take them in for a shine. She saw the navy jacket, replayed the sight of him selecting the red tie and knotting it around his neck.

"And . . . ?" she whispered.

"I'm very sorry, Mrs. Shaeffer, but, according to Ms. Lubrow, the bomb went off within seconds of that. We believe your husband still had to be inside the building at the time. So far we haven't located him, but we wanted to inform you."

Miranda took a step back, almost losing her balance. The detective reached out to steady her. "Are you all right, ma'am?"

Her breath was suddenly coming in short gasps. The detective leaned in to her. "Take it easy," he said gently.

"I'm sorry," she murmured, "I'll be okay. . . ."

She remembered what she had seen on the news bulletin that afternoon, recalling the woman on the stretcher, her arm in its pink sleeve.

Stephen. She thought she might faint. *No, Stephen, oh, please, God, no.*

"Maybe you made a mistake," she said frantically. "You could be wrong."

The taller man nodded. "It's possible, ma'am."

Miranda looked directly into his eyes, and she could see that he didn't believe any mistake had been made. Stephen wasn't coming home that night or any other night. Her husband was dead.

Chapter 12

"Put skim milk in that pitcher, and set it out next to the coffee."

As Miranda ushered her children off the elevator and into the foyer, she could hear Lydia issuing commands. As soon as the memorial service had been scheduled, Lydia had taken control of all the arrangements. That morning, she had arrived at Miranda's apartment to prepare for the crowd of people that would be coming by after the service. Now she was handling the finishing touches. Lydia had slipped out of Riverside the moment the rabbi finished, grabbing a cab back to the Fifth Avenue apartment before anyone else.

That's Lydia, Miranda thought, observing her sister bustling about, barking orders. Rarely a kind word, but great in a crisis. As usual, it made Miranda feel immensely grateful and resentful at the same time.

She turned to her children. Jack was still wearing the same glazed expression that had been on his face throughout the service. Sophie was puffy-eyed from crying continuously for the past week. Ethan just stood there looking forlorn and confused.

Listening to her daughter's sobs during the service, Miranda had thought Sophie's heart would break. She felt her own heart would break at the sight of the girl's suffering. She and the children had sat huddled together in the front row, Miranda keeping her arms around the younger ones, reaching out to stroke Jack's head as he sat, immobile and unresponsive, on the other side of Ethan. It was the longest morning of Miranda's life, requiring all her strength to hold herself together.

She could never have envisioned such a thing, a funeral for her husband, with no casket, no body to bury. The whole day had taken on a surreal air. There were at least two hundred people at the chapel, and when Miranda glanced around the room, she realized that she didn't know a good half of them. Many of those who were strangers stood out as being especially well-dressed. Stephen's new best friends, she had thought with some bitterness, turning away. That was part of what was making it even more horrible. She felt as if, at the end, those people knew Stephen better than she did.

The elevator had been summoned downstairs and now returned, bringing half a dozen people. Stephen's parents, looking pale and shaken, were there, along with their brothers and sisters—the aunts and uncles with whom Stephen had barely kept up. Having already seen them at the service, Miranda gave them a quick nod. She was surprised to realize how much she wished her mother were there, but of course there had been no way to reach her in Alaska; she had left no itinerary.

The apartment would be filling up momentarily, she thought, shepherding the children down the hall.

"Do you guys want to stay with everyone, or would you like to be together in your rooms?" she asked as they walked.

Sophie looked at her piteously. "Together."

Jack gave a derisive snort. "So you can go on being a big crybaby and drive us all nuts? No thanks."

He turned and headed to his own room, shutting the door emphatically behind him. Miranda sighed quietly.

"Soph, Ethan." She kneeled down. Ethan buried his head in her shoulder while Sophie bit on her thumbnail, clearly about to burst into tears again. "How about we all put some cold water on our faces and catch our breath. Then we can go out and be with Grandma and Grandpa." She directed her next words to Ethan, knowing Sophie was too old to care about the food. "I saw cakes and cookies, and all sorts of good stuff to eat."

Her five year old let out a small, muffled cry in response. "I want *Daddy*," he said, anguished.

"Miranda, hon, can I do something?" Joanne Karl came down the hall to join them. Miranda had become friendly with the tall, slender brunette when her daughter, Amanda, and Sophie had been Brownies together in first grade. Amanda was in a different school now, and the girls no longer had an interest in one another, but the two women maintained their friendship.

Miranda stood, still keeping an arm tightly around Ethan. "We're trying to decide what we feel like doing right now. I think we all need a chance to pull ourselves together before facing everybody."

Joanne slipped one hand into Sophie's. "How about if I go with you guys and we let Mom freshen up a minute?"

She gave Miranda a questioning look to find out if she should proceed further in this direction. Miranda nodded gratefully.

"Come on, Ethan sweetheart," Joanne urged, as Miranda gently detached herself from him.

Miranda watched her friend lead them both into Sophie's room. She hated to leave the children, but she could hear the rising volume of voices behind her. Though she wanted nothing more than to run away from the growing crowd, she felt obligated to show her face.

Always the good girl, she thought derisively as she turned and went back down the hallway. If only Stephen were here to act as the buffer—she caught herself short.

The foyer, dining room and living room had nearly filled up with people standing around holding drinks and small plates, eating the catered salads and cold meats. Seeing Miranda, they began coming over to talk to her.

"Oh, darling, it's too terrible. We loved him so, you know."

Miranda stared at the sixtyish woman before her, dressed in a black silk suit and matching turban. "Thank you, yes," she answered distractedly, searching her memory for some clue to the woman's identity and coming up blank.

"And what a dreadful way to go! If there's anything you need, anything at all . . ."

"Miranda, oh God, it's so awful." Emily Light came up to them and the older woman receded into the crowd.

"Thanks, Emily." Miranda returned the hug her friend gave her.

"Listen, I'd be glad to take Ethan for the day tomorrow. Would you want that?"

Miranda couldn't think about the next day, or anything else beyond just getting through the rest of the afternoon. "I appreciate the offer. I'll let you know, okay?"

She turned to face the onslaught of condolences.

"You poor thing . . ."

"We're so sorry . . ."

"He was the best, absolutely the best. . . ."

Miranda stood there, smiling dumbly, barely hearing the words.

She saw Eric and Alida Shaeffer drift by and was struck by how frail they appeared. Their self-assurance, the way they filled a room with their presence, was such a hallmark of their personalities. Miranda was completely unnerved at seeing them so fragile and quiet. But of course, how else would you look after you'd buried your only child, she asked herself.

And not even *buried* him. Just been told he'd been killed in a bombing and his body either so badly burned or buried so deep in the rubble, he would never be found. She shuddered. That was probably the worst part of it for all of them, the open-endedness of it, the inability to say good-bye to him in some final way. That and the nightmare images that Miranda had been living with, images of her husband, trapped and bleeding to death, alone in a black, smoking grave. She could only pray he had died quickly and not endured the kind of pain and fright any other scenario implied.

If Miranda herself could have found a way to stop her terrible imaginings, the constant barrage of the press would have made sure to keep the horror alive. Every time she turned on the television, there were the countless news reports on the bombing and its aftermath. She was besieged by phone calls and reporters outside her building requesting interviews. They wanted anything she would give them—a recollection, a photograph, or best of all, the public sight of her grief. But she had no desire to share her grief with the world. She chose to say nothing at all. Not in the days immediately following the bombing, nor when the terrorists were captured. Sickened as she was by the insane ravings of the Kallifer Five, a self-proclaimed militia that demanded the dismantling of all government institutions, she still chose to remain silent. And she was careful to protect the children from the camera's eye at the special memorial service for the bombing victims, attended by numerous dignitaries and therefore swarming with newspeople.

"Here, dear, eat something."

Miranda's mother-in-law appeared before her, holding out a plate and a glass of soda.

Miranda shook her head. "No thanks, Alida."

"Where are the children?"

"I guess they're still in their rooms."

Alida looked disapproving. "Alone?"

"No. Well, Jack's alone," Miranda conceded. "But that's how he wanted it."

"Nonsense," Alida bristled. "Don't let a child tell you what he wants. Children don't know what they want. I'll go in to him."

Miranda watched helplessly as Alida went off to right this wrong. Alida always thought Stephen didn't know what he wanted either, Miranda reflected sadly. But he *did* know what he wanted. It had taken him a while, but he had finally gone down his own road.

Who would have dreamed that first little manuscript would have led to such fame and success? Well, sort of fame, she amended. It was a shame Stephen could never enjoy the notoriety of being Forrestor. She wondered if that had bothered him much, or if he was content to make the money and keep his privacy. She herself wouldn't have wanted the intrusion of that kind of celebrity, but maybe he hadn't felt that way.

Not that she knew what the hell he felt about anything in the last few years. She was suddenly so tired she was afraid she might collapse on the spot. Ducking out of the room, she went into the study and sank down on one of the two French regency chairs flanking a long table.

She'd always hated those chairs. She recalled how the decorator Stephen had hired insisted they were right for the space, and, as with so many other things that went on in the furnishing of the apartment, Miranda had meekly agreed. She had been afraid of the woman, Elinor something-or-other, so pretty and confident, with her short black skirts and expensive jewelry, every hair in place. There was never any doubt in her mind about what needed to be done, and Miranda quickly realized that her own suggestions were being tactfully ignored. Eventually, she had withdrawn from most of what went on. Stephen, on the other hand, had loved the whole process. He had spent hours with Elinor going over fabric swatches, wallpaper samples, and glossy catalogs of who-knew-what, then running off to look at some antique end table or bid at an auction. The two of them created a home in which I'm a virtual stranger, she reflected.

But that was how pretty much everything had been post-Forrestor. Miranda slumped even further in the chair. That was one of the reasons she felt so isolated and confused today, wanting to cry, yet oddly detached. Her husband, the center of her life, had been stolen from her. She was alone with three grieving children, without the man whom she had lived with since she was practically a girl, upon whom she had depended for everything. But in some ways it was as if he had died several years before. The Stephen she had married had slowly dissolved as the Stephen who published blockbuster novels took over. And she could barely remember that earlier Stephen. He was the one who loved her. The new Stephen was always busy tearing off in fifty directions, none of which seemed to include her. The new Stephen held her in contempt. Death hadn't taken away the love of her life because she'd already lost him.

Tears filled her eyes. She desperately wished she could mourn for him, pound the floor and wail with grief. But she had been shaken to her bones over the past couple of days when it occurred to her that the apartment was actually *pleasant* without him. She noticed that she had stopped watching her every word, waiting for the next insult. It was as if there were suddenly more air to breathe. The realization left her scared and guilty.

"Ran, there you are, I've been looking everywhere." Lydia stuck her head in the doorway, her tone businesslike. "I want you to come back for a few more minutes and see whoever you haven't seen yet. Then I'm taking you in to lie down for a half hour. You look like hell, and you need it."

Miranda rubbed away her tears, smearing her makeup. "Do I have to go back out there?" she asked in a childlike voice.

Lydia nodded, but her face softened with a rueful smile. "I'm sorry, kiddo. You're almost done." As Miranda rose to her feet, Lydia came over to take her arm. "Come on, we'll stop off in your bathroom and brush your hair, throw on some lipstick. Make you a new person, okay?"

"Stephen would have liked that," Miranda answered without thinking as they went into the hallway. Seeing the look on her sister's face, she muttered, "Sorry."

They approached the door to Miranda's bedroom, which was slightly ajar. A woman's voice was coming from inside the room. Lydia made out the words first, and stopped, pulling Miranda back to her.

"Stephen, I just don't understand." The voice was full of pain. "How could you love me and let me think all that?" Her tone grew angry. "This is what you meant by being separated from her? This is the bachelor apartment you never wanted me to see because it was always so messy?" They heard her slam something down on the dresser. "You lying son of a bitch. I never would have found out the truth. You would have strung me along forever."

Miranda felt the blood draining out of her face.

"What on earth—?" Lydia stepped forward and flung open the door.

Jane Connors raised up her tear-stained face at the intrusion, one hand still on a framed photograph of Stephen. Watching her, all Miranda could think about was the day she had taken that picture. It had rained for three days in a row during their honeymoon in the Keys, and by that point Stephen was in a pretty foul mood. But she always felt that photo of him sitting in the hotel bar, rain pelting down outside, a kind of sexy scowl on his face, had been the best one of the entire trip.

Lydia suffered from no such wanderings of the imagination. "And you would be who?" she inquired sharply.

Jane snatched her hand away from the frame and took a step back, flustered. She ignored Lydia. "Miranda. I'm, I'm so sorry about Stephen. When I heard, I wanted to come today." She was clearly uncertain about whether she had been overheard or not.

Miranda stared at her. "Lydia," she said slowly, not taking her eyes off the woman, "this is Jane Connors. Stephen and I used to play bridge with Jane and her husband."

Lydia's eyebrow shot up. "How delightful," she said tightly.

Miranda shut her eyes, unable for the moment to stand what she was seeing, praying none of this had really happened. Then she opened them again. Jane was still standing there, trying to remain composed. Miranda's exhaustion returned, making it an effort to speak. "Why don't you go now, Jane," Miranda said heavily.

Jane, obviously relieved at being dismissed without a confrontation, eased past the two women. Then she paused, reaching out to touch Miranda's arm. "I'm so sorry," she whispered fervently, clearly meaning something beyond her condolences. Miranda pulled back from her touch.

Lydia slammed the bedroom door shut after Jane and spun around to face her sister, her voice growing louder and louder with her escalating rage.

"That goddamned bastard! It wasn't enough he treated you like dirt, and neglected the family so he could go off and do whatever the hell he felt like whenever the hell he felt like it. He was cheating on you to boot."

Miranda sighed. "I see that, thank you, Lydia."

"I swear to God, he belittled you until you didn't have an ounce of dignity or self-respect left, and then he turned around to get his jollies somewhere else because his little brown hen of a wife wasn't good enough anymore."

Miranda heard her own feelings being spat back at her with every word. "Lydia, please stop it."

"You didn't have any idea, did you?" her sister asked, shaking her head at the wonder of it. "God, how he walked all over you."

The truth of Lydia's words felt like a stabbing through the heart. Miranda raised her voice. "*I said stop.*" She took a step back, stunned by her own outburst. It occurred to her that this was the first time she had ever stood up to Lydia in anger.

But Lydia was too consumed by her own outrage to pay attention. "Why did you put up with that shit, Ran? Why?"

"*That's enough*," Miranda shouted. "You may have hated him but he was still my husband and the father of my children."

Lydia looked genuinely startled by the ferocity of her sister's response, but she recovered quickly. "Did that make it okay for him to have affairs? For you to let him reduce you to a sniveling heap? Because that's what he did, you know. I mean, honestly, you can barely take care of yourself anymore."

Miranda's anguish at hearing her own self-loathing coming from her sister's mouth made her explode in fury. "And what have *you* done for me? You've never had a kind word to say, or *anything* other than telling me what I'm doing wrong."

"Oh, that's so ridiculous," Lydia said dismissively.

"It's not!" Miranda was screaming, but she didn't care. "Listen, you've been looking down on me for our entire lives, and then you started looking down on Stephen. I've had all I'm going to stand of it. We'll just have to see if I can't take care of myself."

"Meaning?" Lydia drew herself up, offended.

"Go away, Lydia, just *go away*." Fists clenched, Miranda turned her back on her sister.

"I'm going, you can be sure of that," she snapped.

As Lydia slammed the door shut, Miranda threw herself down on the bed. She burst into tears, a flood of anger and confusion and fear.

Chapter 13

There aren't enough hours in the day. How many times had she said that, Miranda wondered, as she watched the images float across her television screen. Now there were so many extra hours in each day, so much empty space with her alone in the huge apartment, no tasks that really *had* to get done, and, she thought bitterly, no Stephen ever again. At ten in the morning, with the children in school for the next four or five hours, she was still in bed, still lying there in what felt like entirely too much sunlight streaming through the windows.

She'd managed to feed the kids breakfast earlier in the day, but actually getting dressed and going outdoors seemed too great an effort.

The television had been on since five that morning, when she'd awakened. She'd tried to take in the morning news with Katie and Matt and Al, but it was no use. Finally, after switching to the classic movie station, she'd pressed the mute button. Figures dressed in 1940s clothing floated silently across the screen, a dark-haired beauty in a mid-calf-length flared dress being pursued by a man in a low-slung, wide-brimmed hat. The woman could have been Greer Garson or Merle Oberon; the guy might be William Powell. What difference did it make.

She rose from the bed and walked over to the window. Fifth Avenue with its bustle of noisy traffic, the wide green expanse of Central Park, all of it seemed an insult to her state of inertia.

My husband is dead. She mouthed the words, as if not capable of producing sound. "My husband is dead." Okay. She could say it out loud. But the pain that shot through her as she heard her own words was indescribable. It ran in a thin electrically charged burning path from the undersides of her thighs up through her chest.

It wasn't just pain, she realized. Maybe that would be easier to bear. This was loss plus guilt plus anger plus . . . oh, who knows, she thought disgustedly, walking back to her bed and lying down in a crumpled heap. She tried to imagine what Stephen would make of her languor. Would he try to jolly her out of it, or would he be annoyed?

He was always annoyed, a tiny voice in her head said before she could stop it. Ashamed, she turned over and buried her head under a rumpled white pillow. Trying to hide didn't alter the fact that the tiny voice was right. He *was* always annoyed, always angry at her. And, if she had to admit the truth, by the time he was caught in that terrible explosion, she was plenty angry at him.

Did I even love him, she wondered, pulling the pillow away from her head and turning over once again to lie on her back. God, what a question to ask yourself weeks after your husband is killed.

She was spared an immediate answer by the ringing of the telephone. Relieved, she reached across to the end table and lifted the receiver.

"Mrs. Shaeffer?" an officious voice asked.

Miranda shifted her weight to sit up straight, her back against the headboard. "Yes," she said.

"This is Marion Sampler from Clareton."

A clutch of fear found a place in Miranda's belly. "What's wrong with Sophie?"

"She's fine, she's not hurt," the woman answered quickly. "But there is a problem."

Fully alarmed now, Miranda stood up. "What is it?" she asked, her urgency plain.

Mrs. Sampler let out a sigh. "Your daughter caused quite a ruckus in the social studies section of her morning class. She threw an eraser at her teacher."

Miranda couldn't believe her ears. Sophie loved Anne Whitman. She talked about her all the time. "I'm on my way," Miranda said, walking over to her dresser as she spoke and opening the drawer to extract a cotton sweater.

"I should hope so," Mrs. Sampler answered severely before hanging up.

*   *   *

Miranda was at a loss. There was Mrs. Sampler, looking at Sophie as if she were a serial killer, and there was Sophie, the happy extrovert, glowering back silently like something out of *The Omen*. Sophie's teacher, Anne Whitman, stood in one corner of the room, clearly puzzled.

"Honey," Miranda tried gently, "surely you want to apologize to Ms. Whitman."

Sophie looked up at her mother for a split second, then cast her eyes downward one more time. Progress, Miranda thought ironically. Now she not only won't say anything, but she won't look at anyone. The three of them had been trying to extract an apology from Sophie for ten minutes, but by now any word at all, even another expression of anger, would have been welcome.

Anne Whitman cleared her throat before she spoke. "You know," she started, looking as if she'd come to a decision of some sort, "I'm going to go back into the classroom. Soph, when you want to talk about this, I'll be eager to hear what you have to say." She turned to the other adults and nodded. "See you later," she called out to Sophie as she opened the door.

"No you won't," Mrs. Sampler said, her voice laced with iron. "You won't see her later and you won't see her tomorrow. Sophie is going to be suspended for a couple of days . . . until Thursday." She looked meaningfully at Miranda. "By then, perhaps she'll remember the rules of behavior."

Anne Whitman gave a conciliatory nod to Miranda, as if to say, there, there, everything will be fine, just you wait. But Miranda wasn't at all certain that anything was going to be all right. Since Stephen's death, she had a son who barely uttered a word, a five year old who asked when his daddy was going to get home at least ten times a day, the concept of death simply beyond his grasp, and now her daughter, the happy-go-lucky one, turning into a stone right in front of her eyes.

Mrs. Sampler stood up. "I hope you make some sense of this at home," she said to Miranda, clearly meaning it as a signal for them to leave.

Miranda was happy to oblige. "Sophie, run and get your jacket, and we'll get along home, okay, honey?"

The girl didn't look at her mother or give any obvious indication that she'd heard, but slunk outside.

Miranda looked at Mrs. Sampler apologetically. "You know, everything is upset right now."

The older woman smiled sympathetically. With Sophie out of the room, she gave in to a more human face. "I was so sad to hear about your husband. In fact, a part of me feels like letting Sophie off. But I think the sooner we get a handle on it, the better."

She started to walk Miranda out the door, then hesitated. "You know, there's another matter we have to talk about."

"What?" Miranda asked, wishing the woman would just let her go.

"You know the tuition check you sent in two weeks ago? The payment for next fall?" Mrs. Sampler looked embarrassed suddenly. "We got it back from the bank today marked 'insufficient funds.' "

She produced a check. Miranda glanced at her own signature on the bottom, recalling how strange it had felt to be the one paying all the bills for the first time. She felt annoyed. She had no intention of worrying about some ridiculous banking error when Sophie was in such trouble. "I'll look into it when I get home," she said almost curtly.

"I'm sure you will." Mrs. Sampler responded condescendingly.

Miranda left without another word. Right now, all she wanted was to be in her own home with her child.

Getting home, however, provided little relief. Sophie refused to say anything as they walked toward their building, and once inside the apartment, the girl closed herself up in her room, shutting the door behind her. Miranda knew she should try to get her to talk about what had happened that morning, but decided to give her some time alone. She might as well look into the check thing, she thought, sitting down at the desk in her bedroom where she kept her papers.

She rifled through the top drawer, and extracted the checkbook. The balance looked healthy enough. It must have been a mistake on the bank's part, just as she'd assumed. She looked up the number of her branch in the telephone book and dialed. At least she had one problem that had a beginning, a middle, and an end.

She waded through the endless recorded messages before reaching a live voice, then stated her business. When the woman came back on the phone, Miranda was so taken aback she almost dropped the receiver.

"There is a balance of three thousand and forty-two dollars in that checking account," the neutral voice informed her.

Miranda's tone grew more urgent. "But that's impossible. According to my information, there should be over thirty thousand in that account."

"I'm sorry, Ma'am," the woman said politely, "but three thousand and forty-two is the correct number."

Miranda looked frantically through the previous checks paid out, repeating them one by one to the young woman. Totaling them up, there still should have been over thirty thousand dollars remaining.

"So I don't understand why the check was sent back to Clareton's bank," Miranda said heatedly.

The woman on the other end of the phone took on a patronizing tone. "You skipped the withdrawal on the sixth for twenty-five thousand dollars, Ma'am."

"What?" Miranda asked in surprise. "Are you sure?"

The operator was growing impatient.

Miranda couldn't come up with a response. What had Stephen needed twenty-five thousand dollars for? Hanging up, she tried to ignore the uneasy sensation she was feeling. She began searching for their other checkbook, the one from their cash management account. She found it quickly, then realized that the book alone meant nothing. Hurriedly, she dialed the number for Merrill, Lynch, asking for Harry Barnes.

"Harry," she said when their stockbroker came on the line, "can you tell me how much is left in the money market account?"

"Who is this please?" he answered back politely if impatiently.

Miranda tried to slow down. "I'm sorry, Harry, it's Miranda Shaeffer."

"Oh, Miranda, I was so sorry to hear about Stephen. I've been meaning to call, but . . ."

Condolence was the last thing Miranda had time for. "Harry, please, can you tell me the balance in our money market account?"

"Sure," he answered placatingly, "just let me get it up on the screen."

She heard the sounds of a computer in the background.

"Here we are," he said after a minute or so, "there seems to be about a thousand dollars."

Miranda was aghast. One thousand dollars.

"Harry, how much do we have with you in other accounts, in securities and such."

Harry's voice was edged with concern. "Well, Miranda, when Stephen pulled out of the blue chips six months ago, it left only a couple of treasury bills, although there's a penalty for getting out early. All told, you've got about twenty thousand dollars with us."

"What did he do with all the money he took out?" Miranda was almost whispering.

"I have no idea," Harry said.

"Thanks." Miranda couldn't bear to talk any longer. "I'll be in touch with you later."

She lay the phone down on the desk, not even realizing that the receiver was nowhere near the hook. As far as she knew, Harry had managed every cent of their money. If he didn't have it, then it wasn't anyplace she could think of.

There was one more phone call to make. She grabbed her address book and turned to the "T" section. This was a call she had been putting off, figuring there was no urgency. It took a full ten minutes, but she finally got their insurance company on the phone. After quickly acknowledging the woman's condolences upon hearing of Stephen's death, Miranda asked her question.

"Now that I've informed you about my husband, can you tell me how much his life insurance policy is worth and when I might expect it?"

"Mrs. Shaeffer, according to our computer, he cashed it in about four months ago."

Miranda prayed she had misheard. "Excuse me?"

"He cashed it in, ma'am. Are you saying you didn't know?"

Miranda managed to get out a "thank you" and hung up.

Before he died, Stephen had taken his life insurance fund and all their money out of their accounts without telling her. And he had put it somewhere, somewhere she couldn't find it. He had done this deliberately. Decided to do it, planned it, carried it out. He had left her with nothing, and it was because that was what he wanted to do.

How long is twenty thousand dollars going to last, she thought, panic-stricken. The monthly mortgage and maintenance bills alone added up to almost ten thousand dollars. The tuition check for Sophie had been for over five thousand, and she suspected that within a couple of days, she would be hearing from Jack's school as well. If they ate nothing and went nowhere, they would still be out of money within a couple of months.

This was insane. Twenty thousand dollars *was* a lot of money. *Goddamn you, Stephen*, she cursed. Why did you set us up so that we can't survive on a normal amount?

She got up and began to pace. When you lived in the Taj Mahal, bought the best of everything, and put your kids in New York's most expensive private schools, you needed ridiculous sums just to stay afloat. But she hadn't wanted any of this. It was all at his insistence.

And now he had left her without the means to hold this life together, yet with no place else to go.

She sat back down. Oh my God, she thought, laying her head in her hands.

Chapter 14

"I'd like a house salad with that, dressing on the side, please." Emily Light closed her menu.

"Thank you, ladies." Having written down the lunch orders, the waiter reached out for the menus.

Emily gave him a polite smile. But as she turned back toward the table, her smile instantly vanished. Contemplating the bread basket, she let out a long, labored sigh, apparently not conscious of doing so. Miranda watched her, frowning. Emily was usually an upbeat person, but ever since she had sat down for this lunch, she looked as if she had the weight of the world on her shoulders.

"What's up, Em?" Miranda asked with concern. "You're not your usual self."

"I'm not?" Emily looked at her as if startled to be caught. "God, I'm sorry. With all you have on your mind, you don't need to hear my problems, too."

"Come on, I'm not locked in a bubble," Miranda said. "I can still care about somebody else. What is it?"

"Oh, Miranda, you've lost Stephen and you're alone with three children. My God, it's ridiculous to bother you with my petty troubles."

The waiter brought over two glasses of red wine. When he had set them down and left, Miranda immediately reached for hers. Not that I can afford it in this place, she thought. Fancy restaurants like this one had become Stephen's hangouts of choice, and she had always been astounded at the nine or ten dollar charges for a single glass of wine. Emily had chosen the restaurant today, and though Miranda might have asked to switch their meeting place to somewhere less expensive, she had suddenly been seized by a peculiar urge not to let on how financially strapped she was until the very last minute.

But strapped is what I am, she said to herself, savoring the taste of her wine. Which is what I came to see Emily about. So what is this false pride?

Oddly, this wasn't the kind of place the Lights typically frequented either. Miranda guessed that Emily picked it because she thought *Miranda* would prefer it, having so ostentatiously moved up in the world before Stephen died. Boy, whoever said money changes everything sure had it right.

Miranda set down her glass. "Please, Emily, don't treat me with kid gloves," she prodded her friend. "Tell me what's going on."

Emily toyed with her spoon for a moment before answering. "I guess I'm worried. No, actually, frightened." She looked up to meet Miranda's eyes. "Bill lost his job."

"What?"

"I know, I know," Emily said, nodding. "It's not possible, right? Just made chief financial officer last year, nine years with the company, all that good stuff. Well, Cranford merged with another research firm, DBG or GBD or something, and the other company's CFO is in. Bill's out, along with twenty-seven others who got dumped in the, quote, streamlining and downsizing." She laughed humorlessly. "I always think of downsizing as reducing people down to about three inches."

Miranda listened sympathetically, although her heart sank further with each word. Bill Light had always seemed the most solidly employed of anybody she and Stephen had known, and according to Stephen, he had earned several hundred thousand dollars a year. That, combined with their innate good nature, made the Lights the only people she felt remotely comfortable enough with to ask about borrowing money. Now, of course, that idea was out.

"I mean, we've been pretty careful," Emily was saying, "but where on earth is he going to get another big job like that at his age?" She grimaced. "Damn, I *knew* we shouldn't have bought a new car last month."

Tell me about it, Miranda thought. But she said nothing, just continued nodding. She hadn't mentioned anything to Emily about her financial situation, so, like everyone else, her friend naturally assumed Miranda was comfortably set up with life insurance and savings and whatever else a successful husband would normally leave. Of course, *normally* was the operative word here. She had been prepared to lay it all out for Emily, as humiliating as that would have been, to explain why she needed a loan. But there wasn't much point now.

The gnawing sensation Miranda had had in her stomach for weeks had finally eased a bit when she resolved to go to the Lights for help. As she sat there, draining her wine, it returned in full force. What the hell am I going to do? she wondered, only half-listening to her friend's words. For the moment, the kids were safe; they had started day camp the week before, and it had all been paid for back in March. But the school bills for fall were already overdue, and all the other bills continued to stream in.

Jesus, was this all really happening? It was simply too much for her to take in. One minute she had been a woman with a veritable fortune of money at her disposal, a settled wife and mother, albeit married to a man whose soul and integrity seemed to be crumbling before her very eyes. The next minute she was a single mother of three with not a dime to take care of them. She silently cursed her husband for the millionth time since she had learned of what he'd done.

It wasn't just being left penniless that was so upsetting. She had lain awake at night, staring at the ceiling, waves of humiliation washing over her at the thought of how he had abandoned her in every sense of the word before he died. To think that he had actually hidden his money from her, keeping up the pretense that they were sharing a life while all the time planning to go on to something that obviously didn't include her. How long before he was going to ask for a divorce? she wondered. One month? Six months? A year? She cringed as she recollected their last months together, his duplicity in every interaction, her being the idiot who had no clue.

As low as that made her feel, it was nothing compared to her pain for the children. Incomprehensible, inconceivable—she couldn't even articulate her horror at realizing Stephen had stolen what should have gone into raising the three of them. That meant he had been planning to divorce her and try to get out with everything. He didn't even give enough of a damn to provide for his own children. It made her breathless with hurt and anger to think about it.

Stephen Shaeffer had been a total stranger to her, certainly at the end of his life, but probably all along. That was the really scary thing, she thought. The coldness, the calculation that had gone on—it was monstrous. And now, she was left to deal with the aftermath. It wasn't bad enough that the children had lost their father; everything that they cared about, everything that was familiar to them was about to be snatched out from under them. Miranda was damned if she'd let that happen, but she was running out of options fast.

Initially, she was relieved to realize that money would continue to come in from the Forrestor novels, royalty checks from his book sales, and she could retrieve those checks to tide them over. But it had slowly come back to her that Stephen's agent had made him some kind of joint accounting deal, tying up his previous books' income with his new ones. She recalled Stephen telling her that he was getting most of the money for his three-book deal upfront. That meant his profits from all his past and upcoming books would have to be applied against that enormous advance before they sent him anything more. He would get a check every time he handed in a new manuscript, but beyond that it would be years before royalties showed up. Stephen had managed to squeeze every last drop out of Forrestor so there would be fewer assets coming to him in the future that she could point to in a divorce. The realization had made her feel sick.

Her next response had been to sell the apartment. But the real estate agent informed her that selling an apartment in such a high price range could take some time, and she should be prepared to wait it out. That was the day Miranda had forced herself to sit down with a calculator, a legal pad, and a slew of bills to determine how long she could hold out. She sorted and added and made lists. Two hours later, she put her head down on the desk and cried.

Just from what she could see at first glance, Stephen had debts totaling nearly eighty thousand dollars. Apparently, he had been slow to pay his bills, and he still owed on everything from Sophie's orthodontia work to the twelve thousand dollar painting he had purchased for his study six months before. The debt aside, she would need twenty thousand dollars a month just to pay their normal on-going expenses. She was hardly in a position to wait what could be many months to see the money from an apartment sale.

Miranda had been reluctant to share her humiliation with anyone, but she had finally gone to Lydia. The strain between them after their confrontation the day of Stephen's memorial service melted away as Miranda confided in her that Stephen had died without leaving her much of anything. Expecting a lecture and some especially pointed criticism of Stephen, Miranda had been surprised when Lydia simply went to her purse for her checkbook. She wrote Miranda a check for ten thousand dollars and handed it to her with a hug. Miranda couldn't remember the last time she was touched as deeply as by that gesture. Ten thousand dollars was a lot to Lydia, who was far from wealthy. Miranda took it and thanked her gratefully, knowing she could never tell her sister how far it was from enough. In fact, the entire sum had gone to pay Jack's and Sophie's school tuitions.

Miranda's thoughts were interrupted when Emily raised her arm to signal for the check.

"Thanks for listening, Ran," she said.

"Don't be silly," Miranda answered guiltily, realizing she had heard little after Emily's initial revelation.

Emily gave a small laugh. "Despite the unpleasantness of my news, I enjoyed the lunch here. But I guess it's the last time I'll be eating in such a good restaurant for a while." She reached out to take Miranda's hand. "Thank God you don't have to concern yourself with things like that."

Miranda smiled wanly as she pulled her wallet from her purse.

The storm had been going on for over an hour, punctuated by brilliant lightning and fierce, reverberating claps of thunder. Lying in bed, wide awake in the darkness, Miranda listened to the rain pelting the bedroom windows. As the room was brightly lit up by yet another flash of lightning, she finally gave up trying to sleep altogether and got up. Throwing on her robe, she glanced at the clock. Two-fifteen.

Padding barefoot down the hall, she looked into the children's rooms. Ethan was snoring loudly, his face nuzzled against the stuffed monkey who had been his nighttime companion since he was an infant. The top of Jack's head was barely visible beneath his quilt, but she could make out the even rise and fall of his breath. As usual, Sophie had kicked off her blanket and was lying nearly sideways on the bed, one arm thrown over her face. Miranda went in to cover her, amazed that the noisy storm hadn't wakened any of them.

Flicking on the lights in the kitchen, she headed for the refrigerator to pour herself a glass of milk before grabbing the box of chocolate doughnuts that were meant for after-school snacks. She sat down at the kitchen table, opening the box and savagely biting into a dough-nut, which she barely tasted before washing it down with a long gulp of milk.

Stuffing her face this way was hardly going to help matters, she admonished herself. She took another bite of the doughnut, pushing the thought aside. Ever since her lunch with Emily Light the day before, she'd felt as if the top of her head was going to blow off from the strain of worrying about the future. And now the future was really here: Jack's school had informed her that very afternoon that they couldn't extend the deadline any longer than they already had. He would not be allowed to return in September if the balance of his tuition went unpaid past the end of the month. This was what Miranda had been dreading, the moment when it all actually fell apart. And what am I doing to stop it? she asked herself.

Unable to sit still, she got up and wandered around the apartment, turning on lights, straightening up. She tried to think rationally, struggling to control the fear inside her. Going to Stephen's office, she turned on the overhead light and stood in the doorway, gazing at the magnificent cherrywood desk and leather chair, at the still-unpaid-for painting on the wall.

The room was just the way it had been before he died. As always, there were some random books and papers on the desk, but no sign of the activity that had gone on there: the writing of the Forrestor books. Any trace of Forrestor was hidden away in the locked desk drawers. Miranda knew the key to them was in a small ceramic bowl on one of the bookshelves; because she was the one other person who knew what he was doing, Stephen had made no effort to hide it from her.

Forrestor. That was where this whole nightmare had begun.

"I hate you, Forrestor," she whispered fiercely.

She went over to the far corner of the room, where Stephen had kept one copy of each of his books on the shelf. He had told her he couldn't have any more copies around, or any of the numerous foreign editions his agent was always sending him, because that would, of course, look peculiar to anyone who might come into the room.

So there they were, five glossy hardcovers innocently sandwiched between a copy of Stendahl's *The Red and the Black*, and Balzac's *Lost Illusions*. Miranda knew Stephen had never read either of those books, and glancing around, she noticed for the first time how many other titles on the shelves were serious literary works. She shook her head, bemused at the library her husband had set up for himself. In all their years together, she couldn't recall seeing him read even one of these books. In fact, she wondered where all the books she *had* seen him reading were, the paperback mysteries he loved. She almost laughed aloud to think of his hiding them or tossing them out, afraid that someone might discover his less than literary addiction.

She reached out to pluck *After Darkness Falls*, his most recent novel, from the shelf, running her hand over the black cover and silver letters, idly opening the book to read the flap copy on the inside of the jacket.

There would be no more for all the Forrestor fans, she realized. How disappointed they would be when it became obvious that he wasn't going to give them anything else. She paused as the magnitude of the realization sank in. It was the first time she had really thought about it. Everybody knew that Stephen Shaeffer was dead. But nobody knew that Forrestor was, too.

What a mess, she said to herself. It occurred to her that, at some point, the editor Stephen was always complaining about would doubtless try to get in touch with his mysterious author, but would meet with only silence. She turned to gaze at the computer on the desk. Slowly, she put the book down and went over to it. She flipped on the power and accessed Stephen's E-mail.

There were four messages, the first one dated a month before Stephen's death. She shivered as she read them, thinking how eerie it was, notes being sent out into the void.

F—Yes, I realize the outline is late, but we'll work around that. Looking forward to seeing it Monday as we discussed. Stay in touch. Paul

F—Hate to bother you, but haven't heard from you in several weeks. Any problems? I'm here to help. Paul

F—What's going on? Please contact me asap. Paul

F—Are you there? Paul

God, what a strange situation. She stared at the screen. This man would never know what on earth had happened to his biggest author. Forrestor would just disappear, and there would be no explanation, not to his readers, not to his agent, not to his publisher. Just like that, it was all over. Paul Harlow is sitting there in his office waiting for the next manuscript, and it will never come. I'm the only one who knows Forrestor is dead because I'm the only one who knows who he really was.

So I could become Forrestor.

The idea came to her with such stunning clarity, she caught her breath. She stood there, stock-still, almost as if she were afraid that any movement would somehow make the thought disappear.

Stephen was gone. But *she* could write the next Forrestor and send it in to Highland Press. If she could somehow manage to duplicate Stephen's style and actually produce a novel, the editor wouldn't have any reason to think it hadn't come from his author. Paul Harlow could still communicate with Forrestor in the same way he always did. He would never know he was dealing with someone else. No one would know the real Forrestor was gone. It could all continue.

And what was most important, the money Forrestor was owed when he turned in a new book would come as well. Only this time, she would be the one collecting it from the post office box.

No. She shook her head. It was ridiculous, an impossible plan. Who the hell did she think she was, imagining she could write a novel. And in someone else's style, no less.

She dropped down onto the chair behind her. Before she had stopped working, she had written promotional copy. So it's not as if I'm a complete illiterate, she thought. But writing copy is one thing and writing a novel is quite another. How did Stephen do it? She had always read the books when they were completed, but she hadn't had any reason to pay attention to their structure or the complexities of how everything came together in the end. Maybe if she studied them . . .

He plotted the whole story out first, that much she knew. But where would she come up with an idea for an entire book? And the writing of it all—no, no, it was an overwhelming prospect. The editor would spot it as a fraud right away. God knows what would happen then.

Nonetheless, she went back to the bookshelf, gazing at the five hardcovers before her. Without even realizing what she was doing, she pulled out *Stranger from the East*, Stephen's first book. She took it back to the desk chair and sat down, turning to page one.

She began to read.

Chapter 15

It wasn't until she heard Ethan emerge from his bedroom at seven the next morning that Miranda finally looked up from Stephen's first novel. Reluctantly, she put the book down on the desk and went to attend to her son. Despite having been awake the entire night, she found she wasn't at all tired. By the time Jack and Sophie came into the kitchen, their eyes still drooping with sleep, she had already set out orange juice and cornflakes for them, and was in the process of eating with Ethan. Her mind was racing with all she had to do that day.

"Jack, do you think you could go over to Henry's house this afternoon after camp?" she asked her son as he slumped onto a chair.

He grabbed the container of milk just as Sophie was about to pick it up.

"Hey!" she protested.

Jack ignored her, turning a suspicious gaze toward his mother as he poured the milk into his cereal bowl. "Why should I?"

Miranda paused a moment, wanting to hold on to her temper. "Because I need to do a few things. Is that okay?"

He gave a shrug. Miranda decided to interpret that as assent.

"Fine. I'll call his mom after you guys leave. Sophie," she turned to her daughter, "you have gymnastics, right? And Mrs. Wilder will take you along with Samantha?"

She nodded, her mouth full.

"Oh, yeah, the two Olympic champions," Jack said sarcastically, "spazz here and her ugly friend."

"*Mommy.*" Sophie looked to Miranda indignantly for help.

"Jack, that's enough," Miranda admonished sternly. "Apologize to your sister."

"Facts are facts," the boy said breezily.

Miranda raised her voice. "Apologize this minute."

He made a face at his sister. "Sorry for nothing."

Miranda sighed. Since Stephen had died, Jack had been at Sophie without letup. He never lashed out at Ethan, but Sophie couldn't do anything right in Jack's eyes. Of course, he'd always given Sophie a pretty hard time. Still, it was much worse lately.

Well, she thought, I haven't found the answer yet, and I probably won't today either. She turned her attention back to their plans.

"Okay," she said, more to herself than anyone else, "Ethan is in camp until five. So everybody's accounted for."

She rose. "Finish up, guys. Mom's got a busy day."

Jack grunted. "Yeah, doing what? Reading a magazine?"

Miranda tried not to show how hurt she was by his words. "Don't speak to me that way," she said firmly.

This is what comes of not working, she thought.

"I'm ready, Mommy." Ethan drained the last of his orange juice.

She smiled at him. Poor Ethan. He had always been an easy child, but now he was constantly trying to please her. It seemed as if he were afraid of losing her, too, but somehow believed he could prevent it with good behavior. "Nice job, angel."

In the next hour, she managed to get all three children out the door and arrange for Jack's play date before showering and getting dressed. Then she went straight back to Stephen's office. This time, she took a pen and a legal pad from one of his desk drawers and began to make notes as she read. She spent the entire day there, and, after feeding the children dinner and getting them to bed, was back in the chair until midnight. All of a sudden, she was too tired to focus on the words in front of her. She got up and went to her bedroom, tossing her clothes on a chair and quickly putting on a nightgown. She fell into bed, dreaming about a man with a shadowy face, on the run, a gleaming dagger in his hand.

The next day, she realized she would only have four hours alone before Sophie had to be picked up from her camp program. That just wasn't enough time. She hated to change the children's routine, but she had to have more time to work. Besides, she reminded herself, their routine would be a lot more disrupted if they got tossed out of their schools and apartment. She mulled over her choices, then went to the telephone.

Emily Light picked up on the third ring. The two women caught each other up on their news before Miranda broached the reason for her call.

"Em, I have the biggest favor in the world to ask of you," she said. "Feel free to say no."

"Shoot."

"Could you watch the kids for a few afternoons next week? I have a project I'm working on." Not exactly the truth, but not exactly a lie, either, she thought.

"Sure, I'm glad to," Emily answered immediately. "You back at work?"

Miranda hesitated. "Sort of. Listen, I really appreciate it. I owe you."

"Don't be ridiculous. Let me know what days and we'll work it out."

Relieved, Miranda ended the conversation. Now she would have some extra hours. But that night when she informed the children that she had made plans for them to stay with the Lights in the afternoons, Jack was furious.

"I'm not going to be shut up with her," he said savagely, jerking a thumb in Sophie's direction.

"Honey, I've got to do some work and you guys need to cooperate," Miranda said. "It's the first time I've ever asked you to help me out this way. Besides, you'll be with Matthew."

"No!" Jack yelled.

Miranda was momentarily torn, but attempting to write this book might be her last chance to salvage things. "What's the problem?" she asked.

"I won't go with her." Jack screwed up his mouth and fixed Miranda with an angry stare. "I'm not looking at her stupid face all day long."

"Well, I don't want to look at your stupid face either," Sophie shouted at him. She turned and ran into her room.

Oh, Lord, Miranda thought helplessly. "Where *would* you be willing to go?" she asked.

"I don't care," came the sullen reply.

Miranda sat there, thinking. "I guess that leaves us with Joanne Karl. You'd hang out with Michael for a few afternoons, wouldn't you?"

"If I have to."

She got up to go to the phone, thinking how much she hated to ask for such a big favor. But until she got this project under way, she *had* to have more time alone. She just wished her son didn't feel he had to make things so difficult. After she spoke to Joanne, she'd go in to talk to Sophie.

"Jeez, Jack," she couldn't help calling to him, "give your sister a break once in a while."

She didn't hear his muttered reply. "Naturally. She always gets *all* the breaks."

Miranda spent the next day in the library, returning home with two shopping bags full of books. Placing them in stacks on the desk, she stood back to review their titles: books on poisons, the martial arts, guns, mountain climbing, and precious gems. An idea for a story was forming in her mind, and she would build it on these elements. Stephen had actually traveled to research other countries and their customs—and to do who-knew-what else while he was away, she thought grimly—but she could hardly afford such a luxury either in money or time. The books she had gotten on France, China, and Switzerland would have to suffice as her guide.

"Can I really do this?" she asked aloud to no one in particular.

He knew he should be getting to sleep. He would need to be at his most alert tomorrow morning. But the room suddenly seemed unbearably hot and small. He grabbed his jacket, hurriedly leaving the hotel for the deserted street.

Miranda leaned back in her chair and reached out for her mug of coffee, resting on a pile of papers near the edge of the desk. She knew what she wanted to say next, but she couldn't quite find the right way to say it. Distractedly, she hit the up arrow key, returning to the beginning of the chapter, then slowly scrolled down, rereading what she had written so far that day.

She hoped she wasn't making a mistake, trying to insert this little moment in which the main character—a professional assassin named Dirk Findlay—paused for a bit of reflection about the nature of his business. Stephen hadn't been given to having his characters show remorse for all their killing, or even having them give it much thought. But she couldn't help feeling that if you were smart enough to figure out dozens of different ways to shoot, knife, poison, and garrote your enemies and get away with it, you were smart enough to contemplate the moral ambiguities of it once in a blue moon.

But she was only on chapter four. That might be way too soon for

Dirk to be having these thoughts. She drummed her fingers on the table. And exactly what do I have to say on the subject that's so riveting, she asked herself. Maybe Stephen knew what he was doing by staying away from this sort of thing. He got his characters in and out of situations, kept the pace lively, jumped them from one country to another and one bit of intrigue to another. She tried to do the same, but sometimes she felt the scenes were taking control of themselves, as if they wanted to go in a particular direction and she couldn't stop them.

This wasn't the only area where she had problems. She had gone over each of Stephen's books several times, making notes and underlining what she considered to be strong representative passages to help her imitate his style and timing. But it was a lot harder than she had thought to capture someone else's voice on a page. When she had started the actual writing, she had rewritten chapter one six different times, trying to get it right, or at least right enough to feel she was ready to go on.

Tiredly, she massaged her temples. The way Stephen had done dialogue was another trouble spot for her. He kept it brief, the conversations between characters mostly made up of terse, direct sentences. She kept finding her characters talking to each other at greater length; she just couldn't seem to get them in and out of a conversation as quickly as Stephen had.

Maybe she would save Dirk's ruminations until a later chapter. Maybe she would bring in the next guy he was supposed to kill, have him show up here in this scene, but she would make him someone Dirk knew from when he was a boy. An old playmate. He'd changed his name, which was why Dirk hadn't known who he was. It wasn't in her plot outline, but it wouldn't alter anything important.

She smiled, her fatigue lifting. That was the surprising thing: aside from being scary and hard work, this was an incredible amount of fun. It was so exciting to make up these twists and turns, and see them come to life as she built sentence upon sentence, page upon page. She was creating her own little world. She'd had no idea she would enjoy it this much.

Taking another sip of coffee, she looked at her watch.

"Oh, damn," she cried, jumping up out of the chair. She was supposed to pick up Sophie and Ethan ten minutes ago. By the time she got there, she would be a good thirty minutes late. Emily had been nice enough to watch the kids again; Miranda certainly didn't want to be late on top of it.

After the first week when Emily and Joanne had done baby-sitting duty, Miranda had hired a college student to come in four afternoons a week to be with the kids when they got home. But the girl had called to say she was sick today. Jack was off with a friend until dinnertime. Thank God, Miranda thought; he had remained adamant about not going anywhere with Sophie in the afternoons.

She took a taxi across town, racing into her old building and up to the Lights' apartment.

"I'm so sorry I'm late." She was talking almost before Emily got the door open.

"It's no big deal. Come on in." Emily ushered her inside and toward the small kitchen. "Got time for coffee?"

"Sounds great." Miranda followed her. "Where are they and did they behave?"

Emily nodded in the direction of the bedrooms. "Sophie's in with Karen, and Ethan's watching a tape. And, yes, they were fine, as always."

"Thanks, Emily. You don't know—"

"Please, Ran, it's the least I can do for you." She poured coffee for both of them, setting out milk and sugar, opening a drawer for spoons.

"How's Bill?" Miranda asked.

"Pretty good. He's out on a job interview right now, and it looks like an offer is coming in from a place he saw last week. So where's Jack today?"

"A friend's." Miranda stirred sugar into her coffee. Without realizing it, she frowned.

"How's he doing these days?" Emily asked.

Miranda paused, but decided she was glad to have the opportunity to talk about it. "I know losing his father is the worst thing in the world, but I'm kind of worried about how he's taking it out on Sophie. I'm not sure why he's decided to make her his scapegoat, but he's at her all the time."

Emily sipped her coffee. "You mean more than usual?"

Miranda looked at her, startled. "You've seen him do it before?"

"Of course." Emily appeared equally surprised by Miranda's response. "He doesn't make a secret of his resentment toward Sophie, you know. It's always been that way."

Miranda was flustered. "Well, I know he hasn't been the ideal, adoring older brother, but . . ." she trailed off.

"Don't you remember how jealous he was of her when they were little? He used to hit you on the arm all the time when you picked her up. Remember when he threw his shoe at her head when they were here that day of the blizzard?''

Miranda nodded slowly. "It seemed like normal stuff. After all, they're only two years apart.''

"But it's never stopped, Ran,'' she said gently. "I could give you a million examples.''

Miranda took a deep breath. "You're right.''

She put down her coffee cup, painfully saddened by the idea that her son had always harbored such resentment of his sister. And I just haven't wanted to see it, she thought. I've got to get this book done and attend to my children. There's no one else to hold the family together but me.

For the next four weeks, she wrote furiously, staying up at the computer until three or four every morning, scribbling notes every spare minute. And as she got more deeply involved, the story began to consume her, inhabiting her mind day and night. She let everything else slide; the mail would wait, the phone calls could go unreturned. Nothing mattered but the novel.

Then, all at once, it was done. It was nearly one a.m. when she finished the last sentence, and skipped the cursor down four spaces to type THE END. She stared at the screen for several minutes before she got up and went to the kitchen. She retrieved a bottle of champagne from the back of the refrigerator where it had lain, ignored, for months. Placing a dishtowel over the bottle, she popped the cork and poured the bubbling liquid into a glass, an outrageously expensive piece of crystal with colorful flecks embedded in it. She recalled the day Stephen had brought home the set of six, how shocked she had been by the price, the condescension in his tone when he informed her that they were, in fact, *art*.

She took the glass and the bottle back with her into Stephen's office and lay down on the sofa, resting the bottle on the floor beside her and raising her glass in the air.

"Congratulations to me,'' she said softly. "I don't know what the hell I did here, but I did it.''

She downed the contents of her glass. In less than a minute, she was fast asleep.

Chapter 16

"So that's the whole story, Dr. Adamson?" Malachy Albright asked, unconsciously squeezing a corner of the crisp white sheet.

"I'm sorry." Henry Adamson placed his hand over his patient's for a brief second. These conversations never got easier. Years ago, doctors were encouraged to lie to their cancer patients. You'll be up and around in no time, Mrs. Smith. The lump in your groin means nothing, Mr. Jones. Now everything was said straight out.

And Henry was glad. At least being honest with people about to die left them their self-respect, the right to think about how they wanted to leave this world. But knowing it was better didn't make it any easier. Surgeons jokingly referred to themselves as master carpenters, gynecologists as plumbers. And these were not necessarily unfounded as comparisons. When Henry had seized upon his specialty as a resident, he'd seen it as part detective and part philosopher. And, as far as he was concerned, the link between philosophy and medicine remained one of the main attractions of his job.

Henry had never shied away from thinking about mortality. But the price he himself paid every time he watched a patient he'd grown to care about die, or a husband or wife or son or daughter suffer through months of emotional agony—that Henry had never taken into account.

It wasn't as if he wanted to do anything else for a living, he thought as he left Malachy Albright's room and wandered back to the nurses' station. He loved his work. It interested him, it engaged him. It was just . . . just what? he wondered as he marked a notation in the Albright chart. He laid the chart down on the counter, smiling as he watched Marge Henderson, the head nurse, chuckle into the telephone. He and Marge had known each other for over ten years. He'd witnessed the excitement of her first marriage, heard some of the rumors that preceded its ugly breakup a couple of years later, and now had the pleasure of seeing her come alive again. Marge had confided to him about her new affair, this time with a gentle and appropriate man, an internist Henry knew and liked, before the hospital gossip mill had picked up on it. The two had announced their engagement the week before, and Marge was glowing with happiness.

He remembered his own engagement to Mimi fifteen years before. They'd met through his roommate, a fellow resident at Mount Sinai, and their passion had been like a forest fire. Of course, he thought as he walked toward the elevator, everything Mimi was involved in was like a forest fire. She had been bursting with talent and ambition, and their romance was comprised of fierce interludes interrupted by her two weeks as Laurie in the San Francisco summer theater production of *Oklahoma* or her annual three-week stint at the chic Paris supper club on the Right Bank. Their marriage had started on those terms, and they'd both stayed true to them. Mimi was a terrific woman, vibrant, exciting, independent. He was proud of her. But, she just wasn't around much. On days like these, when he had to deliver news of the kind he'd given Malachy Albright, he could have used her warmth at home. He would speak to her later—she usually called after she came offstage—and she would be genuinely sympathetic. And then, he would be alone in their apartment with Blanche and Stella, their Maine coon cats, his copious library, and a glass of bourbon.

Now there's something to complain about, he chided himself, as he pushed the down button. Returning to a beautiful co-op on Riverside Drive, reading a book he enjoyed, and drinking Jack Daniel's. He thought about the three-room apartment on Fordham Road in the Bronx, where he and his sister had shared the bedroom while his parents pulled out the sleeper couch each night. His education had come practically free, thanks to the Bronx High School of Science and City College, and his beverage of choice had been seltzer. He had appreciated Coca-Cola, a special treat served only every now and then, more than he did the finest champagne today.

He shook his head at the memories, starting slightly when he felt a hand clapping him on the back.

"What's with the long face?" Mickey Petersen, the hospital's pre-eminent orthopedic surgeon, said cheerfully.

Henry looked back and sighed. That particular question, addressed to oncologists, had been either the most juvenile joke among residents years before or the most ultimately, ironically, sympathetic. He could never decide quite how he felt about it when he had to listen to it every day; now, years later, he found it remarkably childish.

"And how are things with you?" he replied politely.

"Not so bad," Mickey responded. "Of course," he added with a manic gleam in his eye, "everything costs an arm and a leg."

The ridiculous orthopedic joke left Henry cold, but Mickey Petersen was red faced with laughter. Only when the elevator doors opened and an attractive dark-haired woman in her forties grabbed him by the arm did he stop laughing, replacing his adolescent hysteria with an "I'm in charge here" expression within the blink of an eye.

"I've been looking all over for you," the woman said, clearly upset.

Petersen looked at her with patronizing kindness. "Now, then, Lydia, we'll have your little girl fixed up in no time."

The disdain in the woman's dark eyes would have burned a hole through a more sensitive man than Mickey Petersen, but the doctor was unfazed. He led her back into the elevator, pressing the button for the third floor. Henry got on along with them, smiling encouragingly at the attractive but obviously frantic woman.

She looked at him suddenly. "I know you," she said.

Henry's eyes crinkled as he tried to figure out who she might be.

"The Pediatric AIDS benefit," she said by way of explanation. "I was the harridan on the phone, yelling at my sister. Lydia Greenfield."

Light dawned. Of course, this was the ballet dancer who'd done that nice Tschaikovsky that night. "Well, how nice to see you again," he said, offering his hand. "I gather the circumstances of our meeting again aren't all good."

Lydia looked grateful for his interest. "The 'little girl' in question is Sonya Santarova, twenty-five years old and formerly of the Kirov. She did something in my ten o'clock stretch class, something that seems serious." She glared at Petersen, who simply ignored her.

Mickey spoke commandingly as all three got off the elevator on the third floor. "I'll see to the patient, Lydia. You wait right here like a good girl."

Henry and Lydia both looked at him in wonder as he walked off. They started to laugh.

"I'm not just the biggest bitch in America, am I?" Lydia asked, smiling. "I mean, he is a jackass, right?"

"It was his nickname in medical school." Henry caught himself. "I never should have said that. He's the finest orthopedist in New York. Possibly in the country, or the world for all I know. If my wife or my mother had an orthopedic problem, I'd take her straight to Mickey Petersen."

Lydia grinned. "You don't have to sell me. I've known Mickey for years. His office is a dancer's second home, for better or worse. And since I opened my studio, he's been a real friend. That is, if you don't mind counting a condescending moron among your friends."

They laughed once again, but Henry could see the worry in her eyes. And, of course, she would be worried. If the accident occurred in her gym, who knows what her own liability might be, not to mention the bad press of a former diva getting hurt. Besides, as he had reason to know, performers could be so superstitious. A major injury could keep other clients away in droves.

"Why don't I buy you a cup of coffee?" he offered after looking at his watch. It was the least he could do. And he was getting hungry.

"Are you sure you have time?" His glance at his wrist had not escaped Lydia. "You must have a patient to see."

"Actually, I just finished up." He touched her arm gently and led her into the cafeteria nearby. "And Mimi's in Japan, doing *Sunday in the Park with George*."

He bought them each a cup of coffee, hers black, his with milk and sugar, and guided her to one of the molded plastic seats drilled into the waiting room floor. He sat down opposite her.

"What a jerk," Lydia said, taking a sip of the scalding liquid. "Mickey *is* a great doctor, but sometimes I could strangle him."

"I wouldn't worry about it," Henry said philosophically. "At some point, most people who deal with Mickey think they might strangle him. Luckily, 'indignation is a submission of our thoughts, but not of our desires.' "

She looked at him archly. "Thomas Fuller?"

"Excellent memory," he said, impressed that she remembered the name from their conversation the night of the benefit. "But, no, this time it's Bertrand Russell."

"How do you remember those things?" she asked.

"I was a philosophy major in college. We had to remember those things. After you study all that stuff, it's hard to wipe it out of your mind." He looked embarrassed. "I must sound terribly pompous. Sorry."

She raised an eyebrow. "What would you be sorry about? It's a treat to speak to someone with a brain."

"If months later, you remember Thomas Fuller from a casual exchange, I wouldn't say you exactly want for a brain yourself." He took a long gulp from his coffee cup and sat back as comfortably as possible in the molded chair.

"Please," she demurred, "I've been working toward being a dancer since I was eight years old. I know a *plié* and a *tour jeté*." She chuckled. "And I know how to piss people off. Now there's something I'm really good at."

He eyed her with curiosity. He could imagine a woman with a personality as strong as hers might be hard for some people to take. She certainly knew how to speak her mind, never anyone's favorite trait. But there was a warmth about her, an unpretentious quality, that made her immensely likable. In fact, he recalled his wife mentioning her after that benefit performance. Mimi had admired her professionalism and her skill at helping to organize the event. And his wife was a sharp judge of character.

He kept his thoughts to himself. "You know," he said after a pause, "if you're worried about pissing off Mickey Petersen, I wouldn't. I mean, I don't think it's actually possible."

"I don't think Mickey Petersen would feel a ten-ton Mack truck roll over his head," she said in agreement. "It wasn't him I was talking about." She smiled widely. "It was virtually everyone else I've ever met."

He laughed once again. He was finding this woman very entertaining. And very beautiful, he realized, observing the lean lines of her dancer's body, her dark hair pulled back in the obligatory dancer's bun, the cleanly etched high cheekbones of her face, and widely spaced hazel eyes.

"Everything's terrific," Mickey Petersen interrupted, as he walked through the doorway of the cafeteria.

Henry and Lydia both stood up.

"Our little Sonya's got a slight tendon problem, undoubtedly complicated by a nose candy problem," Petersen said assuredly. "I think the stuff she's been sniffing probably caused the fall."

"Can I take her home?" Lydia asked.

"Nosiree," Petersen answered back. "In fact, it would be better if you left her right here without even looking in." He seemed slightly abashed, even he knowing how amiss his next comment might be taken. "We don't like suspected druggies to visit with their friends."

"Jesus, Mickey," Lydia said disgustedly. "I'm her personal trainer, not her drug lord."

"Yeah, yeah," the doctor said placatingly. "I know that, you know that, Henry here probably knows that, but rules are rules."

Without another word, he walked out of the room.

"My God," Lydia exclaimed, "how the hell do you like that?"

"Listen," Henry said, turning to face her. "How about washing the taste of Petersen away with dinner?"

Lydia looked at him hesitantly, an unreadable expression in her eyes. "Gee, I'm not sure," she said.

"There's a French place on West Eighty-sixth," he said encouragingly. "It's never crowded, and it's really quite good."

"Mirabelle, right?" she replied knowingly. "Well . . ."

He took her arm and directed her toward the door. "Then shall we go?"

She seemed to make up her mind slowly.

"Let's do it," she agreed finally.

Let's do what? he wondered, alarmed and enchanted in equal measure as he took in the graceful curve of her back.

Chapter 17

At the sound of sudden screeching, Miranda looked up from the computer keyboard. Quickly realizing that the commotion was the sound of a car alarm going off beneath her windows on Fifth Avenue, she relaxed, stretching her arms above her head and giving in to a satisfying yawn.

Two-fifteen, she noted with surprise, taking in the time on the grandfather clock in the corner of the office. She'd been sitting there, working without stopping, since nine-thirty that morning. Wow, she thought, standing up for a longer body stretch, I haven't lost track of time that way since . . . Well, since ever, she realized. Perhaps her money troubles were going to be the end of her, but at least trying to solve them was proving to be an engrossing task.

Writing the Forrestor novel and sending it in to Highland Press had been so exciting. But after a few days had passed and she'd recovered from her exhaustion, reality set in. She could never duplicate Stephen's novels. The whole undertaking had been a fanciful delusion on her part.

Of course, it was wonderful to discover how much she loved writing. She'd always enjoyed her writing projects for the bank, but never in a million years would she have guessed that she would revel in writing fiction, just sitting there making up stories. And she had certainly learned about all sorts of things in the course of her research that she would never have known otherwise. Fingerprints, explosives, the back roads through Switzerland—it was completely removed from her life, and so much fun to absorb and write about.

Still, when all was said and done, she would probably be forced to admit that it had been an exercise in futility and a waste of time. She could just imagine the E-mail message that would come from Stephen's editor, Paul Harlow, after he read the manuscript. *What the hell has happened to Forrestor? Why can't he write anymore?*

Grimly, she realized that she couldn't just sit around waiting for that to happen. She'd given it her best shot. But she had to face the odds that her attempts at writing a novel would add up to a big fat nothing. The bills were still coming in, and she needed to find a way to pay them. For one glorious moment she had been a famous author, she reflected, even if it was only in her imagination. But what she really was was a woman who had once written promotional copy. Going back to it wouldn't solve all her financial problems by a long shot, and the notion of trying to get work scared her out of her wits. But she *had* to do something, and it was the fastest, most practical answer she could come up with.

It had taken all her courage to call Fred Salley, her old boss. He'll never even remember me, she'd told herself. And even if he did, why should he send any work my way? What with all those talented people out of work in every industry in the country including banking, why would Fred think he needed the help of Miranda Shaeffer?

But, miracle of miracles, he claimed he did. In fact, he not only assigned her two different brochures to write—one on trust operations, the other on high-interest-yield municipal bonds—but he suggested her to a friend of his at a Japanese-run bank on Park Avenue. That was the work she was finishing up this morning, writing a speech for the bank's chief financial officer, who had to address fifty business executives at a meeting in Scottsdale, Arizona, the following week. She had met with Foro Itami and two of his aides the previous morning, and had left his office with reams of notes on marketing initiatives for the middle market. It had pleased her to realize that she remembered more about the corporate side of banking than she would have thought.

Applying herself to the task for another twenty minutes, she was done. She wandered into the kitchen, grabbing a lemon yogurt out of the refrigerator and eating it slowly. If the speech she'd just finished was acceptable, it would mean a check for fifteen hundred dollars would be in her hands by the middle of next week. Adding that to the two thousand she'd gotten for her work for Fred, she realized she could at least cover part of one month's mortgage payment.

Which only left her about a gazillion dollars short. Yet, she felt lighter about it somehow; there was something she could actually *do* when the novel was turned down. True, she'd have to invent new hours in the day to do enough freelance writing to make a substantial difference. And that wouldn't cover all the money she needed anyway. Still, the feeling of hope wouldn't go away.

God, it felt good. How could she have forgotten how much pleasure there was in performing a task you actually knew something about? What she understood about writing fiction was a big fat nothing. What she had remembered, she realized with pleasure, about writing for banks was, actually, quite a lot.

She turned to look out the window. As her eyes passed over the antique ice chest the interior decorator just *knew* they couldn't live without, she caught sight of a picture of herself and Stephen taken a year after they'd gotten married. There she was, her hair an inch or so longer than it was now, her face smooth and happy, beaming like a typical newlywed. And Stephen looked young and handsome in the first decent suit he'd bought after he'd landed his job in advertising. She couldn't help but recall the happiness of that time, even now that Stephen had become such a mystery to her. She'd loved getting married, felt a kind of perfect pleasure when she had her children.

But, how ironic, she thought as she turned to gaze at the beautiful park view in front of her, she couldn't remember a single minute when she'd felt better about herself than now.

Chapter 18

"But what if nobody talks to me?" Ethan's slow shuffling walk matched the hesitation in his voice.

Miranda held his hand tightly as they walked up Madison Avenue toward Hunter. "Honey," she said reassuringly, "it's the first day of school. Everyone else will be exactly as scared as you are. That's the big secret to life." She smiled down at him. "Honest, sweetie."

At the corner of Ninety-fourth Street, they crossed. There was a large crowd hovering in front of the school building, most of them seeming to be looking in one direction.

"Hey, Mommy," Ethan cried out excitedly. "There's Patty Hetrick!"

Miranda peered into the ocean of people. She recognized the name of the lead singer from the Wreck, a popular rock band Jack had begun listening to. Having seen her on television a couple of times, Miranda recalled her as a tall woman with a wild mane of blond hair and the face of an angel. But when Miranda finally spotted the singer, the invectives rolling out of her mouth were not exactly angelic.

"So what the goddamn hell are you doing here?" Hetrick finally finished screaming at a tall man in a charcoal gray suit.

The man seemed unfazed, standing fast and responding in a quiet voice. "I'm enjoying the sight of my son on his first day of school, just as you are."

The small boy who stood in between them looked shell-shocked, a fact not lost on his father, who leaned down quickly and gave him a hug. "I'm gonna get going, Josh," he said softly, before standing up and nodding a curt good-bye to the boy's mother.

At the sound of a school bell, Patty Hetrick seemed to get herself calm in an instant, planting a kiss on her son's head and sending him inside. Miranda watched the sudden transformation, as did all the other parents.

"Mommy," Ethan said, absolutely ingenuously, as he tugged on her hand, "I bet I have more fun today than that mommy."

Miranda found herself laughing helplessly, as did a couple of the other mothers around her. She scooped her son up in her arms.

"I bet you're going to have the most fun you've ever had." She put him back on the ground and directed him toward the entrance. "See you later, darling."

A short, dark-haired woman in a gray trenchcoat smiled at Miranda. "What a stitch," she said enthusiastically.

Miranda's eyes filled with sentimental tears. "He's pretty great, all right," she answered.

"I'm Claire Bissinger," the woman said, putting out her hand. "How about we celebrate our children's first day with a doughnut and a cup of coffee?"

Why not, Miranda thought. In the rush of getting Ethan ready, she'd forgotten breakfast completely. "That would be good," she said. "I'm Miranda Shaeffer."

The two fell in step. "Boy, Josh Harlow's father must not have an easy time of it," Claire remarked as they walked.

"I think I must have missed something," Miranda said, confused. "Who are we talking about?"

"You know, Patty Hetrick's ex-husband. She seems like a pack of trouble." Claire led them toward a coffee shop on Madison Avenue.

Entering, they chose a booth in the corner.

Claire continued talking as she read the menu. "Josh is a nice kid, although that kind of fighting isn't going to leave him nice for long."

A waitress with a half apron tucked over her blue jeans came over and took their order, pancakes with sausage for Claire, a toasted corn muffin for Miranda.

"Gee," Claire said, eyeing Miranda with interest, "I'm surprised you eat at all. You must be one of those effortlessly thin types."

Miranda broke into laughter. "Me?" she said in surprise. "I've needed to lose thirty pounds since Ethan was born."

"You're nuts," Claire said cheerfully.

Miranda looked down at herself, suddenly noticing that she had lost some weight. The waistband of her tan slacks was awfully loose, and where she used to worry about bulges, her blouse now hung straight. Well, she thought bitterly, the hidden benefits of tragedy.

She wasn't about to discuss her troubles with a stranger. "You sound like you know the boy," she said, leading the conversation back to a subject less personal.

"Josh was in Montessori with my Zoe." She smiled at the mention of her daughter. "You know, those two were the only ones in pre-school to get into Hunter."

"I was proud of Ethan myself," Miranda admitted.

"And Zoe was very friendly with Josh Harlow. Paul Harlow used to call for play dates." She looked at Miranda smugly. "Even Patty herself called once."

Miranda was less interested in the name-dropping than she was in the name itself. So Josh's father is named Paul Harlow. How funny. Here she was, waiting to hear about her novel from a guy named Paul Harlow and here's a guy being berated on the street with the same name.

"What does he do for a living, Josh's father?" she asked, feeling like a small-town gossip.

"I don't know. I guess I never asked. It's the former Mrs. Harlow who's the star. She's Patty Hetrick, *the* Patty Hetrick." The woman's eyes sparkled with self-congratulation, as if she'd just explained the theory of relativity to Miranda in ten easy words or less.

"Is she really?" Miranda replied, managing to look impressed, but actually wondering if she'd just seen Forrestor's editor.

Chapter 19

"I don't want to go! You can't make me!"

Sophie hurled herself across the bed. "I'm not spending the day with a bunch of babies." Her voice was muffled by the bedclothes.

Miranda came in from the doorway where she had been standing. "This isn't supposed to be a vacation, you know," she said flatly. "Children who get suspended from school don't have much of a say in what they do with their day."

"It's not my fault I got suspended," Sophie whined.

"Really? Exactly whose fault is it?" Miranda responded in irritation. "We've spent a lot of time talking about these things you've been doing in school, and I warned you they wouldn't put up with it forever. Copying from Melissa Fowler's paper—honestly, Sophie, it doesn't even make sense." She couldn't help smiling slightly. "If you were going to cheat, you could at least have picked somebody worth cheating off of."

Sophie raised her head and gave Miranda a baleful glare to show how little she appreciated her mother's wit.

Miranda turned serious once more. "Whatever your reason, you'd better be sure it never happens again. In the meantime, I'm going on Ethan's class trip, so you're coming with me."

"Just leave me home," Sophie wailed.

Miranda walked to the door. "Be ready to go in five minutes."

When Miranda and Ethan arrived at the entrance to his school half an hour later it was with a sulking Sophie lagging behind. The three of them went to his classroom, where the children were lining up, a lengthy process that involved pairing off into buddies and a detailed explanation by Mrs. Oliver, the teacher, of the rules for traveling outside the school.

"Come in, Mrs. Shaeffer, Ethan." The teacher ushered them in with a welcoming motion of her arm. "We're nearly ready to go."

Miranda saw another mother standing at the end of the line, and gave her a small wave. This early in the school year she hadn't yet had a chance to meet many of the children or their parents, but she immediately recognized one of the little girls as the woman's daughter by their matching masses of curly blond hair and big blue eyes.

"Okay," said Mrs. Oliver, looking up at the clock above the chalkboard, "we're just waiting for Josh and his dad."

As she finished speaking, the door opened and in walked Paul Harlow and his son. Josh rushed ahead of his father to join a group of boys at the back of the line, the four of them quickly becoming absorbed in conversation over a plastic action figure Josh was holding in his hand.

"Hi, I'm sorry we're late," Paul said to the room in general.

Miranda watched him going over to exchange pleasantries with the teacher. She tried to imagine Stephen taking a morning off to go on a class trip with one of the children. Coming in with a relaxed, cheerful attitude about it, no less. She shook her head at the impossibility of the image. If this actually was Paul Harlow, *her* Paul Harlow, maybe he wasn't as bad as Stephen had always depicted him to be. How can I find out if he's my guy? she wondered, suddenly nervous. If he really was her editor, she was standing next to the person who held her entire future in his hands.

He came over to introduce himself. Miranda tried to conceal her nervousness as she shook his hand. The other mother joined them, and Miranda found out her name was Phyllis O'Malley just as they were all shepherded out of the room. Sophie followed behind her mother, a petulant expression on her face.

"You could try to be pleasant," Miranda said to her quietly as they exited onto the street. "Otherwise, it's going to be a very long morning for all of us."

"You could try to be pleasant," Sophie mimicked her in a singsong voice, screwing up her face.

Miranda gave her a sharp look. "Knock it off, Sophie."

A chaotic bus ride later, the class was on its way into the Central Park Zoo. It was a sunny, warm late September day, and the children

were bubbling over with the thrill of being outside. They went first
to the seals' tank, all the children scattering to find a good spot from
which to observe.

Talking with the children nearest her, Miranda suddenly realized
that Sophie was nowhere in sight. She looked around frantically.
Finally, she spotted her, off in the distance, already a good twenty
yards away. Miranda ran toward her, yelling her name. Sophie turned
around, apparently indifferent to her mother's concern.

"What on earth are you doing?" Miranda demanded angrily as
she caught up to the girl, placing a hand firmly on her shoulder. "Are
you *trying* to get lost?"

"I was looking for a water fountain," Sophie answered carelessly.

Miranda led her back toward the children. "You know better than
that." She deposited her next to Ethan and pointed a warning finger
at her. "Stay with us."

"Mommy, look." Ethan caught Miranda's hand and gestured toward a seal leaping for a fish.

"Yes, sweetheart, I see," Miranda answered.

She bent over to be at her son's eye level, pointing to the seal.
"See how he—"

"Yeow!" Ethan howled in pain as he was propelled almost into
Miranda's arms.

"What, what is it?" Miranda said, alarmed, unsure of what had
just happened.

His eyes were already filling with tears. "Sophie kicked me."

Miranda turned to her daughter, who was watching the seals,
seemingly oblivious to anything else. "Did you kick your brother?"
Her tone was icy.

Sophie gave her an innocent glance. "I don't think so. I stumbled
for a second, so maybe then."

"She kicked me hard!" Ethan was crying in earnest.

"This is the last time I'm going to tell you to behave." Miranda
straightened up. "Apologize to Ethan."

"Sure, sorry." She was unconcerned.

Miranda hugged the little boy as he wiped the tears from his
cheeks, his sobs already subsiding. It had always amazed Miranda
how quickly he recovered from most things.

Mrs. Oliver called out to the group. "Let's go over to the monkeys
now."

Sophie took Ethan's hand and walked ahead with him. Suddenly,
she's the devoted sister, Miranda thought exasperatedly as she looked

around, counting heads, making sure none of the children was straying.

She heard Phyllis O'Malley talking just over her shoulder and turned in the direction of the voice. Paul Harlow was with her, and as they approached, the three of them fell into step together.

". . . Nicholas will be competing in the national competitions next year," Phyllis was saying brightly.

"Oh?" Paul responded politely.

Phyllis leaned over to fill in Miranda. "My older son plays piano. Incredibly."

Miranda smiled. "How nice."

"Yes," Phyllis went on, "and Becky seems to be following right in his footsteps." She laughed. "We never dreamed we'd have *two* piano prodigies."

Glancing over in her daughter's direction, Phyllis apparently saw something that displeased her. With a frown, she excused herself and hurried over to Becky, who was holding hands with a friend, the two of them swinging their arms back and forth as high and fast as they could.

"Gee, I guess my son is a real slacker compared to those two," Paul said dryly. "I mean, naturally, he composes already, but he's always putting two *n*'s in 'sonata.' So irritating."

Miranda laughed. "I have to confess, Ethan doesn't even play an instrument."

"No!" Paul said in mock horror.

"Isn't that terrible?" she asked with a grin.

"Good God," he said, "that kind of lapse qualifies you as a total failure as a parent. Join the club."

She laughed again. He was nice, this Paul Harlow, and witty, she thought. Whether or not he turned out to be hers. She could remember Stephen calling him "a little weasel" when he had made some manuscript corrections that annoyed Stephen. She gave him a more direct look. About six feet, blond. A mighty good-looking weasel, she decided.

Her ruminations were interrupted by the sound of Sophie's yell. Miranda looked over to see her daughter lying on the ground, holding her knee, struggling hard not to cry. Ethan and some of the other children were standing around her, watching helplessly.

"Uh-oh, crisis time," Miranda called out to Paul as she hastened over. "What happened?" She bent down to examine the knee, which was scraped and bleeding.

"I fell." Sophie winced as her mother put a hand near the cut.

"She was walking on the chairs," one of the boys offered to Miranda, "jumping across them."

Miranda turned to see that they were near several outdoor tables and chairs set up for snacking. She looked back at Sophie. "You were doing what?"

"It hurts, Mommy," Sophie whined.

"Of all the ridiculous—come on, we'll wash it off. Stay here a second." She ushered the children over to Mrs. Oliver, explaining that she had to take her daughter to find a ladies' room.

Returning to Sophie, she took her hand and marched her to the nearest bathroom without a word. They stood in front of the row of sinks while Miranda wet a paper towel, then knelt to dab it on the girl's knee. She glanced up to see Sophie watching her with a sullen glare.

"Honestly, Sophie," Miranda exploded, "what's with you?"

Sophie stared at her for a few seconds, then burst into tears. She buried her head in Miranda's neck, hanging on to her for dear life. Stunned, Miranda put her arms around her, gently rubbing her back.

"Honey, there, there, sweetie, it'll be okay," she murmured. "Tell me what it is."

Sophie raised a wet face. "I miss *Daddy*. I want my Daddy."

She put her head back down, her sobs verging on hysteria.

Oh, God, the poor thing, Miranda thought, feeling guilty about how angry she'd been.

"I know, sweetheart, I know," she whispered in Sophie's ear, smoothing back her hair, damp with perspiration from the exertion of crying.

"I w-want him, M-mommy," she managed to get out. "I don't w-want him to be dead."

Miranda's eyes filled up with tears. All three children would be struggling with this for the rest of their lives. To be this young and lose a parent—how could she help them through it? He had been taken from them in an instant, and they were left to find their way alone. For the hundredth time, she wished she could afford to send them for professional counseling.

And she, too, would never have any sense of resolution. Any chance that he might ever have changed, might have gone back to the old Stephen, the man she had once loved so dearly, was also gone forever. She was surprised to realize that she had still harbored that hope.

An image of him at college came into her mind. She saw Stephen sitting in the student union, laughing loudly at something she said.

She recalled how her heart had turned over with happiness at the knowledge that she could make him laugh that way. *Oh, Stephen.* Tears spilled over from her eyes and she clasped Sophie to her, her own quiet crying drowned out by her daughter's choking sobs.

Miranda wiped away her tears and concentrated on Sophie, rocking her gently and stroking her back until the girl quieted down.

"Hey, look at us," Miranda said with a crooked smile, "we're a mess. Let's get cleaned up."

She rose and threw some water on her own face before wetting a paper towel for Sophie, giving her a quick hug as the girl slowly wiped her face, exhausted from her outburst.

"I'll throw that away for you," Miranda said, taking the used towel back.

"Thank you, Mommy." Sophie gave her mother a small smile. Despite her still-red nose and wet eyes, she seemed calm, almost happy, as if the release of emotion had been what she was waiting for.

"All right, my precious," Miranda said, taking her by the hand, "let's go back out and enjoy our visit here."

Sophie put her other hand over Miranda's as well as they walked. Touched by the gesture, Miranda paused to bend over and kiss the top of Sophie's head. She was rewarded with a broad grin as they emerged out into the sunshine. When they rejoined the group, Sophie actually skipped over to Ethan and watched the monkeys with him, the two of them pointing and talking animatedly.

The resilience of children is an astounding thing, Miranda thought, watching her. And God knows, they need it.

After watching the polar bears and the penguins, the class sat down on a row of benches to eat their lunch, the adults helping to get everyone settled. Finally, Mrs. Oliver sat at one end of the row and the three parents sat down together at the other.

Neither Miranda nor Paul had brought anything to eat for themselves, but Phyllis was prepared with a sandwich and a bottle of iced tea. She offered them both a bite of her turkey on pita bread, which they declined.

"So," she said to Paul, opening her drink, "what kind of work do you do when you're not at the zoo?"

Miranda held her breath, waiting for his answer. Thank you, Phyllis, she thought. I can't believe I was so nervous about blowing my cover, I never even considered asking such an innocuous question.

"I'm a book editor at Highland Press," Paul said, reaching over to open a milk container for the little girl sitting nearest him.

"Whoa," Miranda murmured under her breath. So it *was* her Paul Harlow. *You're my editor*, she screamed silently. *I'm your new Forrestor.*

But maybe he wasn't her editor after all; she still didn't know what he had thought of her manuscript. Maybe he loathed it, maybe he thought Forrestor had lost his mind sending in such drivel. *Oh, God.*

"How interesting," Phyllis was saying. "Do you work with any authors I might know?"

Paul leaned back on the bench, crossing one leg over the other and stretching them out in front of him. "Patrick Trent for one. Doris Hennings."

Phyllis brightened. "Oh, yes, Doris Hennings. I like her."

Paul squinted off into the distance at something. "And you might know Forrestor."

"Forrestor? The one who nobody knows who he is?" Phyllis asked excitedly. "My husband loves his books. They're the only thing he reads. If you could tell me who he really is, Larry would be thrilled out of his mind. I swear we would never tell a soul."

Miranda sat very still, not wanting to risk interrupting their conversation with even the slightest movement.

Paul had a bemused expression. "I couldn't if I wanted to. I don't have any idea who he is."

Phyllis looked at him in disbelief. "Oh, you have to."

He shook his head. "Nope, it's the truth. He hasn't chosen to let me in on the secret."

Phyllis digested this disappointing piece of news. "Well, Larry will still be interested to know I met you. Can you tell me if there's a new one coming out soon? And what's it about? That would be a scoop of sorts."

Paul stood up, ready to start collecting the children's empty drink containers and garbage. *Aren't you going to answer her?* Miranda asked silently, feeling frantic. *Tell her if there'll be another one.*

Paul smiled. "Yes, there's a new one, absolutely. And I can tell you that it's far and away the best book Forrestor's ever written."

He turned to attend to the children.

Miranda sat there, too shocked to move. There couldn't be any mistake. He was talking about her manuscript. So she had done it. She had written the new Forrestor. *The best book Forrestor's ever written.* It was almost impossible to believe, she thought, torn between wanting to jump for joy and collapse with relief.

She fought to sort through the jumble of emotions that threatened to overwhelm her. It wasn't just that she had written a book. The truth was she had spent her whole life as a participant in other people's dreams. Her mother, Lydia, Stephen—all of them had carried her along with them, and she had gone willingly. Now, in an instant, she understood that nothing would ever be the same.

Phyllis rose, crumpling up the brown paper bag in which she had packed her lunch. "Wait till I tell Larry who I met today. He'll be so excited."

Miranda could only nod.

Chapter 20

"What's the zip code?" Cradling the receiver between his ear and shoulder, Stephen wrote directly onto the manila envelope as the secretary finished giving him the address. "Thanks."

He hung up the telephone and sealed the envelope with tape. He lightly bounced the thick package up and down in one hand, admiring its compact weight. Two hundred pages of a new manuscript, *the* manuscript, accomplished in less than six months. He'd had no idea the writing would go so smoothly and fast.

And the kicker, he thought with an inward chuckle, is that it's so goddamned *good*.

"If I do say so myself," he said aloud to the empty room. "No need for false modesty."

Smiling, he got up from the desk and stretched. Tomorrow the pages would be on their way to Laura French in New York. As far as he was concerned, no one else even came close to touching her reputation as the premier literary agent for serious books. She was *it*. And she was the one he wanted representing *To the Edge*. He knew her practiced eye would spot it as the real thing. With her clout, he would be on his way.

It was too bad that Stephen Shaeffer would never be the name that got famous, but he would settle for being known under the name he had adopted, Stephen West. His choice had been an homage to the writer Nathanael West; Stephen had always admired *Miss Lonely-*

hearts and *Day of the Locust*, and West had been successful in his day, recognized as a talent before his death, certainly a career to emulate.

He left the bedroom that served as his office and went into the living room, going over to the bar in the far corner to pour himself a glass of Glenfiddich. Then he lit up one of the Havana cigars he had recently begun smoking, and stretched out on the beige sofa, a broad grin on his face. The single-malt Scotch had a smoky taste that went perfectly with the cigar. He smoked and drank contentedly, thinking that he couldn't remember a time in his life when he had felt as satisfied with everything as he did now. He was only sorry he hadn't come to Los Angeles back when he was young and single. Everything would have been so different. But no matter; at least he was here now.

Coming to Los Angeles had been more of an accident than anything else. Wanting to put as much distance as possible between himself and New York after he left, it had seemed the logical choice. The weather was good, and there was plenty to do, so it was the right kind of place to build a new life. Still, he had been unprepared for how much he would love it.

Arranging his own death had been so easy, he continued to marvel at it. He had simply strolled out of the bank building, walked right past the gathering crowds, and taken a taxi to Midway Bank. That was where he kept the bulk of his money, in an account under the name David Ogilvy, one of his earlier heroes in advertising. Now that the moment of his freedom had come, he was sorry there wasn't more money put aside. But he'd done pretty well, considering. *Stranger from the East* had brought in only five thousand dollars, and his second book, only forty thousand. The third book advance had jumped to five hundred thousand, which led to his most recent three-book deal for five million. That was when the real money finally started coming in.

He'd gotten two million of that just for signing the contract. The deal was set up so that he got paid an additional million every time he submitted one of the three manuscripts and it was accepted by the publisher. He'd already collected two million on his fourth and fifth book. God, he thought, what a crime to have to walk away from that last million. But this opportunity was only going to knock once. He couldn't be shortsighted about it.

Unfortunately, taxes had cut his money nearly in half. Then, he'd put down two million dollars on the Fifth Avenue apartment, and was still paying a mortgage of another million. When all was said and done, he was able to put away six hundred thousand dollars in the Ogilvy accounts.

He had his fallback position as well, the other secret account, but he was hesitant to use it. He'd known full well that if a divorce or some other marital problem suddenly blew up in his face, he would be in trouble if he couldn't produce some money. Claiming he had nothing would look far too suspicious. A moderate-sized bank account would be more believable. He had hedged his bets by opening the account using his middle name, Alanson, instead of Stephen. Miranda would probably never have found out about it, but if push came to shove, he could have claimed there was nothing secretive about an Alanson Shaeffer account. He'd say there'd been some kind of administrative mix-up at the bank, and he hadn't seen any reason to correct it since it was still his name. That account held another five hundred thousand.

For now, though, the Ogilvy accounts were his cushion. He had simply strolled into Midway and withdrawn nine thousand dollars, an amount that wouldn't attract any unnecessary attention to him. Another cab ride to Kennedy Airport, and he was on a flight to LAX within two hours. Stephen West checked into the Bel Air Hotel that night, and checked out a week later to move into a furnished, three-bedroom house in Beverly Hills.

The monthly rental bill for the house and its contents was an exorbitant amount, but it was worth every penny. He loved the feeling of luxury that surrounded him, and had even taken up jogging for a few weeks just so he could get a better look at the magnificent houses nearby. Everything about the atmosphere energized him. It felt great to wake up to the glow of the sunshine and sounds of the birds, to throw on his robe and take his fresh-squeezed orange juice outside to admire the palm trees. He hadn't realized how *imprisoned* he'd felt in New York, but it was as if he had suddenly been set free.

He had spent much of his time in the first month glued to the television, following the news. It turned out that the explosion at the bank building was actually a terrorist bombing. He was astounded to think of the randomness with which fate had handed him this choice, and the miracle of his cheating actual death. Fifty-seven people had been killed that day—fifty-eight if you counted Stephen Shaeffer, which, he saw gleefully, everyone had.

It was an incredible experience, watching the reports on the victims with himself included on the list. Three other bodies hadn't been recovered along with Stephen Shaeffer's, an especially tragic note, pointed out the reporters. Two weeks after it happened, rescuers were still digging in the hope of finding any other remains or information.

Stephen had had no idea what a big story this would turn out to be. It was everywhere, in the newspapers, on the cover of *Time*, on the radio when he was driving. It consumed the attention of the entire country. Stephen sat in front of the television every evening, a glass of wine in his hand, mesmerized by it all. Then, little by little, profiles of the victims began appearing. Most of them had worked in the building, but a dozen or so were visiting there as he had been. He sat, rapt, as a picture of him sitting in his office at Colby & Cummings began appearing on various stations when they mentioned him, as descriptions of his life grew more elaborate and flattering, as his friends and acquaintances paraded across the screen. He was alternately touched and disgusted by what he saw. The pious posturing of his old boss from the agency, the crocodile tears of people who barely knew him, escalating their relationship retroactively until they sounded like lifelong buddies, it was all almost surreal. Naturally, there was no mention made of Forrestor, but only of Stephen as a successful consultant—and he was amused to see how much more successful he sounded with every retelling.

The sight of his parents gave him pause. They looked tense and unhappy as they talked briefly to a reporter outside their apartment building one afternoon. He reminded himself that everything had its price, and not seeing them again was the one he had to pay in order to pursue his dream.

When the people responsible for the bombing were captured, Stephen watched, riveted. He studied each of the five men, furious and frightened at how close they had come to killing him. Yet, bizarrely, he owed them a debt; they had given him this second chance at life.

In the parade of grieving spouses who sobbed before the cameras, he soon realized that Miranda was conspicuously absent. Maybe she hadn't loved him as much as she'd always claimed. Or maybe, he reflected, she was annoyed because she'd realized she'd have to get off her duff and earn a living. It made him resent her even more to see that she was above giving interviews the way everyone else did. The newspeople were depicting him as a loving husband and father, but his own wife wouldn't say a few kind words about him on the air or anywhere in print. Clearly she was keeping the kids away from the press as well. How did that make him look? Boy, when it really counted, she sure didn't do right by him. Now he was sorry he couldn't see her face when she found out that there wasn't any money to be had.

"I spoiled the four of you rotten," he muttered to his family as he watched the outside of their building on Fifth Avenue flash on the screen. "Hey, Miranda baby, now you see what it's like to earn a living."

The whole business only confirmed that he had done the right thing by seizing the moment. Finally, the story died down. By the time six months had passed, his life in New York had begun taking on the qualities of an old dream. He rarely thought of it, preferring to look ahead to when he would be established again, this time in a whole new orbit of influence. Living in a place where he felt he truly belonged.

Of course, part of what was so great about being here, he soon realized, was being involved in the action. Sunshine was one thing, but the women and the parties, the whole lifestyle, made him feel twenty again, free and ready to try anything.

And he owed much of that to Toby, no question about it. He couldn't imagine what would have happened if he had tried to break into any kind of social circles without him. If you weren't rich, famous, or connected in the movie business, you were pretty much nothing out here. He'd learned that right away. He'd get as many women being a short order cook as an unknown novelist. None. In fact, he had resolved that after this book was accepted, he would write a screenplay before going on to his next book. He needed the cachet, and if he could excel at both the Forrestor books and serious literature, he figured he could damned well do a commercial screenplay, too. He had frequently lied about having a script in production, but so did plenty of people. It would be helpful to have an actual screen credit. The time spent accomplishing that would be a wise investment in his future.

But thanks to Toby, he had been spared having to struggle along on the social periphery. Back in New York, he would have died before he would have let some twenty-nine-year-old guy show him the ropes. Out here it was different.

Stephen knew it was dumb luck that had brought Toby to him, the day they had backed their cars into each other in a downtown parking lot. Stephen had only been in L.A. for a few weeks, and he was still nervous about the potential of being found. Inside his newly leased BMW, he had cursed savagely, worried about the police attention a car accident might bring if the other guy turned out to be a jerk.

But a tall young man with shoulder-length black hair had gotten out of the Mercedes with an easygoing smile and introduced himself as Toby Wyans. As Stephen would find out later, very little actually upset Toby. It turned out that Toby wasn't the owner of the car, and he said that the friend from whom he had borrowed it was getting rid of it anyway and wouldn't care. They wound up laughing about it and going off to a bar Toby knew of—a very hip one, Stephen could immediately see by the clientele—to drink shots of tequila.

Toby was filled with the kind of information Stephen wanted. Stephen casually mentioned that he was a newcomer, but free and hoping to enjoy himself a bit. Without a trace of condescension, the other man began filling him in on some of the new restaurants and private clubs, subtly dropping them into the conversation as if they both already knew what he was talking about. Stephen insisted on taking him out to dinner, and, afterward, Toby took him to one of the hottest nightspots. Judging by the parade of well-known actors and models, it appeared that only the famous or the super-beautiful were being admitted to the club. But Toby was immediately waved in. At that instant, Stephen realized what this guy could mean for him in getting properly connected.

Over the next few nights, Toby continued leading the way to what seemed like every desirable social scene. When he happened to mention that he had to get out of his current apartment in a week or so, it was a short leap to Stephen's suggesting that he move into Stephen's third bedroom until he got settled.

Stephen was intoxicated by it all, drinking in the energy, the sense of being at the center of the action. Recalling the staid evenings he used to spend with his wife, he cringed. Now, when he chose to, he had brief and wonderfully satisfying affairs with incredible-looking women, blond, tanned, and impossibly thin beneath the swell of silicone breast implants. It was one big fantasy come to life. When he thought of how young he was when he got married, he wanted to bang his head against the wall for being such an idiot. He had missed out on so much. But one of the unexpected benefits of his supposed death was getting another crack at being single again. This time, he was doing it right.

Hiding his identity turned out to be no trick at all. He had dyed his hair blond and grown a beard. But it seemed almost unnecessary. No one pressed for details of his past. In fact, he got the impression most of the people he met were lying about themselves. He had the money to show them a good time, and that was enough.

But, despite the parties and late nights, he never lost track of why he had come to California. He had been determined to stick to a work schedule, and he was proud of himself for having done it. Six hours a day, he blocked out everything else to concentrate on the lives of his characters, a man and woman, married to other people, having an affair that tore apart both their families. He hadn't finished it yet, but he didn't want to appear too eager by doing all the work before showing it to an agent. The two hundred pages were powerful enough to get him a major deal, he knew it beyond the shadow of a doubt.

Getting up, he set his drink on the end table and pulled his wallet out of his pocket. He extracted a slip of paper with a name and telephone number on it. Merilee Summer was an aspiring actress he had met at a party in Malibu the previous week. Aside from being astonishingly beautiful, she was charmingly innocent and had a way of making him feel good just talking to her.

She answered on the fourth ring. ''Hello?''

''Hello.'' Stephen kept his tone casual. ''It's Stephen West. From Adrian Monsey's party.''

He was pleased to note that she made the connection in only a few seconds. ''Oh, hi, Stephen. How are you?''

He engaged her in conversation about her efforts to get acting work, a process she went on about at length while he made encouraging noises. When he finally got around to asking her out to dinner for that Thursday night, she accepted eagerly. Stephen found that refreshing; she didn't have that jaded way about her that some of his dates made certain to display.

He got off the telephone and downed the rest of his drink in one gulp. ''Life is good,'' he murmured.

Toby emerged from his bedroom, where he had been taking a nap, his habit most afternoons, and one he could indulge since he didn't work. Stephen was still unclear about where he got his income from, but felt it was wiser not to press the issue.

He gave Stephen his usual cheerful smile. ''I'm going over to Fred Segal. I need some new pants. Want to come?''

''Sure, why not?'' Stephen retrieved his sunglasses from a small table near the door.

Toby drove the BMW. Once inside the store, the two of them began trying on clothes. Stephen picked out a new black jacket. Most of the clothing he bought now was black, and he tried to restrict his choices to Hugo Boss and Ermenegnildo Zegna. He got a huge kick out of his new look, so completely different from his old wardrobe, the suits and preppy sportswear. Doing the right thing in New York was a serious matter. Here it was equally important, but somehow, it was just so much damned *fun*.

They piled up their selections and waited for the salesman to total them up. Along with the jacket, Stephen had picked out two new shirts, a belt, and a black blazer.

"That will be three thousand and twelve dollars and fifty-eight cents, please," the salesman said.

Smiling inwardly, Stephen pulled out the new Visa card Stephen West had just obtained. He could well afford the clothes. He could afford a whole new life, one better than he'd ever guessed existed.

He handed his charge card over to the salesperson, a suitably bored expression on his face.

Chapter 21

Miranda stood at the back of the chilly classroom, watching Ethan talk to Valerie Ng, whose feet barely touched the floor in front of their shared wooden desk. Early December had turned unexpectedly cold in the past couple of days, and Hunter's heating system hadn't quite caught up. Children were so unaware of temperature, she probably wouldn't have heard a thing about it if parents hadn't been invited in this morning to admire their children's artwork. Miranda had been suitably impressed by the picture of a watermelon, perched atop a bridge, which her young Picasso had signed with a flourish, "Fruit atop the Tappan Zee."

She smiled as she watched him. Even she could admit that his future might not lie in the world of painting, but the fact that he had even remembered the name of the bridge an hour north of their apartment was a sign of his intelligence. "*Ciao, bello,*" a friendly Italian woman had called after him as they left the Madison Avenue bus one day. "*Grazie,*" he'd replied as nonchalantly as if he had just arrived from the streets of Rome.

It was exciting to think where her son's intellectual gifts might lead him as he grew up. She couldn't help thinking about how proud Stephen would be if he had lived to see it. Maybe he wasn't as attentive a father as he might have been, but surely he would have been as thrilled as she was. A sudden gust of wind tore through the classroom. The voice of God chiding her for assuming anything at all about her husband, she thought as she buttoned up her peacoat.

She looked over again to Ethan, relieved that he still wore the bulky green ski jacket she'd bought at his insistence the week before. "I'm too old for a snowsuit," he'd cried when she'd tried to get him into the one from last year. The fact that he hadn't removed the new jacket voluntarily since he'd gotten it was a measure of how much he loved it. And he did look adorable in it, she thought, bemused by her vanity on her children's behalf. But it wasn't just that he was so cute. He was happy.

Happy was not a word she could apply to her two older children. For Sophie and Jack, the months since Stephen's death had been a time of misery. Sophie finally seemed to be coming to some kind of terms with it, thank goodness, she thought, unconsciously holding her hand to her heart, but for Jack every awful day still seemed to last an eternity.

She watched with pleasure as Ethan and Valerie spread a coat of fingerpaints on their enormous square of white paper, eagerly filling in each other's outlines. In her head, Miranda knew that Ethan, too, would bear the repercussions of his father's terrible end, but for now, for this cold, sunny morning, it was nice to see at least one of her children apparently carefree. It was time for her to leave, she realized, relieved to know that Ethan probably wouldn't even notice she had gone.

"But, Daddy, I want to go home with you."

As she turned to go, Miranda heard the bitter protestation from the boy at the desk just behind her. His back to her, he had buried his face in his father's chest. As the father attempted to disentangle himself, she realized that they were Paul Harlow and his son, Josh. She could see Paul's look of recognition as he noticed her standing there, though his smile to her was the wan attempt of a parent under siege.

"We never have a whole day together," Josh continued, his anger turning to the whining noise that comes when losing an argument is inevitable.

Paul spoke softly in response. "Honey, we had all weekend together." He picked his son up and hugged him closely but with finality. Then put him down, settling him in his desk chair. "We'll have all of Christmas vacation, which is really, really soon."

The boy looked up at him sulkily, not yet ready to give in, as his father took a furtive glance at his watch. Miranda could see the slight desperation in his light blue eyes. He probably has a meeting or something, she thought, feeling sorry for him.

"You know," she said, walking over to the boy, "Ethan told me that Mrs. Oliver is doing macaroni math this morning." Her youngest son adored the numbers game the clever young teacher had created, using dry noodles as parts of a makeshift abacus. She hoped it was a bright spot in Josh Harlow's school day as well.

Sure enough, his face brightened. His father picked up on the signs of impending happiness immediately, ruffling the boy's hair and beginning to back away.

"Ready for me to leave, slugger?" he asked, the sweetness in his voice belying the impatience Miranda was sure he felt.

Josh shook his head, not quite willing to look cheerful about it, but already pulling toward him his half of the large white paper and tray of fingerpaints started by his desk partner.

"See you Thursday night," Paul called out from the entrance to the room, holding the door for Miranda, who had followed him out.

Josh waved without even turning around. Already he was engrossed in the thick coat of purple paint he'd laid upon the bare white surface.

Paul looked at Miranda appreciatively as they walked up the corridor. "Without you, I think I might have been there until three or so," he said. "It's Miranda, right?"

"Yes," she answered, feeling awkward suddenly. It was so odd. She knew quite a lot about Paul Harlow. For several weeks, they'd been exchanging E-mail. She'd seen up close how his mind worked, how he dissected a problem, what his editorial instincts were like. But, of course, to him, she was a complete stranger. One more mother from a school trip to the zoo. She felt like running off without saying another word, as if talking to him might expose her. But, just as quickly, the instinct vanished, replaced by an unexpected sense of antic freedom bubbling up.

She pulled open the doors that led to Park Avenue and he fell in step beside her. He stopped as they neared the curb, raising his hand to hail a cab. "Can I drop you off on my way downtown?" he asked.

The "no" was almost out of her mouth when a freezing blast of wind sent the litter lining the sidewalk into a torrent of activity.

"Well, okay," she said as a yellow cab pulled to the side of the street. "If you could just drop me on the corner of Seventy-fifth."

"Easy," Paul replied, opening the door of the cab and holding it for her.

They were silent for a few blocks, but as the taxi stopped for a red light at Eighty-eighth Street, he looked down at the ring on her left hand.

"You must not think much of my fathering skills," he commented, shifting uneasily in his seat. "It's hard with a broken home . . ." He shook his head unhappily. "I guess it's something you don't have to deal with."

She regarded her wedding band. It hadn't occurred to her to remove it. "Actually," she said, "my husband died earlier this year." She looked over at him and smiled in commiseration. "You'd be amazed at how much I've found out about children acting badly in public." She chuckled a little, adding, "and in private. And in the tub. And in the library . . ."

They laughed together, but she understood that the seriousness that underlay her own attempt at wit was matched by Paul Harlow's feeling of helplessness.

"It must be hard for your kids, losing a father. How old are your other kids?"

"Ten and eight. Actually, almost eleven and nine." She continued as she saw the interest in his eyes. "And, yes, it has been very hard for Jack and Sophie."

He looked at her intently. "And, I would guess, for you."

The statement caught her off guard. You could call it hard, she wanted to answer, finding out your husband had somehow divested you of your life savings and was sleeping with an old friend of the family. And, yes, it was hard, having to come up with fifty or seventy-five thousand dollars just to keep your kids in school and the overpriced roof over your heads. Or it had been, she amended, thinking of the enormous check she had received for the Forrestor manuscript just a few weeks before. *You saved my life*, she wished she could say to the man sitting next to her. Unexpectedly, the thoughts of what a roller coaster it had all been made her smile.

He regarded her oddly. "You know, within the last three or four seconds, you've had five different expressions on your face. I would love to know what was going on in your head."

Miranda looked away self-consciously, relieved to see that they'd arrived at Seventy-fifth Street. "Well, we'll have to save it for the next class trip," she said, " 'cause this is my corner."

She began to open the door of the cab, but Paul reached across and lay his fingers on her hand.

"Listen," he said, "I have tickets for a screening of the new Scorsese movie tonight." He had the grace to look slightly abashed. "An editorial perk. Do you think you'd want to come with me?"

Miranda felt the weight of his hand on top of hers, the nearness of his body suddenly overwhelming her. She looked back at him, at the laugh lines at the corners of his blue eyes, the blond hair that was a week or so overdue for a cut. He was remarkably attractive. She felt herself caught up in emotions she hadn't experienced in fifteen years or more. During her marriage to Stephen, she'd never once thought of another man romantically.

It made no sense, but having Paul Harlow so close to her made her feel more threatened than flattered for some reason. Suddenly, she was afraid that if she didn't get out of the cab within the next two seconds, she would faint. Pushing past his hand, she opened the door, bursting out of the cab as if escaping from a fire. "I'm sorry," she managed to breathe, intending to say more but finding she couldn't think of what to add.

Walking quickly up Seventy-fifth Street, she didn't dare look back, didn't want to see the taxi pulling away. She felt like a five year old who'd just made a terrible fool of herself and vowed to put it out of her mind. I have three children to raise and another book to write and . . . She stopped at the stoop of an elegant redbrick townhouse, trying to collect her thoughts. What I have, she acknowledged as her breathing returned to normal, is complete and total terror.

Paul Harlow looked impatiently at his watch. In two minutes he would be taking his place at the editorial board meeting, and he still didn't have the papers he needed. The final accounting of Calvin Lambert's first novel, which Paul had published five years earlier, should have been readily available, but Highland's inefficient conversion from written records to computerized database had made it nearly impossible to find even the most basic facts about any title published more than four years before.

"Got it!"

Paul stood up, relieved at the sound of his assistant's voice just outside. As she always did, Julie Lipson bounded in. Gratefully he reached out for the sheaf of papers in her outstretched hand. Taking another quick peek at his watch, he thanked her warmly and strode out of his office. As he walked down the long corridor, he scanned the royalty statement for *Wider Than A Mile*. He frowned as he took in the numbers. Despite some good reviews, Calvin Lambert's novel had generated sales of only four thousand copies or so.

Paul sighed as he seated himself at the large oak table. As eager as he was to buy *Trust*, Lambert's second novel, he knew these sales figures were not going to make it any easier. Placing the papers on the table, he turned and nodded hello to Jim Calabrese, Highland's publisher, who appeared to be skipping through the last few pages of a proposal for a book on sleep disorders that Paul had read the night before. Too insubstantial, he had thought, but it would be interesting to hear Jim's reaction. The older man often surprised his staff with his idiosyncratic observations. In fact, Paul reflected, Jim's had been the only supportive voice when Forrestor's first novel had come before the board.

Priscilla Mays, Highland's cookbook expert, took the seat to Paul's left. Like so many women in New York, she dressed in black most of the time, and today was no exception. Watching her run a graceful hand through her shoulder-length hair reminded him of something. The image of Miranda Shaeffer came into his mind.

He'd surprised himself that morning, coming on so strong in the cab. Since his marriage had dissolved, he'd been almost immune to beautiful women. With one or two exceptions, that is, he acknowledged disgustedly as he watched Tally Barber slip into the seat across from his. The few dates a couple of months before had left a bitter taste.

Tally had been coming out of a divorce of her own, and begged Paul to help her through a hard time. Their relationship as professional colleagues had never been especially close, but knowing all too well how great her pain must be, he wasn't about to refuse. But after their third dinner, which consisted of very little food and two bottles of wine, they'd fallen into bed together. Overnight, her requests became demands, her helplessness pure entitlement.

Paul felt guilty about their sexual encounter. A woman just out of a marriage was far too vulnerable to treat so casually. So he'd spent more evenings with her, though always in a restaurant. But that wasn't what Tally wanted. "You just *have* to come up," she would murmur hungrily as he dropped her off in front of her building.

As gently as he could, Paul began to turn down her dinner invitations. Neither of them was ready for another relationship, he'd say each time she asked him out. Tally would have none of it. Finally, she'd insisted on one last date, dinner at a cozy French restaurant not far from her apartment. Without warning, she started to berate him for his inattention, blaming him for her unhappiness. As he sat numbly silent, her fury escalated. He was out to ruin her life.

Tally wasn't just lonely, he realized belatedly as he listened to her charges. She was outrageous, highly manipulative, and more than a little crazy. Since that last encounter, Tally had become his enemy, demeaning the projects he brought to the editorial board, scattering innuendos about his personal life among their colleagues, going up against him at every turn. And doing it with the subtle brilliance that made her such a clever editor. Just as she could spot the weaknesses of a manuscript, almost burn them out with the heat of her invectives, so she could set about to destroy someone she'd identified as an adversary.

How nice it would be to have a woman like Miranda Shaeffer at his side. Someone intelligent and attractive. A woman who had clearly gone through pain of her own, yet exuded not just grace but generosity. He hated to think what he and his son would have done without her this morning. He envisioned her face once again. Were her eyes blue or green? he wondered, easily recollecting the particular tilt of her nose, the perfect slenderness of her neck.

Better file it under "never gonna happen," he thought, trying to will himself to reality. But she was such a mystery. So self-confident and competent each time he'd seen her around their children, yet like a frightened deer when he'd reached out to her as a woman.

Not too full of yourself are you, he thought suddenly, almost laughing out loud at his own presumption. What makes me so certain she's frightened, he wondered. More likely, she's just not interested. For another moment, he allowed himself to imagine her there beside him, the fresh scent of her shampoo barely noticeable in the air, the hint of a smile on her lips just before she spoke.

"How many miles away are you right now?"

Embarrassed to realize the remark had been addressed to him, Paul looked up at Karen Schultz, the short, prematurely gray-haired woman who headed up the children's division. She smiled cheerfully at him as she settled herself in a chair at the end of the table.

"I'm right here." Paul smiled at her affectionately. Karen had been a good friend in the last days of his marriage. Without being intrusive, she had managed to be there when he needed someone to confide in. Sure, he would have gotten through the divorce without her, but it would have been with much less understanding and a lot more wasted anger.

Sam Cooper and Morton Vishinsky, both senior editors, sat together as they always did, grumbling about the heavy returns Highland had been experiencing. The fact that bookstores actually bought books on consignment—and those copies that didn't move off the shelf fast enough could be returned to Highland Press, the bookstore's money returned in full—was the bane of every publisher's existence. Sam looked over to Tally Barber in greeting, and she smiled sweetly in return, then went on to acknowledge everyone else in the room.

With the pointed exception of himself, Paul noticed. He wondered if anyone else had picked up on it. It wasn't Tally's style to advertise her animosity. In fact, that the bitterness was so well hidden made it even more effective.

The board discussed several projects before Paul brought up the subject of *Trust*. As was the custom, everyone at the table had read the partial manuscript.

"I thought it was terrific," Sam commented as soon as Paul mentioned the title. "Better even than the first one, and that one was great."

Paul nodded in agreement. "As far as I'm concerned, Lambert's getting better and better. The first book was promising, but this one really delivers. Stronger characters, a more tightly constructed plot." He chuckled slightly. "I'm usually the first one to laugh at reviewers who call writing 'lyrical' but I'll be damned if that's not what this is."

"Here, here," Sam agreed, nodding his head for emphasis.

"How did the first one do?" Tally's low voice was almost inaudible at first.

"What's that, Tally?" Jim Calabrese turned to her, as did everyone else at the table.

Tally looked up at the publisher. "I asked Paul how *Wider Than A Mile* had sold," she replied, her soft smile suggesting sadness that such a question even had to be asked.

"The first one sold about four thousand copies," Paul responded honestly.

Tally smiled once again. "Most of which went to libraries."

Paul regarded her with equanimity. "That's right."

"What are you trying to say?" Jim interrupted their exchange and peered at Tally.

"I guess I have a little less faith in Mr. Lambert's literary future than my esteemed colleague. The line between lyrical and overheated is a thin one."

Tally turned to Jim, the shifting folds of her white cashmere sweater momentarily bringing his attention to her perfectly shaped breasts. "We all know how rough the industry's gotten, how high returns are, how much money we throw away on hopeless projects."

"I would hardly call a second novel by a well-received author 'a hopeless project,'" Paul answered sharply.

"How much does Lambert's agent want for this?" Jim asked,

picking up his pencil and starting to sketch a dollar sign on the yellow pad in front of him.

Paul saw the gleam of satisfaction in Tally's eyes as he answered. When the publisher asked how much something cost this early in a discussion, it usually meant he was ready to reject something out of hand. "Lambert's agent would settle somewhere between forty and fifty thousand," he answered.

"Of course," injected Tally, "that's just the advance. Then there's the production costs, the ads, the tour, the jacket art. And you know how stores do their ordering. If they ordered five thousand books last time out and sold two thousand, this time they'll order only two thousand and return one to us. There's no way this book is going to pay for itself."

Jim cleared his throat, intending to speak, but Paul got there before him.

"As we all know," he said quietly, "very few novels pay for themselves. You have to give an author some room, especially an author this talented."

Paul's eyes sought out the publisher, then took on Tally directly. "Every novel has its detractors. But *Wider than A Mile* was praised by scores of critics. Keeping a guy like Lambert from publishing would be criminal."

"Economically, it's criminal to throw good money after bad. No one wanted to read *Wider than A Mile*, reviews or no reviews, and no one's going to read the new one."

Jim cleared his throat. "I'm afraid Tally may have a point here, Paul," he said soberly.

Tally looked at Paul triumphantly.

Jim continued, his tone conciliatory but firm. "Nowadays, if you don't make it first time out of the gate, you probably don't stand a chance."

Paul sat in silence for a moment, then grinned. "You mean like Scott Turow and John Grisham?"

"Exactly," Sam interrupted from the far end of the table. "Nobody would have bet on *One L* or *A Time to Kill*. Then they came up with *Presumed Innocent* and *The Firm*."

Tally kept her eyes on Paul. "You're not claiming that Lambert has the makings of a Grisham or Turow? For God's sake, they're commercial. I don't see prose this *lyrical*"—she tossed the word out derisively—"becoming a major best seller."

"Well," Paul answered, "Toni Morrison might be surprised to hear that."

He switched his attention to Jim. "Actually, I'd be the last person to claim that *Trust* will sell a hundred thousand copies. But I bet it does a little better than *Wider than A Mile*. And his next one will do even better than that."

He turned back to Tally, who refused to return his glance.

"As we both know, writers with talent build their own constituency." An edge of irony came into his voice. "And, unlike the commercial guys, they don't cost millions. We're talking about less money for Calvin Lambert than Forrestor gets for one sale in Belgium, for Christ's sake."

At the mention of the best-selling author, Jim Calabrese's cheeks reddened slightly. Paul saw that Tally was taking in the change in his expression. Smoothly, she honeyed her words. "Paul, you're absolutely right. The big fish pay for the small fish and they always have. I'd be the last person to stand in the way of a guy like Lambert."

Jim regarded her curiously. "I'm glad to hear it, although I have to admit I'm a little surprised."

"I like surprising you, Jim," she responded, laying her hand lightly on his arm for just a moment. "After all, if you can always predict what someone will say, why have them around at all?" Her musical laugh sailed through the room.

Paul watched the performance with disgust and stayed silent through the rest of the meeting. When it ended an hour later, he was grateful to go back to his own office. He found himself frowning as he reached for the phone. Not that he wasn't delighted to be dialing the number for Calvin Lambert's agent. Lonnie O'Conner would be happy to get the offer of forty-five thousand for *Trust*. But it had been such a ridiculous struggle, none of it really about the book.

Don't ever date a woman you work with, he admonished himself as he waited for someone to answer the phone. The image of Miranda Shaeffer came unbidden into his head one more time. I may never get to date anyone at all, he acknowledged to himself as he heard Lonnie say hello.

As he hung up, he noticed Karen Schultz standing in his doorway. "How about lunch?" she asked.

"You know, as much as I'd love to, I better not," he answered regretfully. "Ed Board ate up all my time this morning and this stuff's not about to edit itself." He gave a vague wave toward the mountain of manuscripts piled on the windowsill.

Karen nodded in understanding. "It takes a huge chunk out of the day all right, but a girl's got to eat.'' She started to walk away, then turned back. "I hope you didn't let Tally get to you."

Paul raised an eyebrow. "Only slightly."

"She's still in love with you."

Paul looked at her in surprise. He'd never mentioned anything about his encounters with Tally. Nor could he imagine Tally having said anything.

"What do you mean?" he finally replied in apparent wonder.

Karen just laughed. "I'm absolutely right and you know it." She hesitated a few seconds, then went on. "You know, if my husband had a few bad moments and you were less of a gentleman, I'd be right there on fantasy island next to Tally. You'd have to beat me off with a stick."

Without waiting for a response, she breezed out the door.

It took hours for Miranda to calm down from her encounter with Paul Harlow in the taxi. Only after a morning of working on the outline for the next Forrestor novel did her pulse return to normal. At three o'clock, she stopped working, feeling unable to concentrate any longer. The baby-sitter was scheduled to stay until six, so she decided to go out food shopping, thinking she might buy something special for the children. They loved the raisin pumpernickel bread and the special Russian coffeecake at Zabar's.

By five-fifteen, she had completed her shopping and was standing on Broadway, hailing a cab to take her back home. The young driver who pulled over eyed her warily, and without much grace started driving east on Seventy-ninth Street. She looked for something to hold on to as he zoomed past a yellow light at the corner of Amsterdam.

"Would you please . . ." she started to say before a black Saab careened into their car, the two cars moving in tandem, their friction making a noise as frightening as the bumper-car ride her body was taking in the backseat.

"You all right, lady?" the driver asked nervously, pulling to a stop. He got out of the front seat and peered in the back window.

Miranda sat stock-still. Her forehead had hit the plastic barrier in between the front and backseats, but she didn't think she was really hurt. She was just completely shaken. Dusk had fallen, and the darkened intersection, one that used to be practically her backyard, seemed oddly strange and lonely. A crowd of people huddled around the accident, their faces filled with what she knew was concern but felt unreasonably as pure menace. Summoning the strength to move, she opened the door and let herself out.

The driver pulled her packages out of the car for her. "You should go to the hospital," he said apologetically, pointing to her face. "You're bleeding."

Surprised, she put her hand to her chin. Sure enough, her fingers came away red. But she didn't want to go to a hospital. She felt fine. In fact, she realized, she didn't feel much of anything except certain that she wasn't up to waiting in the emergency room of Mount Sinai or Lenox Hill for the next two or three hours.

"Please, sir," she said to the driver, then realized she wasn't sure of what she wanted him to do. She didn't want to go home. The kids had gone through enough without having her walk through the door bleeding. She needed to be with someone until she felt like herself, but she was unable to think of anyone she wanted to call. Lydia would have been perfect, but she had left for Los Angeles this morning for some convention of gym owners or something.

It infuriated Miranda to feel so powerless. Then, as if by magic, a picture formed in her mind. She envisioned the one person she wanted to see, as crazy as one part of her knew it was. But she was still too stunned from the accident to let that stop her. Gathering up her bags, she made her way to a phone booth on the corner.

When the physician who was Paul Harlow's neighbor finally left, having given a thumbs-up, Paul seated himself next to Miranda on the black leather sofa. He had bundled her into a blue-and-white-checked blanket and settled a glass of Courvoisier into her hands.

"Satisfied?" she asked, taking a long sip of the cognac.

He gave her a look of paternal disapproval and pulled the blanket higher on her shoulders. "Letting you talk me out of taking you to a hospital was crazy. I wasn't about to let you go completely unattended." He leaned forward to fill another glass with the amber liquid. "When you call someone in an emergency, it is incumbent upon them to actually help."

"Which you did in spades," she said sincerely.

In fact, Paul had gotten there within fifteen minutes of her call and had immediately taken care of all the things she would have forgotten about. The children were covered by his call to Emily Light, whose number she only dimly remembered giving him, he'd taken the driver's name and license number, and when they'd reached his apartment on Central Park West, he'd made sure to have her speak to Jack, Sophie, and Ethan individually, so they'd be absolutely certain she was okay. Miranda allowed herself to be led by Paul as if she were some foggy parade member following an especially trustworthy drum major. Only a couple of hours after the collision did she realize that she'd been in shock.

"I must look dreadful," she said, running her hands through her hair. She hadn't even thought about brushing it since she'd left the house that afternoon. "It was incredibly nice of you to come and get me. I really can't imagine what came over me, calling you like that."

"I'm glad you did," he answered. He hesitated, then finally continued slowly. "I really *am* glad, and I really should be surprised as well, given your quick exit this morning . . . but, it's funny, I'm not really surprised. I feel, well, connected to you somehow." He shrugged his shoulders. "You must think I'm nuts. I mean we only spoke for five minutes in a cab, but I feel as if I know you."

You should only know how well, she thought, taking a quick sip of her drink. In fact, corresponding with Paul by E-mail, even anonymously over the past few months had given her a sense of connection, too. She thought about how strange it should have felt, sitting here in a stranger's apartment, allowing him to take charge of her life, if only for a matter of hours. But it wasn't strange. In truth, she felt more comfortable than she had in months.

No, she realized, in a way, she felt at home as she hadn't in all the time since Stephen had moved them into the Fifth Avenue co-op. She gazed around the room, at the hundreds of books lining the walls, the Navajo blanket tossed casually over an enormous easy chair, the pictures of Paul and his son, even a couple of him and Patty Hetrick and Josh all together as a family. It felt familiar. Well, of course, she said to herself. It felt like her old apartment on West End Avenue.

"Why don't you nap for a few minutes, then I'll take you home." Paul got up from the couch and she stretched her legs out on the cushion.

Surprising even herself, she caught his wrist. "Please, stay here." Hearing her own words, she blushed and released him.

But he didn't walk away. Instead, he sat on the floor next to her, grasping her hand once again, then pushing her hair back with his other hand, comforting her, much as she would have done for Sophie or Ethan or Jack. But the impact of his fingers wasn't restful. She felt electrified by his touch, as if he were a magnet pulling a life force out of her she hadn't even remembered she had. She knew he had to be aware of what she was feeling, her inability to breathe exactly right, her urge to melt into his hands. He withdrew abruptly.

"I'm sorry," she found herself saying, embarrassed at the nakedness of her yearning.

"Sorry?" The word was an explosion. "God, how could you be sorry. Miranda, I want . . ."

He sat with his back against the couch, his shoulders rigid with the struggle to contain himself. How hard it was for him was obvious, even to Miranda. "You're still in shock," he said. "To take advantage of that would make me the biggest schmuck in the world."

Miranda heard the words, but couldn't take them in. It was as if the accident had unleashed all her pain of the past year. She lay her cheek on the back of his neck, nuzzling there like a kitten searching for warmth. She could feel him taking in her heat, his hand coming up to caress the top of her head. They stayed like that until he turned around, facing her now, lifting his mouth up to meet hers, the heat of his lips, the searching of his tongue nourishing her, filling the empty places that had claimed her for so long.

When he came up beside her on the couch, their bodies fit together as if they'd lain next to each other hundreds of times before. He was reluctant to ask anything of her, but she found herself reaching out, emboldened by the need to feel his skin against hers, assuming without reason that his flesh, too, would be familiar. The pleasure that shot through her as he responded made her even greedier with desire. She trailed her hands up under his shirt, drawing strength from the muscular warmth of his back.

It was she who unbuttoned his shirt and let it drop to the floor, she who raised her sweater over her head, hurriedly undoing her bra and guiding his mouth to her breasts. The act seemed to unlock his restraint, as if he could no longer fight the depth of her yearning, the boundlessness of his own. His hands moved down to her essence, stroking, kneading, evoking the flame that had been dormant for so long.

And when he entered her, it was as if they were completing a circle that had begun long before.

"Oh, Miranda, I hope I'm not hurting you," he whispered feverishly, his hand lingering softly over her bruised chin.

"You couldn't hurt me," she breathed back, closing her eyes and feeling him inside her, certain that, for once, she was right.

Chapter 22

"I hate you and I hope you die." Jack's voice carried perfectly all the way from his bedroom.

Miranda looked at her mother, seated across from her, in embarrassment, but Esther just raised her hands as if to say, What can you do?

"I was looking for my book," they heard Sophie explaining to her brother, as her footsteps sounded in the corridor between their rooms.

"The sign saying KEEP OUT means *keep out*," Jack shouted after her, slamming his door for emphasis.

Irv Feldman prowled around Miranda's living room, his red-and-blue-plaid pants an odd contrast to the antique Bukhara carpet. Miranda noted the intensity of his bright blue eyes. As far as he was concerned, she thought, the fight between his stepgrandchildren might never have happened.

"You looking for gold?" his wife Esther asked, coming up behind him.

"Of a sort," he answered, continuing his search. "Here they are," he cried excitedly as he came upon the photo collection on top of the piano, "the you I never got to see." Triumphantly, he plucked one of the old photographs from the group of family portraits.

Rubbing his bald spot, a habitual gesture, Irv examined the photograph carefully. "You *were* a beauty, and you *are* a beauty," he said exuberantly as he focused on the Esther of almost forty years before, seated prettily at the side of Louis Greenfield, her first husband.

Miranda, who'd been observing her mother and her second husband with amusement, felt herself stiffen slightly. Her mother and father had never been able to be in the same room without starting a world war; it was likely that even a picture of the two of them together would evoke some kind of unpleasant reaction from Esther.

But Miranda was happily surprised by her mother's response.

"One thing for Louis," she said, taking the picture from Irv, "he always was a looker." She smiled at her present husband. "Not as good as you, honey," she added flirtatiously, "but he had a certain something."

Miranda regarded her in amazement, a fact her mother picked up on immediately. "Well, he did," she said.

Miranda couldn't keep the skepticism out of her tone. "I can't say you dwelled on Daddy's animal magnetism much while I was growing up." She looked at her mother coolly. "Or for the next twenty or thirty years after that."

"Ahh . . ." her mother said, raising her right hand as if dismissing a royal subject, "you were always too sensitive."

Well, at least her mother was capable of one insightful moment, Miranda thought, irritated.

"Jack's just like you, you know," Esther added with certainty.

Miranda couldn't have been more surprised. "Whatever do you mean?" she asked.

Her mother sat down in the wing chair next to the couch. "Oh, you know, all that mooning around under a black cloud all the time."

Miranda felt her defensiveness growing. What could you possibly understand about it, she wanted to say, coming up here once every five years or so when you take time off from the Bates Motel? And what did you ever know about how I felt as a kid, left alone most of the time, with screaming fights going on whenever there was more than one person in the house?

She felt her face redden in anger. This is crazy, she chided herself, getting up and walking toward the kitchen.

"I'll get some more soda," she called out, hoping her mother hadn't noticed her discomfort. Purposefully, she entered the kitchen and pulled a bottle of Perrier from the top shelf of the refrigerator. She stood there for a few seconds, letting the cold air circulate around her. Almost reluctantly, she shut the door, and as slowly as possible, filled three glasses with the bubbly liquid. Turning to place the bottle in the recycling bin, she caught sight of her face in a small mirror that Sophie must have left on the kitchen table.

Shocked by what she saw, she picked up the mirror and stared into it. Damn, she acknowledged to herself. Her mother had a point. The reflection in the glass was the dissatisfied scowl she always wore when her mother was around. It was the same unhappy face she saw on her son, the one that proclaimed "I've been cheated" with every breath.

She sank onto a kitchen chair, laying the mirror facedown on the table. Just what is the truth here? she asked herself, inhaling deeply and closing her eyes. The Seafarer, the motel her mother owned, was sweet and tidy. Located about three miles inland from the beaches of Fort Lauderdale, Esther had worked hard for over twenty years to buy it. And her marriage to Irv Feldman was another thing to be proud of. She'd finally found a man whose spirit of adventure equaled her own. His little shoe store, filled with Enna Jetticks, might not have lived up to Stephen's standards of class and distinction, but whether they were hanging out at Hialeah or riding around in the spanking new RV that was parked right outside on Fifth Avenue, Esther and Irv had found the joy that Esther and Louis never could.

Somewhere deep inside her, Miranda finally allowed herself to see that her sister's view of Esther was both more charitable and more accurate than her own. There her mother had been, on her own with two kids, financially strapped, filled with dreams, and somehow or other, she'd pulled it off. Both her daughters had grown up to be independent, capable of making their own way.

And I *am* making my way, she thought with satisfaction. Just as my mother made her way. Her eyes searched out the copy of *Stranger from the East* that was one of twenty or so books in a pile on the counter. Thank you, Stephen, she said to herself, for once unambiguous in her acknowledgment. That she had written the new Forrestor novel, and that Paul claimed it to be really good, filled her with pride. And truly she did thank Stephen for providing a map for her to follow. Whatever else her husband had done, he had performed a wonderful service.

And thank you, Mom, she thought, getting up and taking the glasses into the living room.

"I needed that," her mother said gratefully, as Miranda handed her the glass.

"And I need you," Miranda answered unexpectedly, planting a quick kiss on her mother's cheek.

Esther gave her daughter a quizzical glance. "Well, honey, I need you, too. And, I love you. I probably don't tell you that enough, do I?''

Miranda smiled contentedly. So it wasn't so hard to get what she craved from her mother, if she gave a little first. "You do just fine, thank you." She sat back down on the couch, her tension virtually gone. "If you had one guess, what do you think Jack needs?" she asked.

"Hmmm . . ." her mother answered, shaking her head at the request.

Miranda could see that Esther was taking the question seriously, which pleased her. It had never occurred to her to ask her mother's advice before, but she was intently interested in what she would say.

"You know what that boy needs?" Esther said tantalizingly. "I think he needs a long Christmas vacation, all alone with his grandparents. A nice, long trip in a beautiful recreational vehicle, where two people are thinking only about him for twenty-four hours a day."

Miranda looked at her mother in wonder. "Are you serious?"

"Absolutely," she replied, beaming. "He'll do a few chores around the place, we'll take him on some trips, feed him a ton of ice cream. He'll have the time of his life." She turned to Irv. "Right, honey?"

"Of course," Irv said, putting his arm around her. "Jack," he yelled loudly.

They heard the boy's door open, listened as his slow footsteps came toward the living room. He stood in the entrance, not saying a word.

"C'mon, baby," Esther cried, "we're going fishing."

Jack looked at his grandmother suspiciously. "You mean in Central Park? There aren't any real fish there, you know."

"I mean we're venturing out into America in the RV."

"Do I have to sleep with Sophie and Ethan?" Jack responded belligerently.

Esther walked over to him and put her arms around him. "No Sophie. No Ethan. Just you and Irv and me, and the whole outdoors as our destination."

Jack stared at her.

"Now, get your things in a bag, boy, we've got a million miles to cover." Esther strode out of the living room, looking behind her to Irv for a brief second. "You, too, boy," she said to her husband. "Time's a-wastin'."

Miranda watched her son, as Esther and Irv disappeared down the corridor. With amazement, she saw a look of pure joy explode across his face.

"Why does everybody stand for the 'Hallelujah Chorus?' " Miranda asked, as she stirred her eggnog.

"Everybody stands because everbody else stands," Paul Harlow answered, chuckling. "Here's to everybody," he exclaimed, raising his glass and tapping Miranda's lightly.

She smiled back at him and took a long sip of her drink. She felt lazy and happy, seated comfortably right in the window of The Saloon, across from Lincoln Center. The performance of Handel's *Messiah* had been magnificent, and their casual, late dinner was proving to be just as good. They'd already shared chicken wings and were waiting for the main course—for Paul, a cheeseburger, for Miranda, a Caesar salad.

Miranda looked out the window, to the sparkling Christmas lights lining Broadway, the enormous crowds of people and cars not put off by the uncharacteristically snowy New York winter.

"What do you think Santa Claus will have for you this year?" she asked.

Paul reached across the table for her hand. "I think I got my big gift," he answered, grinning. "And you?"

Miranda found herself wanting to be serious. "You know, I think my mother's taking Jack to Florida is about the greatest gift I've ever received." She shook her head in wonder. "My son actually called yesterday to tell me he'd bought presents for all of us at Disney World."

"Sounds great," Paul answered. "He's having fun?"

"The time of his life. Esther's been making the world's biggest fuss over him, and Irv is letting him work in his shoe store the two days before Christmas, which to my son is a pleasure equivalent to a day at the beach."

The waitress came over to their table bearing two large plates of food. Paul reached for the ketchup, pouring a small amount onto the burger and to the side of fries that came with it. "He must miss his father," he observed before taking a bite of his cheeseburger.

"Yes," Miranda answered somewhat uncertainly, "although Sophie is the one who talks about Stephen the most. When I left tonight, she was showing the baby-sitter Stephen's high school graduation picture."

"Josh is fascinated by our early pictures, too," Paul responded. "He's taken to pointing to early pictures of my ex-wife and asking if they were taken before she became Patty Hetrick. He's a little confused by the public persona.''

Miranda took a small bite of her salad. ''A public persona would be pretty confusing for anyone, I guess.''

Paul narrowed his eyes slightly. ''It certainly became confusing for me.'' He picked up a french fry, held it, then lay it back down on the plate. ''I'm not being completely fair. I probably fell in love with Patty partly because of her public persona, and she fell in love with me because I didn't have one. I got to know pretty quickly that the persona bored me silly, and I guess the reality of me wasn't so interesting to her either.'' He finally ate one of the fries. ''What's it like to be in a happy marriage?'' he asked with genuine interest.

Miranda was taken aback. ''I'm not so sure I'm the person to tell you,'' she said uncertainly. ''My husband was attractive and talented, but I think we were both in the process of changing. Or at least . . .'' she hesitated, ''. . . he was changing pretty rapidly, and I'm not sure we would have been so happy if . . .'' She felt an unexpected tear roll down her cheek.

Paul reached across the table and wiped it away with his hand. ''I'm sorry, I don't mean to make you unhappy with these questions. You can tell me or not tell me as much as you want.'' He trailed his finger down her face. ''We have all the time in the world.''

Miranda looked at him gratefully. Even in the restaurant's dimmed lights, his eyes shone with kindness and honesty. Had Stephen ever been completely honest with her? Looking back even on their earliest days, she doubted it.

Suddenly, she felt guilty about her own dishonesty. What would he do if I told him that Stephen had been Forrestor, that I was Forrestor now, she wondered.

She almost came out with it, right there and then, yet something stopped her. Forrestor was a secret. If she told him, if she told anyone who Forrestor really was, might it somehow jinx things? If it ain't broke, don't fix it. She could hear her mother's voice in her mind. It was a phrase Esther used all the time, and Miranda was afraid this was one of the times her mother would have been right.

Forrestor had changed her life. And Paul Harlow seemed to be changing her life as well. They were in two separate worlds, and, she realized with finality, tampering with those worlds might bring her whole universe down around her.

Jack sat impatiently as Esther and Irv started the second halves of their turkey sandwiches. Wolfie's was crowded, most of the clientele elderly and white haired. Jack had eaten his hot dog and most of his french fries at least ten minutes earlier and was looking around impatiently, waiting for his grandparents to finish their meal. At the next table was a family of five, the mother and father dressed almost alike, in chinos and light blue shirts. Both were busily trying to feed their toddler, who was throwing back each piece of food as it was offered.

For a few minutes, Jack watched, almost laughing at the child's resistance. Then his attention wandered to the other two, the younger one a boy who looked six or so, the oldest child a girl, who must have been about eight. There was something familiar about the girl.

The answer came to him quickly. "Hey, Grandma," he said, poking her arm. "That girl looks just like Sophie's friend Erin."

"Who, dear?" Esther asked, glancing around.

"Over there." He pointed.

"Oh, really," Esther said indulgently. "Isn't that nice." She turned back to her husband.

Jack continued to stare at the next table. If Sophie were here, he thought, she'd see it, too. She'd probably go right over there and start gabbing. He picked up a cold french fry. He'd been having a great time with Esther and Irv, but long meals like this were his least favorite part of the trip. He wanted to go outside and explore while they finished up, but it would be no fun doing it alone.

He turned to his grandmother. "Wanna hear a joke?"

Esther and Irv both looked at him expectantly.

"Sure," Irv answered.

Jack leaned forward eagerly. "What does a Chinese cow wear on its feet?"

Esther and Irv spoke in unison. "What?"

"Moo shoes!"

The older pair looked puzzled.

"You know," Jack said through his laughter, "like the Chinese food—moo shu."

Esther smiled.

"That's a good one," Irv said, as he signaled for the waiter.

Jack sat back, deflated by their reactions. Gee, he thought, Sophie would have fallen off her chair laughing at that one. He pictured his sister back in New York. What would she be doing tonight? Thinking back, he remembered the Friday night that marked the beginning of Christmas vacation just before he left on this trip. His mother had put in a tape of *Willy Wonka and the Chocolate Factory*, and he and Sophie had watched it together, sharing a bowl of popcorn.

He felt an unfamiliar sensation in the pit of his stomach as he admitted the impossible to himself. He actually looked forward to seeing his sister. Sophie was the person he spent the most time with, the one who knew what made him happy and what made him miserable. Aside from his mother, Sophie was probably the person who cared about him most in the world.

A shocking realization dawned.

He missed his sister.

Stunned, he sat there, turning the incredible fact over in his mind.

"Jack," Esther said, "do you want some dessert?"

Jack didn't answer, so lost was he in his thoughts.

Chapter 23

Hurriedly coming around from behind the desk, Lydia grabbed her shoulder bag. She turned to see her path was blocked by Katherine Woodland, who had suddenly materialized in the office's doorway, a woeful expression on her face. Lydia groaned inwardly. Although she was only twenty, Katherine was one of Lydia's best exercise instructors. But she had a flair for the dramatic, and, according to her, nothing in her life was ever less than a complete catastrophe. Normally, Lydia was willing to take the time to do the necessary hand holding, but right now she didn't want any part of it.

"Can I talk to you for a minute?" Katherine asked in a somber tone, indicating the importance of her request.

Lydia smiled brightly at her. "Hon, I'm rushing off, but I'll be back in a couple of hours. We can talk then."

She approached the doorway, hoping the woman would get the message, but Katherine didn't move.

"I sort of need to do it now." Katherine gazed at her with sad eyes. "I might be too upset to teach my twelve-thirty otherwise."

Lydia glanced impatiently at her watch but tried to keep her tone even. "Of course, dear, I'm all ears. What can I do for you?"

"It's about my boyfriend. . . ." Katherine's eyes filled with tears.

Oh, jeez, Lydia thought, here we go again. Whichever boyfriend it was this month. "Yes?" she said as sympathetically as she could.

"He wants to break up." Her lower lip began to tremble. "But he said we could talk about it because he's not totally sure. The thing is, he's going to Boston on business tomorrow. He wants me to come with him.'' She hesitated. ''I'd be gone three days.''

''Tomorrow?'' Lydia arched an eyebrow. ''So you'd miss teaching tomorrow and Saturday?''

Katherine nodded. ''I know you're not supposed to ask for time off less than a week ahead. But this is such an emergency. I don't know what I'll do if we break up.''

Lydia was beginning to feel frantic. Under any other circumstance, she would have said no. The only replacement possibility was Mindy, and she was out sick with the flu. But Lydia knew a refusal would lead to a long discussion in which Katherine would explain why this was so crucial to her well-being, and Lydia didn't want to waste another second. She would just have to deal with it later.

Gently, she put a hand on the small of Katherine's back to usher her out. ''This once it's okay. Please don't ask again on such short notice.''

The girl nodded solemnly. ''I appreciate it.''

''Good.'' Lydia rushed off toward the exit. ''See you later.''

As she stepped off the curb to hail a taxi, Lydia knew she would regret her decision. But right now she didn't care. All she cared about was getting to her apartment so she wouldn't waste another minute of her time with Henry.

He was already there when she got out of the elevator on her floor, leaning against the wall outside her apartment, reading a medical journal. At the sight of her, he immediately dropped the magazine into his briefcase and, smiling, came forward.

''Hello, you.'' He took her in his arms and they kissed deeply.

''I'm sorry I'm late,'' Lydia said almost breathlessly when they finished. She fumbled in her purse for her key. ''How long do you have?''

''I have to get back for a one-thirty meeting.''

''Damn.'' Lydia gave him a radiant smile as she opened the door. ''Not enough time.''

''Never enough time.'' He followed her inside, depositing his briefcase and jacket onto a nearby chair.

She had set the table and prepared the curried chicken salad that morning, so she was able to put out their lunch in only a few minutes. Henry broke off a piece of French bread while she poured sparkling water into two wine glasses.

''It's a hard choice, this or the hospital cafeteria,'' he said, smiling, as he bit into the bread.

"I know I can't compete with the nameless gray luncheon meat they serve there," Lydia replied with exaggerated humility. She sat down next to him and put her hand over his. "You're very kind to pass it up to eat with me."

"It's a charity thing, really." He took a forkful of salad. "Delicious. But you're an amazing cook. I've never had anything here that wasn't great."

Lydia looked at him, knowing she was practically beaming. I can't believe I'm acting like a twelve year old, she thought. And I don't care.

They ate and talked, catching up on what had happened since they had last gotten together the previous week. When Henry's wife, Mimi, was in town, they only saw one another for lunches like this one, with an occasional evening thrown in if he could manage to get away. Mimi might be preoccupied with her career, Lydia knew, but that didn't mean she would accept her husband having an affair. Fortunately, she traveled frequently, even if it was only for a night or two at a time, and they made up for it then.

Lydia had never been so happy. It astounded her to realize she was even capable of this much happiness. When they made love, she responded with more passion than she had felt for any other lover. In Henry's arms, she could finally let down her guard and relax, losing herself in him. This was the love she hadn't dared hope for all these years, and she still couldn't get over the fact that she had actually found him.

They finished lunch and got up, wordlessly coming together and walking into the bedroom, already unbuttoning their clothes as they went, anxious to be next to each other, skin against skin. Naked, they lay down on the bed, Lydia giving a sigh of contentment as she pressed the length of her body against his. Slowly, langorously, they made love.

Afterward, they lay there peacefully, his arm around her, their fingers interlaced, relishing the final few minutes they had. They talked softly about unimportant things, just enjoying the sound of each other's words.

"By the way, Henry, I made the reservation at Le Cirque for eight-thirty on Saturday." Lydia was taking him out for a birthday dinner, delighted that Mimi was scheduled to be in a special benefit performance of *Brigadoon* in San Francisco. This was the first important occasion on which Lydia was able to have him to herself, and she planned to make it a special night.

"Oh, damn it." Henry made a face of regret, remembering.

"Sweetheart, I forgot to tell you. Mimi informed me this morning she's making a dinner party for me." He raised himself up on one elbow to look at her. "It seems I got the dates mixed up, and the show isn't until the following week. I can't tell you how sorry I am."

Lydia gave him a weak smile, trying to hide her immense disappointment. She hated herself for feeling this way. In the beginning, she had been fine about the time he had to spend away from her. In a way it was a relief; it kept them from getting too close. But the more she loved him, the less sanguine she was becoming. It was a new feeling for her.

"Well," she said at last, "we can celebrate the next week when she goes to Madrid."

He lay back without responding. There was a long silence.

"Henry?" Lydia asked tentatively. "Is she not going to Madrid?"

He took a deep breath. "Her friend Elise canceled out at the last minute. She doesn't want to miss out on the whole trip, so she's insisting I go with her instead."

"Oh." Lydia hoped her voice didn't betray how upset she was. Henry and his wife would be enjoying the sights and foods and finest hotels of Spain while she sat waiting for him back in New York. "Can you take that much time off from work?"

"We've agreed that I'll go for a week, and she'll do the rest alone." He turned to her unhappily. "Lydia, I realize this is awful for you. It's not what I want either."

"I know, I know." Lydia swallowed.

"It's just what I was afraid of." He reached for her. "I don't want to go. You must know how much I love you."

They were interrupted by the ringing of the telephone. Grateful for the excuse to break away, Lydia leaned over to answer it.

"Hello?" She turned her back to Henry, glad he couldn't see her misery over what they had agreed was inevitable when they first became lovers.

"Lydia?" Miranda's voice was startled. "I didn't expect to find you there. I didn't want to disturb you at the studio, so I was going to leave a message. What are you doing home? Are you sick?"

"No, no, I'm fine. You caught me as I was running in and out." Lydia swung her legs over the side of the bed to sit up as she wrapped the quilt partially around her. "I forgot something I needed."

"Oh. Well, I just wanted to remind you about coming over for dinner tomorrow. Seven o'clock?"

"Fine, fine."

"Good. I won't keep you. See you then."

"Bye."

Lydia hung up, and lay down once again, still clutching the quilt around her. She was aware of Henry's eyes on her but didn't look at him.

Miranda knew nothing about Henry's existence. Lydia had considered telling her several times early on, but she could never bring herself to do it.

How tawdry, Lydia, an affair with a married man. She could practically hear Miranda's reaction. *Gives you a few of his stolen hours and you accept that. After all your talk about standing up for yourself, about how I used to let Stephen walk all over me.*

It was true. Lydia had always browbeaten Miranda about letting her husband treat her so badly. And Lydia had been justified in doing so. It was incredible the way Miranda was coming back into her own since Stephen had died. Lydia felt terrible for the children, losing their father. But, as brutal as it might have sounded, Stephen's death was probably the best thing that could have happened to her sister. Miranda had gone back to work, doing some sort of freelance copywriting or something. She looked better than she had in years, and she seemed so much more confident.

Lydia would never have wished for Stephen to die or for her sister to have her life thrown into such upheaval. But there was something about him that Lydia had never trusted, and a small corner of her was perversely satisfied to learn she had been right about him. Not only had he been such a bastard that he left his wife without any money, but Miranda's blossoming was proof that he really had been holding her down the way Lydia had claimed.

But now Miranda was the one gaining control of her life while Lydia was voluntarily relinquishing it. For a woman to adjust her life around the schedule of a married boyfriend was the kind of thing Lydia had always held in utter contempt.

What the hell am I doing? she asked herself.

At that moment, Henry leaned over and gazed at her with sad eyes. "I love you. I don't want to lose you."

He kissed her gently. Lydia wanted to cry as she brought her arms around his neck, knowing that being without him was simply too terrible to contemplate.

When Henry returned from Madrid, he and Lydia spent every night of the following week together. She felt as if having that much time with him was like finding a treasure chest, filled with wonderful things. They went to the theater the first night, but the chances of running into people that Henry and Mimi knew made it too difficult to enjoy being out. After that, they camped at Lydia's, cooking lobsters, watching rented movies, sharing a long bath with champagne. Lydia had a masseuse come to the apartment one evening to give them both massages. Best of all, every night they were able to make love, sleep wrapped in one another's arms and wake up together every morning.

Lydia didn't care whether they went out or just relaxed on her sofa; being with him for such an extended period made her drunk with pleasure. Somehow, this time felt different from any of the other times Mimi had been away, each moment more precious. It was always hard to readjust when it was over, but now she couldn't even bear to think about it. The more she was with him, the more she wanted—needed—to be with him.

The day before Mimi was scheduled to return, they decided to venture out to SoHo for Sunday brunch. It was neither one's neighborhood, and for Henry to be seen having brunch with a woman in broad daylight seemed pretty innocent anyway. They had just sat down at their table by the window and ordered Bloody Marys, when Lydia happened to look out onto the street. There was Miranda, passing by with her friend, Emily Light. In that split second, as if feeling the gaze, Miranda glanced Lydia's way. Their eyes met.

Miranda smiled in surprise, and turned to say something to Emily. The two of them went toward the restaurant's door.

"Oh, God," Lydia said with dread.

Henry looked up from his menu. "What is it?"

"My sister. She's coming in." She paused. "I didn't want to get into, you know, all this with her."

Henry started to speak, but Miranda was suddenly at their table, her friend in tow. He rose as the three women quickly exchanged greetings.

"Please don't get up," Miranda said to him. She turned to her sister. "Isn't this funny, seeing you. Emily and I are going shopping. Normally, I'm never down here." She turned back to Henry. "I'm Miranda Shaeffer, Lydia's sister."

Lydia introduced Henry to both women. They made some small talk, then Miranda excused herself. "We've got to run. I'll call you later," she said brightly, as she led Emily away.

Lydia watched her go. Actually, she thought, there was no reason for Miranda to think there was anything going on between her and Henry. They could be business associates or casual friends. Miranda would have no way of knowing. Still, Lydia was unusually quiet during most of the meal.

She and Henry were lying on her bed, drinking coffee and reading the Sunday *Times* at about five-thirty, when Miranda called. Hearing her sister's voice on the other end, Lydia got up and took the portable phone with her so she could talk in the living room, out of Henry's earshot.

"Did you enjoy the shops?" she asked Miranda.

"A lot." Miranda got right to the point. "I didn't realize you had a guy. You haven't said a word about it."

Lydia realized she was as nervous as if she'd been caught doing something illegal. "Who said I had a guy?" she replied, trying to sound casual.

"Lydia, for God's sake, it was so obvious. The way the two of you looked at each other—only a total idiot could have missed it."

"He's kind of nice," Lydia said, knowing how ridiculous she sounded, but hesitant to say anything more.

"And kind of married. He was wearing a wedding band."

Lydia bristled, not wanting to hear what she knew was coming. "Am I about to get a lecture?" she asked sharply.

Miranda's tone was even. "Not at all. Of course I hope you don't get hurt." Her voice softened. "To tell you the truth, I'm happy you finally let someone into your life. You've been so hard on yourself all these years. It's exciting to see you let a man love you for once. God knows, you deserve it."

There was a pause. Lydia was too taken aback to say anything.

"Oh, Ethan's yelling for me. I'm sorry, I better get off. Talk to you soon."

Miranda hung up.

Lydia pressed the telephone's off button but remained where she was, gazing out the living room window. Oh, shit, she thought. A lecture would have allowed her to get angry with Miranda, to combat her warnings with self-righteous protests.

Lydia sank down onto the couch. She stared straight ahead, thinking, facing what had to be done.

After several more minutes, Henry emerged from the bedroom.

"Hon, where'd you go?" He came over, sitting down beside her and running his hand along her hair. "You okay?"

She shook her head. "We have to talk."

He put his hand back in his lap. "Uh-oh. This doesn't sound good. All right, what do we have to talk about?"

Her eyes were full of pain as she turned to look at him. "This isn't the role I want to be playing in life. I'm not going to be your girlfriend on the side or your mistress. Hiding like this—I've been pretending to myself it's okay, but it's not, not at all.''

He pursed his lips. "I know."

She got up and began pacing. "I love you so much. More than I ever hoped I could love someone. But you've got to decide if you want to have a life with me. Not this way. A *real* life."

He rose and moved to put his arms around her. "Lydia, we talked about this when—"

"No." She stepped back, out of his reach. "I think you understand me. You should go now, Henry."

He stopped, and she saw her own pain reflected in his eyes. But he said nothing. Then he turned, picked up his jacket from where it lay slung over a chair, and was gone.

Chapter 24

Stephen lay back on the bed, shoving a couple of pillows behind his head as he watched Merilee cross the bedroom to where her clothes were piled on a chair. As much as she was beginning to bore him, he never got tired of looking at her body, so young and firm. Right now she was wearing a short black silk robe trimmed with lace. He had made her leave it on, open, while they were having sex. Now she absentmindedly belted it again as she rummaged through her enormous purse, searching for something.

"Got it." She held up a white box tied with a red ribbon. Smiling, she returned to the bed and handed it to him, leaning forward to kiss him on the nose. "Happy Valentine's Day, Stephen. I didn't want to wait till after dinner to give it to you."

What lovely thing did I buy myself, he wondered as he pulled off the ribbon. Giving Merilee her own credit card had originally seemed like a good idea. It was a new experience, really doing the mistress thing, as he thought of it. Of course, his wife had bought whatever the hell she wanted and he had paid for it, but this was different. He liked seeing Merilee preen in a sexy new dress or a piece of jewelry that he had paid for. It made him feel oddly powerful, basking in her enjoyment and gratitude. And she didn't use his money for pots and pans or dish towels; she somehow sensed that it was to go for those things that gave him pleasure as well.

Unfortunately for her, the spending was coming to an end. She didn't know it yet, but yesterday he had canceled her credit card. That was when he had reviewed his financial situation and faced the bad news.

In less than a year, he had gone through over two-thirds of his money. What was amazing was how easy it had been. The house, the car, the clothes, the three-hundred-dollar dinners several times a week—he had been having a great time, but it had cost him. He'd already dipped into his backup, the Alanson Shaeffer account, which made him very uneasy. And with the way things were going, he might need to make his reserves last longer than he had expected.

He parted the white tissue paper inside the box to reveal a silver flask. Very nice, he thought admiringly. It must have set me back a few hundred.

"It's terrific," he said aloud. "Perfect for me."

He went to his closet, grabbing a large, flat box wrapped in silver. "And I have something for you."

Her eyes lit up with anticipation. "Oh, thank you, honey."

She tore off the paper eagerly and eased off the top of the box to reveal the red teddy inside. He saw the disappointment appear in her eyes for a split second before she recovered to give him a wide grin. She held up the garment by its spaghetti straps. "Beautiful. You know just what to pick," she said sweetly.

Sure, I do, baby, he answered silently. Except you were hoping for a big-ticket item or maybe even a diamond ring. Such is life.

He gave her a peck on the cheek and went into the bathroom to shower. Turning on the faucets, he tried to ignore the tension in his stomach. It had disappeared during sex, but now it was back. Over the last several weeks, the dull ache had become his constant companion. A combination of fear, anger, and apprehension. He vacillated between attempting to ignore it, and giving in, letting his emotions get the better of him until he'd downed enough Scotches to dull them.

He stepped under the running water, closing his eyes and letting it wash over him. His mind began to drift. He pictured himself at the Waldorf—conjured up white tablecloths and gleaming silverware, the sights and sounds of an elegant dinner in progress. The crowd was erupting at the sound of his name being announced. Stephen saw himself looking momentarily stunned. He rose from his chair, accepting the congratulations of his editor and the other executives from his publishing company who were sitting at the table. Gently smoothing down the front of his tuxedo jacket, he began making his way through the crowded room toward the dais, surveying the sea of faces, all the important publishers mixed with famous and respected authors. Everyone was clapping, smiling at him, admiring his talent, recognizing how right it was that he should be this year's winner of the National Book Award for fiction.

Off to the left, he saw his parents leaping to their feet, jubilant, applauding louder than everyone else. He gave them a broad smile and a wave. Jauntily, he bounded up the three steps to the stage, moving past the men and women seated behind the podium so he could get to the chairperson of the fiction committee, the woman who had just announced his name. Her eyes filled with admiration, she had one hand outstretched to give him his award. He put out his own hand to accept it, reaching for the—

Stephen groaned, opening his eyes, the picture in his mind going black. *Jesus*. He couldn't believe it. His reverie had come to an end because *he didn't know what the goddamned National Book Award looked like*. Was it a plaque or a statue? Maybe a scroll? Of course that was the irony of it. He *should* know what it looked like, because he should have one. But he didn't. And his parents should witness him winning it. Wouldn't that be something?

Embarrassed at even having had the daydream, he got out of the shower and yanked a towel off the rack, pulling it across his back savagely.

"You almost done?" Merilee opened the door and stuck her head into the bathroom. "I wanted to know what you think of these shoes."

Stephen glanced at her, annoyed. "They're fine."

Her tone sounded hurt. "You didn't even look." She smiled. "My feet are in a different room."

"I can see them from here," he said curtly. "I said they were fine."

About to speak, she seemed to think better of it and retreated, shutting the door once more. Maybe it was time to get rid of Merilee anyway. She was becoming more of a financial liability than anything else. What he'd considered her sweetness in the beginning, he had come to view more as simplemindedness. Besides, he'd never intended to get hooked up with one woman in the first place. The sex with her was great, but he could get sex elsewhere. It was time to cut her loose.

He felt a sensation that was becoming familiar, the same feeling he experienced whenever he had dropped a woman that he was dating. After being tied down in a marriage for so many years, he was both amazed and supremely satisfied that he was now able to walk away from any relationship with such ease. Of course, in a sense he had just walked away from Miranda, he reminded himself with a chuckle, but that had been quite a bit more intricate. Now he was completely free. When he decided something was over, it was over. That simple. He loved it.

When he emerged from the bathroom, Merilee wasn't there, but he could hear her talking to Toby out in the living room. He took his time getting dressed. Merilee had made reservations for a Valentine's Day dinner, but she was keeping the name of the restaurant a surprise. As if I cared, he thought.

He stopped in front of the mirror, reaching for a comb to fix his hair. Standing there, he suddenly remembered the collection of valentines that Miranda had kept in the back of his top dresser drawer in their bedroom. Every year when they were small, the children had made him valentines, and she had rescued them from being deposited in the trash, placing them in his drawer as if he were going to want to pore over them in his old age. Jack had stopped when he turned six, but Sophie and Ethan had continued the tradition, clumsily decorating red construction paper with the same hearts and lace year in and year out. He doubted he could have told which card was from which kid in which year, they were all so similar. But he had done his best to act surprised and grateful when he got them. I was a damn good father, he thought. He paused. It had been nine months since he'd seen the kids. He wondered if they'd changed much. He wondered if Miranda had thrown out the valentines.

A pang of longing shot through him, surprising him in its intensity. He recalled the feel of Ethan's small hand clutching his as they walked down the street. He thought of Jack's smile, so rare but so brilliant when it finally appeared. And his Sophie, his jewel—she would no doubt be getting prettier with each passing day. Damn, he wanted to see them.

He picked up the comb and slowly ran it through his hair. It was a mistake to go down this road, he told himself. He couldn't accomplish what he needed to if he got all caught up in the past. The children were part of what had to be left behind, and there was nothing to be done about it. It was far too risky to contemplate having any contact with them.

But maybe that wasn't altogether true. He could still have contact with them in a sort of indirect way, he reflected. There was nothing to prevent him from sending them something, some little present, assuming he did it in a way that was untraceable. He'd have the stuff mailed from a catalog or a store in another state. It would be a mystery for them, each one receiving something special from an unknown admirer. He smiled at the notion, already starting to consider what he might choose for each one, feeling almost cheerful.

Stephen slipped on a jacket and went out to join Merilee and Toby. They both looked up from where they were sitting on the sofa, drinking Margaritas. The half-full pitcher from the blender and an empty glass for Stephen sat on the coffee table.

"I didn't realize you were home," Stephen said to Toby, moving to pour himself a drink.

"I came back to pack up my stuff," Toby said casually. "I'm moving tonight."

In the process of lifting the pitcher, Stephen stopped, his hand frozen in midair. "What do you mean, moving?"

Toby downed the last of his drink. "Remember? I told you," he said easily. "That couple from the gallery who live in Bel Air. They've offered me the guest house for a couple of months."

"No." Stephen tried not to sound panicked. "No, I don't remember. We never talked about this."

"Really?" Toby seemed genuinely surprised. "Well, this is what's doing. And I want to thank you. You've been great."

Stephen stared at him. Without Toby, there would be no more parties or private clubs. Stephen didn't have to be told he wasn't connected solidly enough yet on his own to gain access to the places that counted. And of course he hadn't made himself a name as Stephen West, the novelist, yet. He would be just another nobody, hanging around with not a lot to do.

"Will you be coming back after a few months?" He tried to sound unconcerned.

"Hard to say." Toby rose. "I'll leave you a phone number, and we'll definitely get together, okay, man?"

Then Stephen understood. Toby was going because he sensed that Stephen's ship might be sinking. But how did he know? He had never told Toby anything about the manuscript or the rejections from the dozen or so literary agents. During those weeks, he had been excruciatingly careful not to let on that he was virtually in shock over the form letters he received in which agent after agent thanked him for his submission and politely declined to represent him. He was reduced to scraping the bottom of the barrel, submitting his manuscript to newcomers and has-beens.

And he certainly hadn't breathed a word about how stunned he was when Bruce Baines turned out to be the one agent willing to take him on as a client. To think that this twenty-three-year-old moron at the mediocre Messinger Agency was the only one willing to handle *To the Edge* made him nuts. Stephen was banking on the fact that the good editors at the publishing houses would recognize his work for what it was. He only hoped this Baines kid had some way of getting it to the right people.

Maybe Toby read my mail and saw the rejections, Stephen thought. Or maybe it was the day a few weeks back when Toby had been standing nearby as Stephen opened his American Express bill and cursed aloud at the amount due. Could Toby be that tuned in, could he just sense when it was time to move on? I'm getting paranoid, Stephen told himself. But, hey, it was probably that instinct that enabled this guy to live the way he did.

Stephen forced himself to continue pouring his drink, acting as if he were completely unconcerned. "Sounds good, Toby. Yeah, we'll see you around."

Toby flashed them both a dazzling grin before disappearing into his room. Stephen drank his Margarita in one long gulp. The tension in his stomach had turned into a hard knot.

"We should get going." Merilee stood up, smoothing the front of her dress.

Stephen hurriedly poured a second drink and drank that as well before turning to her. Maybe breaking off with her tonight wasn't such a good idea after all.

"Right, honey, let's go."

They were almost to the door when the telephone rang.

"Hang on a second." He went over to pick up the portable phone on the end table. "Hello?"

"Stephen, hi. Bruce Baines here."

Speak of the devil, Stephen thought. He hadn't heard from Bruce in nearly two weeks.

"Yes, Bruce, what is it?" Stephen made sure he sounded friendly but businesslike. He didn't want Bruce to think they were going to be buddies, or, worse, that Stephen actually needed him. Cool and professional was the way to play him. God, how Stephen longed for Michael Armand, his old agent, who fell all over himself to please his invisible but highest-earning client, the mysterious Forrestor.

"Let me get right to the point," Bruce replied. "You're not going to like what I have to say. Both Winthrop and Highland turned it down."

Stephen felt his stomach drop. Highland was Forrestor's publisher. He had certainly expected them to fall into line with an offer.

"Who did you send it to?" he asked through clenched teeth. "Did Paul Harlow see it at Highland?"

"No, I know Martha Finegarten over there."

"Who the hell is that?" Stephen snapped.

"She's an editor, and she definitely read it. She was nice enough to get back to me pretty fast, too. But she's passing."

"What about at Winthrop?"

"Sean Harris. A good guy. But he says no."

Stephen closed his eyes, struggling to stay calm. "I told you to send it to Myra Kahn, didn't I?"

"It was assigned to Sean to read. Once he rejected it, she wouldn't look at it."

Stephen held the phone away from his ear for a moment and rubbed the bridge of his nose with his forefinger and thumb. "I don't believe this," he muttered.

Merilee was watching him, one hand on the doorknob. "Everything okay?"

Stephen got back on the line without answering her. "Why are they passing on it? Did they give a reason?"

Bruce paused. "Let's see what a few others have to say."

"What does that mean?" Stephen yelled. "Tell me what they said."

Bruce sighed. "All right. Martha said it wasn't commercial, but she didn't think it was . . . how did she put it? 'Not particularly literary.' Neither fish nor fowl, she said. Sean just didn't like it. Thought it wasn't original enough, didn't grab him, that sort of thing."

"Jesus," Stephen breathed.

"Now, listen," Bruce said comfortingly, "don't get upset. We have other people to try, and they may have something completely different to say. Fiction is completely subjective, and you know how much I liked it."

Stephen wanted to explode at the thought that this kid was patronizing him with his little pep talk. "Call me when you have something else, Bruce," he said tersely before pushing the off button to disconnect the call.

He put the phone down. That incompetent jerk had given his manuscript to some lowly editors who didn't know anything about books. Now the more senior people wouldn't give it the time of day. That had killed his chances permanently at two of the top publishing houses. But, of course, this Baines flunky didn't have access to the senior people.

Shit. Shit. *Shit.*

Merilee began tapping one foot. "Stephen, are you ready to go? I'm just standing here."

He whirled to face her, anger blazing in his eyes. "Oh, am I keeping you?" His voice dripped with sarcasm. "Perish the thought. You have so many important things to do."

In a few quick strides, he was at the door. He yanked it open and gave her a rough shove, sending her stumbling outside. As she cried out his name in hurt surprise, he slammed the door shut as hard as he could. Then he headed to the bar, grabbing the bottle of Scotch and a glass. He was going out to the garden as Merilee pounded on the front door, calling to him over and over.

Chapter 25

Miranda entered the tall gray building, trying to take in every detail without calling undue attention to herself from the security guard seated in front of the elevator bank. So this was the home of Highland Press, she thought, awed by the large numbers of people coming and going. She made her way over to the directory, although she remembered the floor Paul had told her his office was on. Eighteen. The place from which he'd been E-mailing her for months. For some reason, actually meeting him at his office, seeing the desk where he'd edited her very words, was nerve-racking to her.

For the past few weeks, she'd been working on the first four chapters of the new Forrestor novel, but it was daunting. She found herself wanting to travel further from the formula Stephen had used in all his books, tracking the emotional ups and downs of the protagonist, a disaffected former spy, searching back through a past she was making up to explain all the choices he made. And she liked the results. But there was no way to guarantee that Paul would like them. Or that readers would like them.

In fact, she thought, for perhaps the hundredth time that week, readers might not like her first attempt either. *Into Thin Air* would be coming out in a few days. Sure, Paul claimed to like it, but he was the editor, and pleasing a big author, which Forrestor assuredly was, must be a part of his job. What if *Into Thin Air* was really a lame imitation?

God, what if reviewers picked up on the differences between Stephen's writing and her own? Not that critics had been terribly kind to Stephen. Formulaic trash, several of them had called it. But his fans liked the books, and that was all that mattered in the end.

Uneasily, she shifted the large bags she was carrying. She had written for a couple of hours that morning but left the word processor before noon, too restless to work any longer. She'd expected to feel worried all day, but the rest of her afternoon had actually cheered her up considerably. She'd been to Saks Fifth Avenue and Bloomingdale's, mostly buying things for the kids, but picking up a dress and a pair of slacks for herself. Imagine me a size six, she thought, walking over to the guard. She was right on time to pick up Paul for dinner.

"I have an appointment with Paul Harlow," she said to the neatly bearded young man.

"Your name?" he asked.

She had the urge to answer *Forrestor*, but controlled it. "I'm Miranda Shaeffer," was all she said.

The guard lifted the phone and dialed Paul's number, then allowed her to pass by. The receptionist on the eighteenth floor was warmer. Curious even. The middle-aged woman, dressed in a polka-dot shirt tucked into a pleated skirt seemed to be wondering just who she was to Paul—business or social.

"Mr. Harlow is coming out to get you himself," the woman said, her emphasis on the last word making it sound like a royal privilege.

When Paul emerged from behind a closed door to the right of the reception desk, his affectionate kiss hello evoked a raised eyebrow from the woman that made Miranda smile.

"I have a few things to do before we can get out of here. Do you mind?" he asked, walking Miranda down a long corridor leading to a spacious office at the end, its two walls of windows facing down on the darkening streets.

"What a beautiful view," she exclaimed, walking over to look out on Madison Avenue. "You must spend all day looking out the window."

"If I looked out the window all day, I wouldn't keep this office very long," he answered, chuckling. He sat down behind his desk and started to look through a pile of papers. "I'll be just five or ten minutes, I promise."

She sat down near a small table chockablock with newspapers and magazines, and started leafing through a month-old copy of *Publisher's Weekly*.

Paul noticed the cover of the magazine and reached across his desk to pick up a section of the *New York Times*. "Here's the Book Review for next week," he said, lobbing it over to her. "You can be the first on your block . . ."

Miranda looked at the date on the front page of the advance copy. Sure enough, March 11. Almost a full week in the future. She looked at the headline on the first page. A new study of William Faulkner was coming from Knopf. Then she combed the teaser copy on the right-hand side. An essay on deconstructionism by some Harvard professor would be found on page twelve, and some established author making a major breakthrough on page four.

Idly, she turned the page, reading quickly through the review of a memoir by an old Civil War hero uncovered by his great-great nephew from an attic in Virginia. With more interest, she noted a full-page advertisement on the right-hand page for a new family encyclopedia, one that sounded perfect for the children.

Turning the page once more, she let out a gasp. WHO KNEW HE HAD IT IN HIM? the headline read. Underneath the head was a twenty-five-square-inch photo of *Into Thin Air* by Forrestor.

Paul looked over to her curiously. "You look like you've seen a ghost."

"Just a book about a place I once visited," she said quickly.

Holding the paper in front of her face, lest her shock give her away, she read through the full-page review, hardly believing what she was seeing.

When you're a professional reviewer, here are the things you usually get: free books, multiple deadlines, and not much cash. Here's what you usually don't get: any real surprises. But today I had one, and it was a beauty.

Forrestor, that master of the predictable, has become a writer. Leaving the shock, shlock world that has made him a multi-millionaire, he has finally delivered a work of imagination and writerly flair. A work of genuine literary merit.

Miranda read the review through to the end, then read it over again. The reviewer extolled everything from the action sequences to the emotional underpinnings that had been missing from the previous Forrestor books. *If the first few Forrestor novels were produced with a pickax*, the reviewer concluded, *this one was hand delivered by a laser beam*.

Oh my God, she thought, finally daring to put the paper down.

She stood up and turned once again toward the window. In its reflection, she saw Paul get up from behind his desk and walk around to where she'd been sitting. He picked up the review she'd been reading, and glanced through it, an expression of satisfaction setting his handsome face aglow.

"You know," he said softly, "after all these years in publishing, I don't put that much stock in critical opinion, but it is nice to see the reception to the new Forrestor."

Miranda didn't dare to speak.

"It's amazing," Paul declared, coming over and laying his arm lightly around Miranda's shoulders. "This writer, whoever he is, has so much more range than I would have thought. I mean, trust me, most guys with multi-million-dollar contracts do not bother to go any deeper. Most of them write the exact same book every time, and America doesn't mind a bit."

Miranda covered his hand with her own, as the two of them watched the evening lights go on all over Manhattan.

"Most writers probably don't have it in them to get any better even if they wanted to," he continued thoughtfully. "But this guy . . . well, I'm his editor, and even I'm amazed."

He leaned over and planted a kiss on the back of Miranda's neck.

"Now, if I were Forrestor," he said, playful suddenly, "I'd take all that cash and run." He turned her around and held her tightly. "I'd bundle you off to Hawaii or Tahiti, and feed you piña coladas and make love to you day and night for the rest of our lives."

Miranda glowed within the warmth of his arms. The lights of New York City seemed to be shining just for her. *I did it*, she said to herself exultantly. She thought back over the pages she'd written for the next Forrestor novel. *I did it once, and I'm going to do it again.*

Chapter 26

Even before he opened his eyes, Stephen felt the intense pounding of a headache. He rolled over in bed, a wave of nausea making him immediately regret the movement. His mouth was bone-dry, and it was work to pry open his eyelids.

Christ, he thought, now I have to get through a hangover, too. On top of everything else, I'm going to feel like crap for the rest of the day.

He turned to the clock radio beside the bed. It was three-thirty in the afternoon. Normally, a good long sleep should have taken him past a hangover. But then again, he reminded himself, he hadn't even gotten to bed until seven that morning. And maybe it had something to do with the fact that he'd been drinking a lot harder than usual.

He slowly extricated himself from the tangle of covers and made his way to the bathroom. Three extra-strength aspirin and a long shower helped only a little. As he yanked a T-shirt over his head, he wondered what he would do with himself all day. Toby was long gone, as was Merilee. He'd been hanging out at the bars, but there was certainly no one from there that he wanted to see during the day.

In the kitchen, he quickly drank a glass of grapefruit juice before going to make a pot of coffee. Extra strong today, he decided, opening the freezer to get the bag of ground beans. Lifting it from the shelf, the bottom of the bag split in half, coffee spilling all around him onto the floor. For a moment, he just stood there, regarding the mess, his frustration building to an unendurable pitch. He realized tears were actually forming in his eyes. It was all too much, he thought. Just too goddamned much.

He walked away, sitting down heavily at the kitchen table. Despite having thought about little else in the three days since the last conversation with his agent, he was still at a loss to explain the rejection of his manuscript.

Not even in his worst nightmares had he entertained the notion that no one would want to publish *To the Edge*. It was a wonderful book—poignant, well written, insightful. He knew that as sure as he knew he was sitting there. People would definitely want to read it if they could only get their hands on it. Whichever publishing company brought out the book would have that golden combination of literary worth and popular appeal. He had been virtually stupefied when Bruce Baines informed him that there was no one in any of the major publishing houses left; everyone of any consequence had seen it and passed on it.

And it wasn't bad enough that his book was being ignored. He was running out of money. In another couple of months, things were going to get pretty dicey. The house and the car would be the first to go. Where he would go and what would happen after that he couldn't bear to contemplate.

The hell with the coffee, he decided. He got up and poured himself a tall glass of vodka, drinking half of it in one gulp.

It *had* to be because that jerk Bruce was the agent, he thought angrily. I should have waited, not let myself be talked into giving it to him. I could have come back with the manuscript completed in six months, sent it around New York again. Things might have been different when editors gave it a second reading. Or I should have tried to wear someone down, gotten them to see how good the book is. What the hell was I thinking, letting a cretin like Baines handle my work?

But there still was his ace in the hole, and Stephen was banking on it. He didn't know why he hadn't thought of it right away, but a couple of weeks after Baines informed him that Highland Press had passed on his book, Stephen had gotten the idea to send the manuscript directly to Paul Harlow. Baines wouldn't have done it after his own contact there had turned the novel down, but that didn't mean Stephen West himself couldn't put a copy in the mail. Paul Harlow probably wouldn't even know, much less remember, that someone else at the company had read it. And once it was in Paul's hands— assuming Stephen got lucky, and Paul was willing to pick up an unsolicited manuscript from some name he'd never heard of—Stephen had no doubt that his old editor would shepherd it to safety.

Still sipping at his vodka, he idly picked up the stack of mail from the end of the kitchen counter where it had lain since he'd brought it in the night before. He'd been too drunk to read any of it. He set down his glass to flip quickly through the envelopes. And there it was. A letter with Highland Press's return address, with P. Harlow typed in above it.

"You came through, Paul, baby," he muttered, tearing off the envelope and letting it fall to the floor. "Now make me proud of you."

He unfolded the cream-colored piece of stationery and began to read.

Dear Mr. West:

Thank you very much for your submission of To the Edge. *I know that one of our other editors previously read it and passed on it, so when I saw it on my assistant's desk, I was curious about the author who was persistent enough to make an end run around a formal rejection. Part of me says good for you; that kind of persistence is what we all need in this business. Unfortunately, after reading it, another part of me says that our editor was correct in her original assessment, and this letter will bring you only additional disappointment.*

You most definitely have a strong sense of narrative drive, and the book travels along at a brisk pace. Recognizing this, I believe you are entitled to a fuller criticism of the manuscript so that you may incorporate this valuable talent into your next writing attempt. Indeed, I do feel you should go on to a fresh attempt, as this book's problems are so deeply rooted that fixing them would require virtually starting from scratch anyway.

I'm going to give it to you straight. The characters are two-dimensional; their dialogue is stilted; their motivations remain unclear all the way through, and their emotions never ring true. These are not real people. They are conveniences, being moved from one place to another by an author to suit his purpose. With no character development, there is no psychological depth. And, while, generally speaking, your rapid forward motion is a positive note, the plot development is utterly linear, A to B to C, without surprise or complication. That kind of predictability does not make for an emotionally gripping read. Put all of this together and you have a manuscript that does not engage the reader. (By the way, the quote "In the spring a young man's fancy lightly turns to thoughts of love" is Tennyson, not Blake.)

Thank you very much for thinking of us at Highland. I wish you the best of luck in your future literary endeavors.

Sincerely,
Paul Harlow

Stephen put the letter down on the kitchen counter, and picked up his glass, downing the vodka that remained in it. Then, the glass still aloft in his hand, he gazed up at the ceiling.

Paul had certainly given it to him straight. *You have no talent, schmuck.* Narrative drive, well, yes, that made sense; that was probably what pushed the Forrestor novels along, the reason people enjoyed zipping through them. But the painfully clear message was that he couldn't write anything even remotely serious or real. *And thank you, Paul,* he thought bitterly, *for so kindly pointing out about Tennyson. In case I wasn't absolutely certain that I was a total intellectual lightweight.*

This had been his last chance. Now that Paul Harlow had turned him down, it was truly and completely over for *To the Edge.*

He slammed the glass down on the table, overcome with impotent rage.

"Take it easy," he muttered. "There's an answer somewhere. Just keep cool."

For a few moments, he didn't move, awash in his despair. Then, taking several deep breaths, he tried to block it all out. He would read the paper, eat something, go to a movie. Later, something would come to him. Like Scarlett O'Hara, he thought sardonically, as he went to the front door to retrieve the *L.A. Times.* I'll think about it tomorrow. That's it. End of story for today.

He grabbed a bag of cinnamon raisin buns from the kitchen counter on his way back to the table. Savagely biting into one, he perused the paper's first section, then started flipping through the rest. His method of reading the Sunday paper rarely varied, and by habit, he stopped at the Book Review section and pulled it out to see what was going on in the business.

The front page was devoted to some important book on computer technology. He quickly scanned the approving review and turned the page as he licked his sticky fingers. The new novel on page two didn't fare as well; the reviewer's assessment was scathing.

Sorry, buddy, he said silently to the book's author as he reached for another bun, but at least you got your damn book into print. And reviewed on page two of the *L.A. Times Book Review*, no less. You ain't gettin' any sympathy from me.

He shifted his gaze to page three. About to bite into the bun, he stopped, his hand suspended near his mouth. He stared at the words in front of him, a sudden stabbing pain in his chest. Putting down the bun, he realized he was having trouble breathing. He looked away, shutting his eyes, trying to calm down. A mistake, he told himself. A weird, impossible mistake.

He looked back at the page. AN ENIGMA AT THE TOP OF HIS GAME read the headline. Below it, in smaller print, there was the book's title and author: *Into Thin Air* by Forrestor.

"No," he whispered. *"Christ, no."*

He raced frantically through the review. It was written by a university professor who proclaimed to be a longtime fan of Forrestor's. Stephen realized his hands were trembling.

> With this novel, Forrestor moves from the ranks of enjoyable, but typical male adventure writer to join the likes of Le Carré and Forsyth.
>
> The top-notch dialogue, pacing, and unexpected twists make *Into Thin Air* a welcome leap forward in this writer's career. That a top-selling author—who could easily coast on his popular success—has honed his skills to this level makes the mystery of Forrestor's real identity even more tantalizing. I myself am more frustrated than ever that he/she/they won't reveal him/her/themselves.

Reading to the end, Stephen felt as if the blood were slowly draining from his body. Who had written the book and how had it happened? Someone had co-opted Forrestor's name for his own benefit. He couldn't imagine who was smart enough to come up with the idea, or how he knew Stephen was out of the picture so that it could even be done.

Worst of all, he had beaten Stephen at his own game. They were proclaiming this impostor's book better than Stephen's. What in Christ's name was happening?

The *New York Times*. That was the review he had to see. That was the one that mattered.

He leaped up, grabbing his keys as he tore outside, running to the car and yanking open the door. Careening out of his driveway, he tried to think how he could find the New York paper. It came to him: the Beverly Hills Hotel, at the place where they sold cigarettes and magazines.

When he got there, he didn't wait to buy the paper, but rifled through it until he found the Book Review section. Grabbing it, he went through the pages roughly, both desperate to find a review and petrified that one might actually be there.

It was there, on page four. His mouth went dry as he read.

. . . he has finally delivered a book of imagination and writerly flair.

Dropping the section, he ran out of the hotel and back to his car. Half an hour later, he was at a bookstore, paying for a copy of *Into Thin Air*. He was sickened by what he saw there, the copies of the book in the window, the huge spread of them on a table up front near the registers. It wasn't until he was home alone again that he permitted himself to take a closer look at the glossy blue cover and raised gold letters, the book jacket's style so typical of all the Forrestor novels.

He read the flap copy, the print on the inside cover describing the book's plot. It sounded like one of his, no question about it. But better. He could see right away that, even without his level of writing talent, just playing out the story would make a more complex book than his other ones. And the reviewers had carried on about the high quality of the writing. Who had come up with this? Seething, he sat down on the sofa and started to read.

By the end of chapter one, he had his answer. For a long while, he just sat there, staring into space. An iciness was spreading through him, the combination of rage and hatred so powerful he didn't think it could be contained.

Then, finally, he went back to the book, not getting up until he was finished, hardly moving other than to turn the pages. When at last he reached the end and closed the cover, he leaned back, shutting his eyes.

Her voice was so clear, it was as if she were in the same room with him, telling him the story in person. How anyone could think it was the same narrative voice that had told the other Forrestor stories was beyond belief.

And she had used everything she knew, details from their past, their travels, their conversations. She must have been paying closer attention than he'd realized when he had idly discussed how he structured his books, or whatever he might have said about his technique.

It was all there in front of him. The most staggering betrayal, the most shocking display of duplicity he could ever imagine.

"You fucking *bitch*," he spat out.

He threw the book as hard as he could across the room. It smashed into a table, knocking over a porcelain vase that hit the ground, shattering with a crash.

Miranda had stolen Forrestor from him. Outright *stolen* him. And there wasn't a goddamned thing he could do about it.

Chapter 27

Jack held his remaining three cards carefully, his face a mask of disinterest. In the past ten rounds, he had picked up all of the available hearts, making sure to act unhappy as he accumulated point after point. Now, all the while knowing that no one else at the table had any clubs left, he threw out the ten. Sure enough, Sophie put down the four of hearts, while his mother and his aunt Lydia deposited the six and the queen, respectively.

"Gosh," Ethan said, as he passed by the table and grabbed a handful of grapes, "you're gonna end up with a thousand points."

"He's shooting the moon!" Sophie cried, as the truth suddenly dawned.

Jack picked up all four cards and deposited them in the large pile in front of him. Smiling slightly, he played his second to last card, the king of diamonds.

Happily, he picked up two more hearts, as the other three players did what they had to. His final card, the queen of spades, drew gasps of horror from Lydia and Sophie. Only his mother smiled as he gained the final thirteen points in his fatal assault.

"That's it," Miranda said, holding her son's hand up in triumph.

Lydia gave a smart salute, as she rose from her chair and began collecting the dirty snack plates. Sophie shrugged, then offered her brother a high-five, which he responded to gleefully.

"How about the three of you coming with me?" Paul asked, getting up from the easy chair in which he'd been reading a manuscript. "Your aunt was incredibly kind to have us all over. But her food is altogether too healthy. I think a Häagen Dazs run is called for."

"Okay!" Sophie squealed. "C'mon, Eth," she said, taking the *Highlights* magazine he was holding out of his hands peremptorily.

Ethan ran to get his jacket, while Jack walked over to the pile of Lydia's CDs and began shuffling through them distractedly.

"You, too, Jack," Sophie said.

"Yeah, yeah," he said indifferently. But within seconds, he had picked up his own jacket and wandered to the front door.

Left by themselves, Lydia turned to Miranda. "How many miracles was that exactly?" she asked, shaking her head in wonder. She went into the kitchen, putting the dirty dishes in the sink before pulling out a large bowl of fruit from the refrigerator. Setting it out on the kitchen table, she turned to Miranda, who had walked in behind her carrying three dirty glasses and an enormous bottle of spring water.

"Let's see, there's Paul and the kids. That's one," Lydia continued, holding up her index finger. "And then there's Jack agreeing to play Hearts with Sophie and never once threatening to kill her." She paused. "Then there's you, not even seeming surprised by any of it."

Miranda grinned. "Actually, the kids really seem to like Paul. He took all of us to the Bronx Zoo last Saturday, including his son, Josh."

"How'd that go?"

"Not so bad," Miranda responded. "Josh kept to himself for the first couple of hours. By the time we got to the Big Cats, everybody had bonded like glue."

She started to rinse the dishes. "Ever since Jack's trip to Florida over Christmas, he's been slightly less horrible to Sophie."

She applied soap to a yellow sponge and began to vigorously scrub the pan in which the buckwheat pancakes for their brunch had been cooked. "Now what was the third miracle? Oh, yes, my lack of shock at my own good fortune." She rinsed out the pan and placed it on the drying rack, then picked up one of the dishes, poking at the dried pancake remains with a corner of the sponge. "Well, I do feel fortunate." She put down the plate and looked around at her sister. "That's about it for me and miracles."

Lydia leaned forward suddenly and placed her arms around her sister.

"Gee," Miranda said, rubbing Lydia's back affectionately. "What's all this about?"

Lydia held on for a moment, then let go. She walked to the small kitchen table, drew up a chair and sat down.

"I don't know, honey."

"Honey?" Miranda said lightly. "What happened to fatty? Or lazy? Or dopey?" She laughed. "Or even Sneezy or Doc?"

Lydia looked down at the floor, keeping her sister from seeing the expression on her face. When she raised her head, Miranda was shocked to see tears in her eyes.

"Hey, what gives?"

Lydia's expression was one Miranda had never seen before on her sister's face.

Finally she spoke. "You know, Ran, I can't believe I really call you those things all the time. I shouldn't. Not now, not ever. There's nothing lazy or dopey or anything like that about you."

Miranda jokingly grabbed at the area over her heart. "Now, this *is* a miracle, and I don't think my body can stand it."

"I'm not kidding." Lydia put her hand out beseechingly.

In response, Miranda turned off the water and joined her sister at the table, taking the seat next to her and grabbing the hand Lydia held out to her.

"You've come through a terrible time amazingly well, Ran, and I'm really proud of you." Lydia squeezed Miranda's hand before letting it go. "That's the *real* miracle."

Miranda smiled slightly. "You just approve of me 'cause I've gotten thinner."

"No," Lydia replied emphatically. "It's much more than that. You don't begin to know how apologetic I feel." She leaned forward, looking into her sister's eyes. "We haven't talked much about Henry, but there are a few things I should tell you. One is, I've broken up with him. Which," she smiled sardonically, "may just about kill me."

Miranda smiled in response, but the look of real pain on Lydia's face was nothing to take lightly, she could tell.

"I'm sorry—" she started to say, before Lydia interrupted.

"It was really you who gave me the courage. The fact that you didn't yell at me about his being married, and trusted me to handle it the right way, meant everything to me. It was like a challenge to actually be my own person. The kind of person I always yelled at you about becoming. But, it turns out, you always were that person. A great person."

The tears started running down Lydia's face in earnest. "Jesus, when Stephen was alive, I was at you day and night about what a louse he was. Like it's so easy to be clear-sighted when you're in love." Lydia tried to wipe away the tears, but they were replaced quickly by new ones. "I haven't had a clear thought in months."

"You really love this guy, don't you?" Miranda asked.

Lydia's voice lowered to a whisper. "So much, I feel like my heart is breaking. It's ironic, isn't it?" she said ruefully. "Here I kept accusing you of being the weak one, and you're the one who comes out like a champ, while I act like a jerk."

Miranda stood up and came around behind her sister, hugging her from the back, as she had done so many times for her children. "Loving someone doesn't make you a jerk. And breaking up with someone you love that much takes all the strength in the world."

Lydia grabbed a napkin from a pile on the table and dabbed at the mascara that was now smeared under her eyes. "I wonder if he even misses me," she said, blowing her nose into the napkin and tossing it into the wastebasket a couple of feet away.

"Two points for Shaquille Greenfield," Miranda said, smiling. She gave her sister another hug. "Of course he misses you."

Both of them were surprised when the telephone rang. Lydia stopped to blow her nose one more time with yet another napkin before answering.

"Hello," she finally said, her voice as normal as possible.

Miranda turned around when she heard her sister gasp, then stared as tears appeared once again in Lydia's eyes. But this time, the look of pain had become a transcendent glow.

"What?" Miranda asked, as Lydia whispered something unintelligible into the receiver, then put it down on top of the table.

"That was Henry," Lydia said in wonderment. "He just asked me to marry him."

Chapter 28

Stephen slowed his car down as he passed a large bookstore. He let his eye wander over the window display of *Into Thin Air*. The stacks of the new Forrestor seemed to multiply, scores of books becoming hundreds in his mind's eye.

Enough, he told himself, pulling away and driving toward the Saks Fifth Avenue on Wilshire Boulevard. As he walked away from his parked car, a young couple, both dressed all in black, the husband holding a baby, bumped into him, the man muttering about loiterers as they unapologetically rushed past him. Loitering? Stephen thought furiously. You've got a goddamned nerve. I lived in New York, he wanted to scream at them. I practically *invented* being busy.

Realizing how crazy he was beginning to sound even to himself, he stopped at a bench, taking a seat. I have too much time on my hands, he thought, inhaling deeply, then letting the air out. He glanced at his watch. Only two in the afternoon, with the rest of the day looming like a big empty balloon over his head. He'd made a lunch and tennis date with Toby a few days before, which his former roommate broke over the telephone machine while Stephen was in the shower. When he called Toby back a few minutes later, he didn't even bother picking up the phone, although Stephen was certain he was there, just listening on the other end. Well, screw you, Toby. He scowled as he realized that a little girl, her mother holding tightly to one hand, her father to the other, was staring at him as if he were a creature from another planet. God, was everybody here part of a family, he thought, watching as couple after couple trailed by with their young children. All of them made him sick, he thought, his eyes coming to rest on another family. He noticed the son, maybe a year or two younger than Ethan would be by now, looking at his father adoringly. It was a look he remembered, and not just from Ethan.

How old was Jack that day I played catch with him in the park, he wondered. Maybe five or six, he decided, remembering with pleasure what unusual agility his oldest child had shown. I should have done it more often, he reflected guiltily. By now, the kid would be in Little League. Probably playing first base. No, with those reflexes, maybe shortstop.

Two identical twin girls strolled by, dressed in matching white sailor suits, their hair pulled back in pigtails affixed by blue-and-white polka-dot ribbons. Like the ribbon Sophie had used when she dressed up her Tiny Tears doll.

The force of his sudden loneliness made Stephen spring up from the bench. You're thinking crazy, he told himself, heading toward the entrance of the department store. He walked past the perfume counters, taking in the scents, enjoying the reed-thin young women offering all the female customers a spray of this, a whiff of that. It would be wonderful to take one of those young women home with him, to plug away at her firm flesh until all the bad feelings went away.

Uncomfortably, he recalled Tuesday night. He'd gone to see a movie. Sure enough, he'd gotten into a conversation with the two young women beside him. They'd all gone for a beer after the film, and one of them, the gorgeous one, in fact, had come home with him. He shuddered as the rest of the night came back to him.

Christ, he thought, it wasn't so serious. It happens to every man. If it didn't ever happen, I wouldn't be human. Besides, I satisfied her plenty. Her leaving before midnight had nothing to do with that. She works, for God's sake. She had to get a few hours' sleep.

Stephen brushed his thoughts aside as he searched for the men's department. Socks, he decided. I need socks. He'd stopped the daily maid service, and now had a woman coming in to clean four hours every Wednesday. It was adequate, but it didn't allow time for laundry, and he'd awakened every day this week stuck for a pair of clean socks.

He made his way to the men's department, knowing that the brand of socks he liked would be there. And maybe he'd pick up a new tie. He paused at a glass counter entirely covered by paisley ties. One by one he held them up to his neck. Finally, he found the perfect print. Shades of red mixed with navy. Perfect, he decided, admiring the glow it brought to his face when he checked in the mirror.

He called over a young salesman, clearly inexperienced, who was rearranging striped ties on the other side of the counter.

"That's a beauty, sir," the young man said, clearing his throat like a high school junior on his first date. "You know," he added, "the same pattern is available in shades of purple and green."

Stephen paused. He didn't really need two ties. Actually, he didn't really need one, but it was a nice print.

"And they're on sale for only one hundred thirty-nine ninety-five," the salesman added enthusiastically.

Stephen hesitated. That was almost three hundred bucks for two pieces of clothing he didn't need at all. How could he justify that, he wondered, thinking of his dwindling bank account. The high six-figure bonanza he'd started off with had turned into five figures. With his apartment and car payments due on the first, it was about to plunge into the low five figures.

Damn it, he thought, furious, I hate worrying about a few hundred bucks. "I'll take both," he said grandly, pulling out his gold card and handing it to the clerk. He imagined how envious the young man must be.

He walked out proudly, the ties in a bag under his arm. It was only ten minutes later, when he stopped for coffee at a nearby Starbuck's, that he realized how foolish the purchase had been.

"Regular or decaf on the latte?" the bored middle-aged woman behind the counter asked as he gave his order.

Stephen felt paralyzed by anxiety suddenly. A latte was three-fifty. Three-fifty was almost five. And five was almost ten. Ten was a major piece of a hundred. He felt as if the room were beginning to spin around him.

The woman looked at him oddly. "You all right?" she asked.

"Yes." He tried to keep the feeling of panic from overpowering him. "Decaf," he answered, then caught himself. "No, just a decaf coffee." That was only a buck. The wave of dread lodged just below his breastbone eased slightly.

Stephen grabbed the cup the woman offered and made his way to an empty table. Just breathe, he told himself, aware that the woman was watching him. Audaciously, he looked back at her. God, he thought after a few seconds, she looks like my mother. The same gray hair. The same expression of pity on her face.

My mother didn't pity me, he corrected himself, getting up and going toward the exit. My mother loved me, he assured himself, walking crookedly down the cement path that led to the parking lot. He realized his tread was rocky, and purposefully slowed down, making straight for his BMW. Get hold of yourself, he thought, as he opened the door and eased in behind the wheel. Unbidden, images of his mother and father filled his brain. Him, as a little boy, watching them prepare their lectures in their shared office. The pleased expressions on both their faces when he received his high school diploma.

Suddenly the pictures metamorphosed into images of his wife and children. Jack, graduating from that silly Montessori preschool Miranda had him going to. Sophie, his beautiful Sophie, throwing sand into a bucket that summer in Maine in her little pink flowered bathing suit, that beatific grin on her face. And Ethan. Would he even recognize Ethan? He must have changed so much in the past year. At five, he'd been just a baby when Stephen had left. Now he was six, going on seven. A real boy.

Stephen felt sick to his stomach. I want it back, he screamed silently. I want my life. I want to be Forrestor, making millions of dollars, not Joe Schlub worried about the price of a cappuccino.

With horror, he realized he was about to vomit. As quickly as he could, he opened the car door and whirled around to hang his legs out and plant his feet on the pavement. Humiliated, he hung his head. You're not going to puke in an open parking lot, he promised himself, looking up to see if anyone was watching him.

Relieved that no one seemed to be looking, he breathed evenly, the feeling of nausea receding. Not daring to close the car door again, he stayed as he was, his eyes boring into the white line delineating his parking space.

I have to go back. The realization came to him with certainty.

But I can't go back.

Finally, he sat up straight once more. I'm not going to let them beat me, he decided. I *can* go back. I *must* go back. He thought about the shocked delight that would fill his parents' faces when he walked up to their door.

But what would he say in response to the questions they would have? Amnesia. That's what I'll tell them, he decided. I was in the bombing and I lost my identity. They'll be happy to believe me. And I can get back to writing my books.

With horror, he realized that he no longer wrote the Forrestor books. He was no longer Forrestor. That scheming bitch Miranda was Forrestor.

He turned the situation over in his mind. If he reappeared, Miranda would want money, Miranda would want revenge, and Miranda would no doubt want to continue being Forrestor. She would also keep him from the kids. With her in the picture, he really couldn't go back.

But he'd figure out how to deal with that later. Right now, getting back was the only thing that mattered.

Chapter 29

Sophie threw the tiny rubber ball into the air, then, with her other hand, swept up the ten jacks that lay in a large unwieldy formation on the floor in front of her. Holding on to the tiny metal clusters and lifting them high, she smiled in triumph.

"Gee, Sophie, that was great," Josie Frommer exclaimed, her red curls bobbing around her angular face. "Maybe when my mom gets here and we go back to my house, we can play some more and I can beat you."

Lucy Driscoll, stroking one of her dark braids, threw Josie a look of disdain. "Yeah, you'll beat Sophie . . . when refrigerators fly."

"It's 'when pigs fly,' moron," Josie shot back at her.

"Don't you think it's time we looked for your mother?" Sophie asked, intercepting, as she often did, the constant sniping between the girls who had become her best friends.

The three of them had been waiting inside the Clareton school for fifteen minutes. Eda Frommer's lateness was so commonplace, her daughter routinely carried reading matter with her to stave off the boredom of waiting.

"Yeah," Josie said, looking at the Mickey Mouse watch she'd pointedly asked for on her last birthday. "We might as well go outside."

Sophie was the first out the front door, her eyes adjusting quickly to the bright sunlight, a surprise after the dim corridor of Clareton.

As she held the door for her friends, she noticed a man rise suddenly from the steps of the apartment building across the street. Tallish, with a blond beard and blond hair, he stared at her for an intense few seconds, before turning and striding quickly into the crowded city street.

Transfixed, Sophie let the door go, paying no attention when Lucy yelled in annoyance as it hit her in the shoulder. With both her friends now looking at her in bewilderment, Sophie took off down the steps that led to the street, running as fast as her legs could carry her.

"Sophie, where are you going?" Josie yelled after her. "My mother's going to be here any second."

The two girls watched Sophie disappear around the corner.

"Mommy!"

Miranda heard her daughter's cry all the way from her office. Rushing out to the living room, she scooped up Sophie in her arms.

"What is it, honey?" she asked, setting her back down on the floor and examining her closely. Aside from the girl's bright red face there were no injuries that Miranda could see.

"I saw Daddy!" Sophie exclaimed with a huge smile. "I was coming out of school with Josie and Lucy, and he was waiting across the street."

Miranda felt an almost physical blow to her stomach. Horrified, she sank onto the sofa. Sophie had seemed to be so much better, she thought, as she took her daughter onto her lap and enfolded her in her arms.

"Baby," she crooned softly, "I know how wonderful it would be if Daddy were still alive. But he's not. You know that, sweetie."

Impatiently, Sophie tore out of her mother's grasp. She stood up, facing Miranda, her face contorted not in grief, but in frustration.

"Mommy, listen to me. Daddy was right there, sitting on the steps of the red building across from school." Sophie's eyes implored her mother to believe her. "Only when he saw me, he got up and walked away."

Miranda felt helpless. "You saw a man who *looked* like Daddy, honey," she said, smothing back an unruly strand of hair from her daughter's forehead.

Sophie rolled her eyes. "He didn't look like Daddy. In fact, he had long blond hair and a beard. But it *was* Daddy." She saw the disbelief in her mother's eyes. "I'm telling you," she said belligerently. "I *know* my daddy!"

Miranda had no idea what to do. For lack of a better idea, she led

Sophie toward the kitchen, pulling a carton of milk out of the refrigerator and a box of Mallomars out of a cupboard.

"Okay, sweetheart," she said, settling herself and Sophie around the kitchen table. "Tell me all about this guy."

Twenty minutes later, Sophie was in her room, her mother's promise to look into things ringing in her ear. Look into what, Miranda asked herself disgustedly as she sponged the cookie crumbs from the table. Stephen was dead, and all the wishing in the world wasn't going to bring him back.

She rinsed the sponge under the cold water and laid it on the rim of the sink. It was disheartening to think that Sophie was still in denial about her father's death. She had seemed like herself in the past few months, behaving properly at school, more cheerful around the house. She'd gone back to picking up complete strangers on the street, a habit that filled Miranda with fear. But it was a fear she could handle more easily than the helpless dread she'd experienced as she'd watched her daughter self-destruct just after Stephen got killed.

That Sophie could cut class or act like a brat, those things had been upsetting. But that Sophie could dream up Stephen, pining for his daughter like some hero in a fairytale—that was devastating. Miranda wandered around the kitchen aimlessly, pushing in the silverware drawer that hadn't been entirely closed, straightening a pile of papers Ethan had drawn on with a green magic marker. Finally, she stopped moving and stood, her back against the refrigerator door, her eyes closed. How could she not have noticed how damaged her daughter still was? The guilt exploded inside her like water bursting through a pipe. Her extroverted, happy little girl had succumbed to delusions. What Miranda thought had been set right was proving to be terribly, horribly wrong.

Miranda opened her eyes, reassured momentarily by the ordinariness of the room in front of her. The sight of the bright kitchen, the slight messiness exactly as it always was, the annoying drip of water falling into the sink, as it almost always did—all of it seemed to clear her mind.

Sophie was not a fanciful child. Not a liar, not a girl who imagined demons in her closet or monsters under the bed. Of all her three children, Sophie was the most practical, the most closely wedded to reality. She certainly hadn't seen her father, but she must have seen a man who looked a lot like him, whose mannerisms resembled Stephen's.

As if out of nowhere, the phrase Paul had uttered carelessly when he was taking about Forrestor's astonishing recent success came into her head. *I'd take the cash and run.* Those had been his words.

Suddenly, she felt the blood pulsing through her body, a rush of electricity that almost made her lose her balance. It couldn't be, she said to herself, hoping the words would fight the riot of emotion that was threatening to overwhelm her. She made her way to a chair, sitting as calmly as possible, taking one deep breath after another in an effort to focus.

She forced herself to consider the things she actually knew. Stephen Shaeffer had disappeared. His body was never found. Their savings were gone. All these months after the bombing, not one piece of direct evidence of Stephen Shaeffer's death had ever been uncovered.

"Oh my God, is it possible he's still alive?" Paralyzed by horror, she said the words aloud without meaning to.

The notion that Stephen had survived the bombing was as difficult to believe as a river changing its course or pieces of the sky falling to the ground. He couldn't have just disappeared. He couldn't have done such a thing, she assured herself, thinking of the man she married, a responsible person with three children, the only child of two aging parents who'd spent the last year shattered by grief.

But no matter how impossible it seemed, there was a thread of fury building through her chest, telling her just the opposite. Stephen Shaeffer hadn't been the man that she married. He'd become a stranger. Who in God's name knew what that Stephen could have done.

The presents. The memory flashed into her mind as if out of nowhere. The three presents that had arrived for the children awhile back with no card, no indication who had sent them. Miranda shut her eyes, trying to recall them. A peach leotard and matching sequinned tutu for Sophie, running shoes and a football jersey for Jack, a cowboy outfit complete with boots for Ethan. All obviously expensive, all with the tags removed, all in the wrong sizes.

The return address on the box had been a department store in Florida, and Miranda had immediately assumed the gifts were from Esther, although it didn't seem like something her mother would do. And she certainly wouldn't waste her money buying things that wouldn't fit; she would have consulted Miranda first. But her mother denied sending the gifts anyway. Miranda meant to follow up on it, but without any tags she doubted the store would be able or willing to track down the buyer. The whole thing hadn't seemed all that important anyway. She had quickly forgotten about it.

Until now. It wasn't hard to imagine Stephen picking out things he believed the children would like, not knowing their sizes, blithely figuring he would be in the ballpark with his guesses. A chill went up her spine.

Miranda walked out of the kitchen and went to her office, closing the door behind her. She needed time alone to think this through.

The Forrestor money, gone from the bank accounts—had that been his preparation for leaving? But how could he have planned his method of departure? Her next thought almost brought her to her knees. Could Stephen have been involved in the bombing?

Numbly, she sat down at her desk, staring at nothing. Could the Kallifer Five have lied about their responsibility for the terrorist attack? All five members of the radical group were in jail. At least four of them were expected to be sentenced to death. Her mind reeled. There was no way they would have confessed to a crime of that magnitude if they weren't guilty.

No, she decided, Stephen couldn't have set that plan in motion. But might he have taken advantage of their actions? Was that so crazy? After all, he'd been taking money from their accounts for months. He must have been planning to leave. She'd known that in her heart since she'd found out about the missing funds, though she hadn't let herself dwell on it. But now she had to. Stephen had been unhappy for months. No, she admitted to herself, for years. Would he have been willing to put his children, his parents, herself through the torment of the past year? Yes, she suddenly knew. That wouldn't have been beyond him at all.

That bastard, she thought, incensed. Stephen Shaeffer. A man who could leave three children in tatters. That was exactly who he was. And now, he had chosen to come back. Oh, maybe he didn't expect Sophie to see him. Certainly, he hadn't wanted to go public. This time, anyway. But what about next time? What about the day he decided to seek out Jack and Ethan?

She felt her body coming back to life. One thing she knew for sure, she was not going to sit around, powerless, waiting for him to alight. She was going to use everything she'd learned about him in fifteen years of marriage to find him herself. She pulled a yellow pad and a thin black marker from the top drawer, and started jotting down her thoughts.

Stephen must have left New York after the bombing; it was the most logical move for someone going into hiding whose face was on the local nightly news for weeks. She started pondering where he might have gone but quickly realized it didn't matter. If that very day her daughter had seen Stephen, it meant he was somewhere in Manhattan. But where? The old Stephen would have been impossible to locate, she thought ironically. He might have been anywhere from Staten Island to the Bronx. But what about the new Stephen Shaeffer, the guy with the fancy suits and first-class taste. If he was still running true to form, she bet she could guess where he would stay within five or ten minutes.

She reached back and pulled the thick Yellow Pages from the shelf. Turning to "Hotels," she started making a list of the fanciest places in town. Her husband would probably be at the Plaza or the Four Seasons. Or maybe the Regency or the Parker Meridien. It was just a question of a few phone calls.

She started by dialing the Plaza, asking for Stephen Shaeffer. Told there was no one by that name registered there, she asked for Stephen Forrestor. She could well imagine her husband using his former pseudonym to put a little distance between him and the life he'd left behind. When there was no Stephen Forrestor either, she went on, calling eleven other hotels. At the end of half an hour, she had spoken to Richard Schaeffer, who must have been at least seventy-five years old, and Michael Forrestor, who turned out to be a woman. No one else by either name was staying at those hotels.

She'd come up with the names of the best hotels she could think of. Frustrated, she wondered which ones she'd missed. She reviewed her notes, wondering if any of her scribbles would provide a clue. Nothing, she thought irritably. Most of what she'd written resembled graffiti and nothing more, arrows going nowhere and dollar signs with angry slashes through them. That was just what her husband's life had turned out to be about. The almighty buck. What her father always referred to as the root of all evil.

But another phrase occurred to her. Follow the money. Watergate. That was what Deep Throat told Woodward and Bernstein. Well, if they could do it, so could she. After all, large sums had been deducted from their accounts. They must have ended up somewhere. He certainly hadn't had a million dollars on him when he disappeared from Central Bank. He must have set up another account somewhere. Maybe multiple accounts even.

Sorry, Stephen, she said to herself, as she reached for the phone one more time, but now you're in my neighborhood. She dialed a number she knew and waited impatiently for it to be answered.

"Fred Salley," the familiar voice of her former boss answered after three rings.

"It's Miranda. Thank goodness you're still there," she said. "I have a tremendous favor to ask. An essential favor, actually."

Fred's easy yes came immediately.

"I need to find some very large transfers my husband made from a couple of our accounts to another bank. They may have gone to several different banks."

"Hmmm . . ." Fred said dubiously. "That's not so easy."

Miranda knew she had to tell him the rest. "It may also have been deposited under another name. Stephen would have been hiding this money from me, and possibly from the government as well. I just don't know."

"Whew!" Fred said, obviously surprised. He was quiet for a few moments, then continued. "Were these deposits for over ten thousand dollars?"

Miranda considered the question. "Yes, I would think they were for a lot more than that."

"Well, then, we've got a shot. Deposits that large are monitored for tax purposes. Not that I can do it without pulling some major strings, but from what you're saying I gather this is really important."

"You can't imagine how important," Miranda sighed.

"Okay, then," Fred said in a more businesslike tone, "give me your husband's full name and his social security number, and let me see what I can do."

"Stephen Alanson Shaeffer," she responded, adding her husband's social security number.

"The middle name, spell it for me," Fred replied. "It's unusual."

Miranda laughed bitterly. "A-l-a-n-s-o-n. It was an homage to the William Alanson White Institute, where his mother wanted to take analytic training before she met her husband and moved to Ann Arbor to join him in graduate school. Stephen considered his middle name his mother's way of making his father feel permanently guilty about forcing his wife to give up her dreams."

"Well," Fred said in response, "let me make a few calls and see what I can come up with."

It was only an hour later when he called back.

"You owe me big, kiddo," he said as soon as Miranda picked up the phone. "I found what you're looking for at Midway Bank. Alanson Shaeffer is the proud owner of just over twelve thousand dollars. It's deposited in the branch on Madison and Fifty-sixth Street. By the way, from what my source told me, there was a whole lot more at one time."

Miranda thought about what Fred said. "Is there any way at all that I can get into that account?" she asked finally.

"Hey," Fred laughed, "just walk in. After all, you're his widow. Take the death certificate with you when you go, and you shouldn't have a problem." His tone grew more serious. "Miranda, are you okay?"

"Now there's a profound question," Miranda said, trying to laugh off his concern. Abruptly, she realized she didn't have to avoid the issue. "You know what, Fred? Things have been up and down for a long time now, but as of today, I believe I'm on the road to full recovery."

"I don't know what's going on," Fred said, "and you don't have to tell me. But I'm here if you need me."

Miranda felt moved by his words. A casual acquaintance for all these years, yet Fred had come through each time she'd called on him. "Thank you, Fred. I'm grateful," she said sincerely.

The next morning, Miranda showed the death certificate to a receptionist at Midway Bank and was seated opposite Wanda Prince, the assistant manager. Within fifteen minutes, she was staring at the printout of Alanson Shaeffer's banking records for the past two years. Incredibly, there had been large withdrawals on December 10th, March 12th, and April 10th. Amazing, she thought, clutching the paper to her chest. Stephen Shaeffer had completed at least three major banking transactions months after he died.

"Can I do anything more for you, Mrs. Shaeffer?" the petite brunette offered.

You can buy me a rifle, Miranda thought bitterly, but said instead, "No, thank you. You've been very helpful."

Prince rose from her chair. "Well, then . . ." she said with finality.

Miranda rose also, but instead of walking away decided to ask one more question. "Is there any way of knowing whether these funds were withdrawn in person?"

"No, not really," the woman answered hesitantly. "It could have been by mail." Her eyes reflected sudden worry. "Are you suggesting there's something wrong here?"

The woman had looked at the death certificate for mere seconds before giving Miranda the information she'd asked for. There was no way she would have taken in the date of Stephen's actual demise. Miranda thought briefly about taking the death certificate out of her bag and pointing out the date but decided against it. Whatever steps were to be taken would be taken by her, not by a bank or any other organization. For better or worse, Stephen Shaeffer was the father of her children. She didn't want them to have to live with a father in prison. On the other hand, she wasn't going to let him get away with this.

"No, Ms. Prince, everything looks just fine."

Miranda had to rush off to work at Jack's school's book fair for most of the day. She arrived back at her apartment just in time to greet Ethan as he returned home from school, quickly followed by Jack and Sophie. After feeding them a snack, she settled them in front of the VCR and turned on *Star Wars*, a movie all three of them loved.

"How come you're letting us do this?" Ethan asked.

He was quickly shushed by his sister and brother. Watching television in the afternoon was generally forbidden, and the two older children knew better than to question their luck.

Miranda had no time to feel guilty about breaking one of her most steadfast rules. Stephen Shaeffer was alive, and living somewhere in New York City, and she was going to find him in the next two hours. She went back to the yellow pad she'd been using the day before, returning to the list of hotel telephone numbers. Now, she tried them all again, but this time she asked for Alanson Shaeffer or a Mr. Alanson. From the Pierre to the Stanhope, they all announced that no such person was staying there.

Then she began to write down anything she could think of that Stephen might use as the basis of an alias. Stephen Morris, she thought, remembering the first name of her husband's beloved grandfather. Stephen Goren, maybe, utilizing the name of the bridge expert whose book Stephen had used as a bible when they'd first played in college. Then she added several other names: Colby and Cummings, plucked from his old ad agency; Callowell, his aunt Sarah's second husband, who'd taken him to ball games when he was in junior high school; both Nathanael and West, the author whose work Stephen idolized.

She combed her mind, coming up with seven more surnames, easily rejecting any that tied into the early years of their marriage. Surely Stephen wouldn't have bothered dredging up any sentimental memories to help him hide from her. Then she picked up the phone and started dialing yet again. She began by asking for only one name per call in order not to rouse any suspicion, but quickly raised it to two. Still, it took an hour to get through every name at every hotel.

Nothing, she thought, panicked by the notion that he might not be staying at a hotel at all. Maybe he had friends she didn't know anything about, someone willing to put him up, someone she couldn't find if she had decades to do it instead of mere hours. Or maybe he was staying outside the city. New Jersey or Westchester. He could be anywhere.

I will do all I can, and I will not panic, she lectured herself silently. She looked once more at her list. "Okay, Ran," she said aloud, "time to fire up the imagination." Now she added all the names he might have chosen from the happiest period of their lives. It was hideous to think of her husband employing their favorite moments together in service of his betrayal, but maybe Stephen was capable of even that. God knows, she thought grimly, he had proved capable of just about everything else.

Stephen Keys, she wrote, thinking of their honeymoon in the Florida Keys. Stephen Jack, Stephen Sophie and Stephen Ethan, she noted as possibilities. Horrifying to think he would utilize his children's names, but not impossible.

Then she thought back to their wedding and added Silver, Emanuel, and Jordan, which represented the names of the rabbi who'd married them, the temple in whose small chamber they'd exchanged their vows, and the name of the restaurant where they'd shared any number of exultant toasts to their future together. Searching her brain, she thought of one more possibility. Frederick. That was the name she'd given to the bear he'd won for her at that silly carnival in Maine the summer after Sophie was born. She'd wanted to give it to the baby, but Stephen had insisted she keep it. It was such a silly gesture, but oh, so sweet. Screw sweet, she thought, turning once more to the telephone and dialing the Plaza, whose number she now knew by heart.

She got it right on the ninth try. Stephen Frederick was staying at the Sherry Netherland.

It took only seconds for the operator to connect her to his room. Miranda gripped the receiver tightly as she waited. When the phone was picked up on the second ring, she could barely breathe.

"Hello. . . . Hello." The man who answered hung up quickly when he got no response.

Miranda stood there, frozen, as the dial tone clicked in. She knew she should hang up as well. But she couldn't. All she could do was replay the voice over and over in her head. The voice she wasn't supposed to hear ever again.

Chapter 30

Miranda finished brushing her hair and left her room to join Paul in the kitchen. On her way, she paused outside the half-open door to Jack's bedroom. She could see her two oldest children inside, sitting cross-legged on the floor opposite one another, a game of Stratego set out between them. Jack was explaining how to play the game, and Miranda listened, amazed and grateful to hear the patience in his voice as he told his sister how the pieces moved across the board. Sophie, obviously aware of her good fortune in obtaining her older brother's attention, responded eagerly to his instructions.

"No, the Colonel can't move that way," Jack said, reaching out to put a hand on Sophie's arm as she was about to do something against the rules.

"Oh, yeah, yeah." Sophie adjusted the game piece. She looked hopefully at Jack, pleased with herself for remembering. "Like this, right?"

He nodded. "Right."

Miranda saw Sophie's face light up, although she instantly altered her expression to keep her brother from seeing how thrilled she was by his approval.

Boy, Esther, I've got to hand it to you, Miranda told her mother silently, continuing on her way down the hall. I don't know how the hell you did it.

She entered the kitchen to see Paul searching for something in the open refrigerator. He had come over nearly an hour before, the two of them planning to go out for dinner. But the baby-sitter had called to say she would be late, so they were still waiting to leave.

She took a step forward just as Paul realized she was there. He turned his face to her. "Did you say there was some homemade lemonade in here? I had a sudden craving for it."

Miranda gave him a smile of regret. "Sorry, Ethan just finished it off. Will you drink something else?"

"Certainly not," he said, feigning outrage. "How dare you even suggest such a thing."

She laughed. "I must have lost my mind."

He peered into the recesses of the refrigerator once more. Moving closer, she reached down to put her hands on his shoulders and gave him a few quick massage strokes. She loved to touch him, relishing the combination of sexual desire and comfort she experienced, taking any opportunity to run her hand up his arm, or through his hair.

If anyone had told her she would be able to reawaken the intense sexual feelings she recalled from her teens and twenties, she wouldn't have believed them. But this was just as powerful. In fact, it was even better, because along with the passion was the knowledge that this was so absolutely *right*. The solidity of that feeling seemed to make her desire even greater. Is this what they mean by being a grown-up, she wondered. I can't say I ever had these feelings in the last ten years or so of my marriage to Stephen.

She dropped her hands to her sides, chilled by the thought of her husband. Alive, out there, about to make his move—whatever the hell it was. She made herself relax. She couldn't let Paul see that anything was wrong.

Sophie appeared in the doorway. "Mom, what am I giving Lucy for her birthday tomorrow?"

Miranda turned to her, startled. And quickly as she could, she adopted an expression more appropriate to her daughter's concern. "Tomorrow? It's not tomorrow. The party's next Sunday."

"No, it's not," Sophie said, shaking her head. "It's tomorrow."

Miranda opened the pantry closet to consult the large calendar that hung inside the door. She had always been fastidious about noting all their activities on it, knowing it was the only way to avoid chaos in a household with three children. "See, here it is. Next week."

"No, Mom." Sophie was starting to sound panicked. "I don't know why you wrote that, but I swear to you, it's tomorrow. Lucy and I were talking about it yesterday." She had an idea. "Wait, the invitation's on my desk."

The girl raced back to her room. Paul removed a can of Coke from the refrigerator and stood up, popping the top and taking a drink. "Calamity, huh?" he asked mildly.

Miranda grinned. "The end of the world may be only narrowly averted. But it's true that I don't have a gift yet."

Sophie returned bearing the brightly colored invitation featuring a girl on a skateboard in mid-spin. She thrust it at her mother. "See? Twelve o'clock."

Miranda looked at it. "Right." She handed the invitation back to her daughter. "So we need to think present. Given what everybody else has going on in the morning, there's not going to be much time to take care of it."

Sophie paled. "What are we going to do?"

"Take it easy, sweetheart, we can deal with this," Miranda said soothingly.

Paul took another swig of soda from the can. "Would this Lucy be interested in a book? The Barnes & Noble should be open now. You could run over for something while I wait for the sitter up here."

Miranda looked at him gratefully. "You're a genius and a saint both." She turned to her daughter. "What do you say to that?"

Sophie's face brightened. "Maybe an American Girls book? Lucy just got *Molly*, but she doesn't have too much else to go with her."

"Sure." Miranda went to get her purse from the counter and the navy blazer lying there beside it. "You want to come with me so we can pick something together?"

Sophie nodded.

"Okay. We'll be right back," Miranda called over her shoulder as they headed out. "You're great and I love you madly."

Paul smiled. "You'd better."

The thing of it is, Miranda thought, smiling, I really do love him madly. Whoever sent him to me—thank you, thank you, thank you.

Unbidden, a voice inside her head asked when she was going to tell Paul that Stephen was still alive. Or what the connection had been between them. Or that she herself was the new Forrestor.

The smile instantly disappeared from her face as she rang for the elevator. She hadn't foreseen what a mess this would become. Keeping it all from him for such a long time as the two of them fell more and more deeply in love transformed what had once been a simple secret into a major deception. To tell Paul now seemed almost impossible.

"Talk about a tangled web," she murmured.

Sophie looked at her. "What'd you say?"

She gave her daughter a thin smile as the elevator doors opened and they stepped inside. "Nothing, honey."

Still carrying his can of soda, Paul wandered over to Jack's bedroom, sticking his head in to see the boy lying on the bed, reading a book. "Everything okay in here, sport?" he asked.

Jack moved the book slightly to one side so he could see Paul. "Yup."

Paul saluted. "Aye, aye. I'm going to your baby brother's room. Any messages for him?"

Jack shot him a look.

"I didn't really think so," Paul said sotto voce as he turned to go.

The house phone buzzed, and the doorman informed him that the baby-sitter had arrived. Paul greeted her at the elevator, explaining that Miranda and Sophie were out for the moment, then continued on his way to see Ethan.

He found the little boy in the playroom, seated at a table whose surface was nearly buried under paper, markers, glitter, glues, crayons, and assorted other art supplies. He was in the process of cutting something out of red construction paper.

Paul had a special feeling for Ethan. He had realized that early on. Ethan was in the same class as his own son, and the two of them had been growing friendly lately, which was a special bonus as far as he and Miranda were concerned. But when Ethan looked at Paul, there was that same expression in his eyes that Josh sometimes had. It was happiness at having a dad, or, in Ethan's case, Paul thought, a dad-like guy, around. That expression tore Paul's heart out when he saw it on his son's face. There was no way he could have stayed married to Josh's mother, but that didn't make him feel any less bad about his son growing up in a separate household. With Ethan, it was equally heartbreaking, because the boy's father was gone completely, snatched from him, brutally and forever.

"What'cha doing?" Paul asked. "Mind if I come in?"

Ethan turned to him eagerly as Paul came over to examine his handiwork. "Very nice. Can you tell me about this?"

"In a second."

Ethan resumed cutting, concentrating intently. When he finished, he held up an unidentifiable shape for Paul to see.

"It's a card for Mother's Day." He gazed up into Paul's eyes. "When is Mother's Day?"

"Pretty soon, actually. A few more weeks."

"That's what I thought." Ethan gathered the other colored shapes he had already completed, busily explaining and gesturing. "I put this together, and these parts make, like, a fan thing, and this is a heart, but three-dimensional. You know, sticking out." He looked around at all the supplies spread before him. "I need some Scotch tape. You see it?"

Paul reached out to move some piles of paper around, feeling to see if tape might have been buried beneath anything there. "I don't."

"Hmmm . . ." Ethan slid off his chair. "I'll go find some."

Alone in the room, Paul took another look at Ethan's art project. The little boy had drawn a likeness of his mother on a sheet of white paper and colored it in. Paul admired his thoroughness; the figure was clearly recognizable as Miranda, the colors well chosen and applied neatly within the lines. Ethan was both sweet and bright, Paul thought, a very nice combination.

He suddenly spotted the tape out of the corner of his eye, on the floor, half-hidden behind one of the table legs. He knelt down to retrieve it. There was no sound of Ethan returning, so he went to look for him.

Paul could hear the boy moving around in Miranda's office, although he knew she had designated it as the one room in the house that was off-limits to the children.

"Hey, buddy, I don't think Mom would find this too cool," he said, finding Ethan rummaging through her bottom desk drawer, the two above it pulled halfway open as well. "Besides, I found the tape after all." He brandished it in the air.

"Great." Ethan looked up from what he was doing and started toward Paul. "I know I'm not supposed to be in here, but I couldn't find any tape anywhere. Please don't tell Mom."

Paul went to close the drawers. Glancing down, about to push the top drawer shut, he stopped, oddly disoriented, uncertain that he was actually seeing what he thought he was seeing.

A puzzled expression on his face, he slowly pulled the drawer open all the way.

He was looking at a manuscript. On the cover sheet was typed "Into Thin Air by Forrestor." And protruding from the sides of various pages of the manuscript were yellow Post-it's.

With his handwriting on them.

Like many book editors, when he read through an author's work, he made notes on the actual pages themselves, but he also stuck Post-it's on the pages with other comments or questions. At the end, the manuscript had the little yellow flaps sticking out in all directions. Was it possible that that's what he was looking at now, the actual manuscript of Forrestor's last book?

He reached in with both hands to lift up the heavy stack of pages bound by a rubber band. Supporting it against one arm, he flipped through at random, seeing his own red pencil marks and queries, rereading some of his comments.

Continuity problem—it's noon when they get into the car, yet they're going for lunch when they arrive. But that trip takes at least six hours.

I don't believe these two would resolve the situation so peacefully. They're both egomaniacs. I feel as if there should be threats, conflict. Can you build this up?

I wonder if this would work better if Mark drove off before Alex had a chance to respond.

"Come on, Paul. Let's go back."

Ethan's voice startled him. Still stunned, he looked over at the boy, but didn't answer.

What the hell was Miranda Shaeffer doing with the edited manuscript of *Into Thin Air?*

He heard the elevator doors open, heard Miranda and Sophie laughing about something as they entered the apartment, heard Miranda calling his name as she came looking for him.

Ethan hurried out, not wanting his mother to catch him in forbidden territory. Paul listened to him greet his mother and respond to her question about Paul's whereabouts. He was still standing there, the manuscript in his hand, when she entered the room, already talking before she saw him.

"Okay, we can finally get go—"

She froze where she was, taking in the open desk drawer, the thick sheaf of paper in his hands, the expression on his face.

He gazed down at the manuscript. "Ethan and I were looking for some tape," he said slowly and deliberately, as if unsure whether what he was saying made any sense. "Ethan opened this drawer." He raised his eyes to look directly into hers. "Unless I'm crazy, this is the manuscript my author sent to me. Which I marked up and returned to his P.O. box. Which, unless something really peculiar is going on, no one else in the world other than the actual Forrestor should have possession of."

"Oh, God." Miranda took a fast, deep breath. "This isn't the way for this to happen."

He set the manuscript down on the desk and turned to her. "For what to happen? Miranda, what's going on? Why do you have this?"

"Paul, I wanted to tell you . . ." She trailed off, knowing the situation was about to go from bad to worse and there was nothing she could do about it.

The expression on his face was one of utter bewilderment. "You *know* who Forrestor is? You're in contact with him and you never told me? Why do you have his manuscript?"

Miranda looked down at the floor, trying to figure out the best way to tell him.

Before she could speak, shocked recognition flashed in his eyes. "Jesus Christ! *You're* Forrestor."

"I . . . well, it wasn't . . ." She struggled for the words, not knowing where even to start the story.

He slammed the manuscript down on the desk and advanced toward her, rage and hurt evident on his face. *"You're Forrestor!* I don't believe this. All that stuff about copywriting—that was just a load of crap!"

She could see his anger overtaking the hurt. "Paul, please, let me—"

He wasn't listening. "You're my author. Yet you never saw fit to clue me in to this little fact. You let me fall in love with you. What, were you laughing the whole time, hearing me talk about my job? You're pretending to be some little freelancer when you're one of the top-selling writers in this whole damn country. And you're certainly the most powerful writer in my whole goddamned publishing house." He turned away. "And *I'm your editor*. I feel like the biggest fool in the world."

She came forward, reaching her hand out to touch him. "I wanted to tell you. But the way it happened, I couldn't figure out—"

"Oh, for Christ's sake!" He pushed past her and stormed out.

Miranda stood there, too stunned to know what to do. This was exactly what she had feared. She heard the elevator open and close behind him, and the noise galvanized her to action. She couldn't just let him walk away.

"Paul," she cried, running out to the entryway, knowing he couldn't hear her.

She pressed the elevator button frantically, but when it returned, he wasn't inside. She rode down, racing through the lobby. The doorman saw her running toward him, and opened the door for her.

"Mike," she said breathlessly, "did you see which way Paul went?"

The doorman pointed left. "Mr. Harlow went that way. I was outside and I saw him going downtown, walking fast. Then the house phone rang, so I came in."

"Thanks." Miranda ran outside.

* * *

From the bench across the street where he'd been waiting, Stephen watched Miranda emerge from the building. He stood up, startled by the actual sight of her. She began to walk south at a rapid pace. Crossing over to her side of the street, he followed her, keeping a sizeable enough distance between them so that she wouldn't spot him. It wasn't hard to do. Wherever she was headed, she seemed intent as hell on getting there, never once looking back in his direction.

So there she was. Right in front of him was the ticket to reclaiming his old life. He didn't yet know how he was going to accomplish his goal. But he wasn't worried. He would watch and wait, and it would come to him.

Miranda stopped on Sixty-ninth Street and waited for the light to turn green. Stephen stopped as well, looking more carefully at her now. The fitted navy blazer she wore lay loosely on her hips and the narrow blue jeans hugged her legs.

He moved up and slightly to the side to get a better view of her. There was no danger of her looking back toward him. In fact, in all the years he'd known her he couldn't recall seeing her look as focused as she did tonight. Jesus, he thought, she's completely different. She looked almost beautiful—slender, neatly put together, with an air of vitality totally unfamiliar to him.

But beautiful or not, this was the woman who'd stolen his dreams and left him with nothing. So what if she had lost a few pounds. She still was in the way of everything he wanted. Everything he deserved. Now, she had it all and he had nothing. He felt rage bubble up inside him. Somehow her beauty made him even angrier. What right had she to *his* success? What right had she to anything at all?

Miranda hurried across the street. Stephen continued to follow close behind. When she got to the next block, she stepped off the curb, but stopped suddenly when a parked car unexpectedly roared to life, the driver racing to make the light.

I'm sorry she stopped herself in time, Stephen thought, as he watched the car careen around the corner. I'm sorry he didn't kill her outright.

The thought almost stopped him in his tracks. How perfect that would be, he realized. Miranda's death would solve everything. He'd have his career back. His children. His parents. But that was too much to hope for.

Or was it? Thoughtfully, Stephen moved even closer. Still, she didn't look back. She has no idea that anyone's behind her, he said to himself. Absolutely no idea.

*   *   *

Where would Paul have gone? He lived on the West Side but he usually took a taxi or the Seventy-ninth Street crosstown bus, which was in the opposite direction. Maybe he just needed to walk because he was so angry.

Tears stung her eyes. How could I have been so stupid? she asked herself angrily. Sooner or later, it *had* to come out, and anyone would have known he'd be furious. Hell, I'd be furious if I were Paul. I sleep with the guy, but I lie to him about what I do, who I really am.

Miranda cringed inside, fully grasping for the first time how humiliating that part alone must be for him.

"No, please, no," she whispered miserably as she hurried along the street, hoping there was still a chance she might find him a few blocks ahead. Dear God, she loved him and she was going to lose him over this.

She quickened her pace, but there was no sign of him. Finally, she slowed, realizing it was a waste of time, that he was long gone to wherever he had decided to go. But she didn't feel like turning around and going home. The sitter was with the children, so she didn't have to worry about them.

Her head down, she continued along Fifth Avenue, replaying the events of the past few days, what she had learned about Stephen, what he had done to her and the children. She thought about how lucky she had been to find Paul, and how foolish she had been not to realize that the secret she possessed was a time-bomb waiting to go off.

As she approached Sixty-first Street, she noticed a crowd in front of the Pierre Hotel, men and women dressed in tuxedos and evening dresses. She stopped at the corner before crossing the street, wanting to observe them from a distance. Most seemed to know one another, and they were milling about, talking and smiling. A wedding, maybe, she thought, or a special anniversary celebration. But then she saw that the crowd was breaking up, groups going in different directions.

More people were leaving the hotel, so whatever it was had been for quite a large group, she realized. Thirty or forty people crossed Sixty-first Street toward her. She remained standing there, her mind traveling back to the charity benefits and fancy dinner parties she used to go to with Stephen. She watched the faces of the people around her, some genuinely carefree and happy, others slightly strained. That's what I must have looked like, she reflected, observing a woman struggling to maintain a serene expression while she was obviously desperate for her husband to stop talking to a fiftyish man smoking a cigar so they could leave.

The large group that had crossed the street swirled around her, and her mind was bombarded with a flood of images from her marriage. She was about to resume walking when she observed that the light was turning red. She stopped and looked left to see if she could ignore the red light and cross anyway. A green Buick was practically flying along Sixty-first Street, evidently in a hurry to catch the green light and make the turn onto Fifth Avenue. She waited.

As the car approached, Miranda suddenly felt two hands pressed flat on her back, and the shove she got was hard enough to send her out into the middle of the street. Instinctively, her arms went up to break her fall. Stumbling, she went over onto her side, smashing her left forearm and hip against the blacktop. The momentum rolled her onto her stomach, and her chin painfully smacked into the ground. She shut her eyes. There was no time to move.

The car's brakes screeching, the driver tried to stop. But the car was too close, traveling too fast. As if in a dream, Miranda could hear the terrified screaming of the crowd on the street.

Miranda was still stretched out in a straight line as the car passed over her. The bottom of the car just cleared her as the wheels went by on either side. Stunned, she realized that the car had stopped a few feet beyond her, and she was still alive.

Immediately, people rushed over to kneel beside her, shouting to ask if she was all right, barking orders to each other to stand back and give her air, to call an ambulance, find a doctor. Groggily, she rolled over, feeling the pain shooting through her arm and side, the throbbing in her jaw. It was a miracle she hadn't been killed.

She opened her eyes and looked up, past the anxious faces staring down at her, up into the night sky, twinkling brightly with stars. As she turned her head, she saw a familiar figure hurrying down Fifth Avenue. His hair was blond, but, just as Sophie had, she knew him when she saw him.

Stephen.

Now she knew why he had come back.

Chapter 31

Miranda spent much of the next day on the sofa in her office, resting her aching arm and hip, applying compresses to her swollen lower jaw. Josie's mother had agreed to take Sophie to Lucy's birthday party along with her own daughter and offered to take both girls out to a movie afterward. Jack and Ethan went off on play dates, which Miranda arranged to have extended into the afternoon.

Her bruises weren't that serious, and she knew she was physically capable of going about her regular day had she chosen to. But she had to be alone to think. Think about why her ex-husband was trying to kill her. Think about how she was going to save her life. Her problems with Paul would have to wait.

It was odd, she reflected. As long as she was resting her aching body, she preferred to spend the day in her office instead of her more comfortable bedroom. She found that she wanted to be around Forrestor—or, rather, all the things that suggested Forrestor. Forrestor was the key to her survival.

The day passed as she continually rearranged the pieces of the puzzle in her mind. By the time all three children were back home and ready for their dinner, she knew what she had to do.

Calmly, she cooked and served lamb chops, carrots, and baked potatoes, then sat down at the table to inquire about each child's day, skipping her usual argument with Sophie about eating her vegetables, immediately agreeing with Ethan that ice-cream pops were indeed a fine idea for dessert.

When she had finished getting the children to bed, she went back into her office and shut the door behind her. She sat down at the desk, then reached over and picked up the telephone, setting the entire instrument on her lap. She stared at it for a few minutes, not certain she could go through with this. Then, her hand shaking slightly, she picked up the receiver and dialed.

"Sherry Netherland," an operator answered.

"Stephen Frederick's room, please," she said firmly.

"I'll connect you."

Her heart was beating so hard in her chest, she thought it would burst through.

"Hello."

She desperately wanted to hang up, but she forced herself to speak.

"Stephen. It's Miranda," was all she could get out.

There was a long silence. Of course, she realized, he's wondering how I knew he was still alive, much less how I knew where to find him.

"I'm a good guesser, huh? I always did like that teddy bear." Her attempt to keep the conversation light sounded ridiculous to her own ears. She wondered what he was thinking, but he said nothing. Maybe she'd better stick with the simple facts, she thought, and cut out the witty banter. "Sophie saw you at school."

She heard him exhale.

"Well, well," he finally said.

She waited, but there was nothing else. Okay, she said to herself, taking a deep breath, here goes.

"Stephen, I don't know why you disappeared. I don't understand any of it. But now I know you're alive. And, no matter what, we have three children together. Your children need you. You can't imagine how much."

"How are they? What are they up to?" he asked casually but with seemingly genuine interest.

I can't be hearing this, she thought. He abandons them, makes them think he's dead, tries to murder their mother—and now he wants to chat about soccer and ballet.

"They're fine, really," she responded, trying to keep her tone even. "It would mean the world to them to see you."

"And?"

He was telling her to get to the point.

"I think it would be best if we talked a bit first." Miranda shifted in the chair, nervous perspiration making her blouse stick to her back. "You know, to set it up in a way so when they see you it won't be too sudden. That could be overwhelming, having you appear out of the blue."

"What did you have in mind?" The terse, annoyed tone was one she remembered well.

"Why don't you come here to the apartment tomorrow at around one o'clock. They won't be back from school yet, so we can talk in private for a while. Is that possible?"

Stephen was evidently turning her proposal over in his mind. Finally, he answered her. "Fine, one o'clock tomorrow." He paused. "Same apartment, I take it."

He must be wondering how I managed to hang on to it after he took all our money, she thought incredulously. But she spoke sweetly. "Same one."

"Will you be glad to see me?"

He laughed as he put down the receiver on his end.

Miranda hadn't known that she was capable of feeling as intense a fury as the one that threatened to consume her now.

Why don't you just come and find out, you son of a bitch.

Stephen started to hum as he walked away from the telephone and over to the dresser where he had a bottle of Scotch. He poured himself a drink, feeling better than he had since he'd returned to New York.

It would be all right, he could see that now. After the fiasco the night before, he hadn't been so sure that would be the case. But Miranda was as dumb as ever, too stupid to realize he had pushed her in front of that car.

It had been a momentary impulse, something he thought he'd regret the moment after he did it. The funny thing was, he didn't regret it. In fact, in the light of day, he realized it was sheer brilliance. The only thing to do.

It had been such a surprise seeing Miranda. He almost hadn't recognized her. There had been a thin, well-dressed and very attractive woman in place of the overweight hausfrau he remembered. She looked as good as when he'd married her, but in a different way. Back then, she'd been merely pretty; now she was polished, sure of herself. It was downright sexy.

She never bothered to look that good for me, he thought, annoyed. How come she waited until after I was dead to get herself together?

He shook his head, still amazed at her luck in escaping what should have been a fatal accident. At least he had gotten away un-noticed; the crowd in front of the Pierre had been an unexpected bonus. It had been a simple matter to give her a shove, then melt away behind all those people. But of course she couldn't go down like any normal person and die, he thought. Miranda always was a pain in the ass.

He laughed softly at his own humor, going over to the window and looking out at the street below. What was really priceless was that she had invited him over. Tomorrow he would just waltz right into the building—via the service entrance that he knew led to the basement, so the doorman wouldn't see him—and kill her at his leisure, making it look like a robbery. And there were fifty million ways he could do it, considering he knew every inch of that building and where he could find all sorts of appropriate weapons. Just to protect himself in case of some unforeseen hitch, he would bring the gun he had purchased two months before. This time, nothing would go wrong.

He raised his hand to his forehead in a salute. "Here's to you, Forrestor. I'm coming back."

Chapter 32

Stephen's appointment with Miranda was for one o'clock. Just after twelve-thirty, he approached the building, making sure no one saw him before hastening in through the service entrance. Quietly, he made his way down a dark and damp hallway to the basement. Having once spent the better part of an hour down here with the superintendent trying to locate the source of an electrical short in his apartment, Stephen knew just where to go.

There was a second intercom system located outside the doormen's locker room through which they could call up to the apartments. Stephen had stuck his head into the room that day with the super, observing the faded red lockers that held the men's uniforms, and the odd assortment of sofas, card tables, and lamps—cast-offs from the building's tenants. Little did I know how handy this would be, he mused as he picked up the intercom receiver and pressed the buzzer to signal his old apartment.

After a pause, he heard Miranda on the other end. "Yes?"

Stephen lowered his voice and did his best imitation of the daytime doorman's Greek accent, trying to sound abashed. "It's Al, Mrs. Shaeffer. I'm in the basement." He hesitated meaningfully. "I'm very sorry to tell you this, but there's been an accident, a small one. Your Jack—well, he's here, in the doormen's lounge."

"What?" Miranda's shock was clear through the earpiece. "Jack is in school."

"No," Stephen said in an embarrassed tone. "He's playing hooky today. He does this, only sometimes."

"I don't believe it," Miranda muttered. "Wait a minute, did you say there was an accident?" Her voice rose in alarm. "You're not talking about Jack, are you?"

"Yes, ma'am. Jack cut himself on some broken glass. He's bleeding."

"My God, why didn't you say so! I'll be right down."

Stephen replaced the receiver, smiling grimly. Couldn't have gone any smoother, he thought. She'd waltz right into his waiting arms. He reached into his pocket to touch the gun nestled there, reassuring himself that he was ready. This was a great plan. A botched robbery attempt that turned violent in the basement of a big New York City building. No one would question it for a minute. He didn't relish the idea of shooting Miranda at close range, but it would be over quickly, and then things could get back to normal. He went into the laundry room to wait for her.

Miranda tapped her foot impatiently as she rode down in the elevator. Of all times for this to happen! This was definitely not the moment for her to have to leave the apartment. But Jack was bleeding. Of course, he couldn't be hurt that badly, she reasoned, or Al would have sounded a lot more panicked. She didn't know whether she should be upset that he was hurt, or furious that he was cutting school. Pursing her lips, she stabbed at the button marked B, knowing it wouldn't actually get the elevator to move any faster.

The doors finally opened and she stepped into the silent hallway. She'd always hated coming down here. No matter what the time of day, it was invariably dark and deserted.

"Jack?" she called out. "Al? Where are you?"

No answer. She had assumed they would be waiting somewhere close by to meet her. Maybe they were in the doormen's lounge. She turned left and started walking hurriedly, her heels clicking on the cold linoleum. In the dimness, there was one well-illuminated spot just up ahead, the fluorescent bulbs inside the laundry room casting light out onto a patch of the hallway's floor. As she approached it, she heard movement from inside the room.

"Jack, is that you?"

She stopped, startled, as a man emerged from the laundry room to stand in the puddle of light. When he turned to face her, she let out a loud gasp.

She had known she would be seeing Stephen today, but she was still unprepared for the sight of her husband, alive, up close. He was, just as Sophie had described, blond and bearded. Somewhere in the recesses of her mind, she registered that he looked peculiar, the light hair so clearly unnatural on him. He also looked older, a good five years older, she realized, his face far more lined and slightly puffy. The glint in his eye suddenly reminded her of the jungle animals on Ethan's favorite nature show, the predators eyeing their prey.

And she was not supposed to be meeting him in the basement.

She took a step back, fear coursing through her.

"Where's Jack?" she asked urgently. "Is Jack with you?"

A smile slowly spread across Stephen's face. "Is that the way you greet me after all this time?" His eyes traveled up and down her body in a slow appraisal. "You look good, Miranda, really good. I, frankly, am amazed."

Miranda fought to hold back her terror. "You haven't hurt Jack, have you? Where is he?"

"I assume he's in school, where he should be," Stephen said mildly.

Oh, God, she thought wildly. How could I have been so stupid? But of course Stephen had known that any threat of danger to one of the children would bring her flying immediately.

She started to turn, but Stephen's arm shot out and grabbed her, his grip bruisingly tight. He dragged her, stumbling, the few steps into the laundry room.

"Stephen, stop, don't do this," she cried out.

She managed to break loose, but, pulling back sharply, she smacked up against one of the washing machines behind her. His arms instantly encircled her, trapping her there. Desperately, she pushed against him.

His eyes bored into hers, and his tone was low with fury. "Did you think you could steal Forrestor from me? I created him with my sweat and hard work. Did you really believe I would let you take credit for what I did? Steal my talent, steal my *life*?"

Her heart was pounding wildly in her chest. "You were dead! You wanted us to think that!" she cried, almost more frightened by his irrational words than his force.

"You lived off me all those years, Miranda, like a parasite." He gripped her hard by the shoulders, forcing her to look directly into his face. "You were lazy and fat, and now. . . ."

With horror, Miranda saw the expression on his face change, saw the sexual gleam in his eyes.

"Finally, you're worth having in bed. But you wouldn't have done it for me, would you? *Would you?*"

He pushed her backward onto the washing machine as he brought his lips to hers, his kiss brutal. "I think you owe me," he whispered harshly in her ear. "One last time."

"I owe you?" For the moment she forgot her fear as fury rose in her chest. "What do I owe you? You broke your children's hearts. You took all our money and left me with no way to take care of them. I survived in spite of you." She paused. "In fact, I did better than survive."

He slapped her, the force of the blow stunning her. *My God*, she thought, panicked, *he's completely crazy*. She had no idea where the strength came from, but she shoved with all her might and kicked out with one leg, sending him sprawling onto the floor. She rolled off the washing machine, putting a hand out to steady herself.

"You bitch!" he spat out.

Miranda ran, her breath coming in frantic gasps. If she didn't get away, he would kill her right now, right here. She raced down the hall toward the elevators, realizing as she went that she couldn't stop to try to get one.

Stephen's footsteps grew louder; he was coming up quickly behind her. With his longer legs, he would overtake her in another few seconds. She *had* to do something. The stairs were at the far end of the basement. Could she make it?

She screamed as she felt his hand grab on to a hank of her hair. Her own hand went back to hold on to the hair herself, closer to the scalp, so he wouldn't be able to pull it right out. Feeling the flesh of her hand against his only escalated her terror. She turned, nearly losing her balance, and kicked him as hard as she could. Her shoe made contact with his shin. He cursed, hobbling a few steps, his grip on her hair involuntarily relaxing.

She broke free. Casting about wildly as she ran, she saw a small wooden sidechair up ahead, left up against the wall. She practically dove at it, lifting it with both hands as she turned back once more and threw it at him. It was then that she saw the gleam of a gun in his hand. A guttural cry of fear escaped her.

Please, God, help me, she prayed. There was the exit door, just a few steps away. She yanked on the doorknob to pull it open, waiting to hear the gun go off, to feel the bullet tear into her. She was afraid her heart would burst right through her chest as she tore up the stairs, two steps at a time. Was he there behind her, pulling the trigger? She didn't dare look.

Stephen watched Miranda frantically open the exit door and race into the stairwell. He stopped short and ran back to the elevators. The stairwell door to the lobby was always kept locked, so she wouldn't be able to get out there. She would no doubt continue up, all the way to the apartment. But he could easily beat her there in the elevator.

He pressed the button. An elevator arrived almost at once. Riding up, he smoothed his clothes and ran his fingers through his hair. It had been stupid to let himself get distracted that way in the laundry room, although he was more than entitled. But now he would deal with her and take off. Enough fooling around.

The elevator stopped, and the doors slid open quietly. Stephen glanced down at the gun in his hand, preparing himself, then looked up.

He was momentarily blinded by the glare as more than a dozen bright lights swung around in his direction, held up at various spots within a crowd of what had to be at least forty people. Most of them were holding cameras or notebooks.

Stephen froze, his eyes darting from side to side. *What the hell . . . ?* He quickly moved the hand holding the gun behind his back, hastily trying to shove the weapon into his pants' waistband.

There was a silence, then the people in the crowd suddenly seemed to find their voices. He heard questions being shouted at him.

"Are you Stephen Shaeffer?"

"Did you actually walk out of that bombing alive? And nobody knew?"

"Where have you been all this time?"

Stephen inhaled sharply, suddenly understanding. It was a press conference. Miranda had called all these people to come here at one o'clock, to greet him on his arrival. Far from having no idea that he was trying to kill her, she knew he was coming here today for that very purpose, and she had been prepared. Well prepared.

It was as if everything were happening in slow motion. He saw Miranda enter from the far side of the foyer, trying to catch her breath, her face flushed from her exertion. She would have come in through the back door to the kitchen. If they had been alone, he would have been standing at that door, his gun at the ready, the moment his.

Instead, he was finished. She had won. The press was about to take the whole story and tell it to the world.

From opposite ends of the room, Stephen and Miranda locked gazes. He had no doubt she could see the icy hatred in his eyes. What surprised him was that he saw in hers, not the anger or fear he had expected, but mostly sadness.

Chapter 33

"Miranda, honey, stop pacing like that. Sit down, or call him, or do something. But you can't go on roaming around the room like a caged lion."

Lydia spoke gently, coming up next to her sister. She put a hand on Miranda's arm. "Look, to say it's been a long day is a ridiculous understatement. You should take it easy."

"I can't." Miranda bit her lip. "I messed everything up. I've got to do something about it."

"So you keep saying. But what?"

Miranda paused, making up her mind. "I'm going over to Paul's. He can yell and throw me out, but I need to see him, to talk to him in person."

Resolute now, she strode to the closet and grabbed her jacket. Slipping it on, she looked back at her sister. "I love him, Lyd."

Lydia smiled. "Not a news flash. That's what I've been sitting here trying to tell you—go to it."

Hurrying uptown on Fifth Avenue, Miranda kept an eye out for a vacant taxi. Every taxi seemed to be already occupied, the lights on all the cab roofs turned off. She would have to catch a bus, she decided, picking up the pace to a near run.

She had been such an idiot. How else could he have. . . .

She glanced up to see Paul, less than ten feet away, striding purposefully in her direction. *He had been coming to see her.* She stopped short, her eyes filling with tears of relief.

When he spotted her, a smile spread across his face. She smiled in return, and hurried, nearly running, into his arms.

"I saw the six o'clock news," he said, burying his face in her hair. "My God, Miranda, I can't believe what he put you through. Letting you and the children think he had died, hiding out. And why didn't you tell me he left you without any money?"

"Oh, Paul, that wasn't your problem." She pressed her cheek against his, lowering her voice. "What they didn't say on the news was that he had come back to kill me. That was the reason he turned up again."

He held her at arm's length, searching her eyes. "Are you serious? The son of a bitch."

She nodded. "That's why he was at the apartment today. He'd tried once before. Today, he brought a gun."

"Jesus Christ," Paul breathed.

"I finally realized what he wanted," Miranda said. "He wanted Forrestor back. And he had to get rid of me to get him back. I was the only thing in his way."

Paul wrapped his arms around her, more tightly this time.

"I invited him to the apartment," she went on, "but I had the press there, TV, newspapers, everybody. It wasn't hard to get them. After all, we were talking about a victim of the bombing come back to life."

"Miranda, I don't know what to say."

"You forgive me? You understand?" she asked breathlessly.

He bent his face down to kiss her. "Do I forgive you? For God's sake, I love you. I love you as Miranda, I love you as Forrestor. I'll love you under any name you choose to call yourself."

Miranda raised her lips up to his once more, shutting out all the sights and sounds of everything but him. Now, she would be the one starting a new life. But this time there would be no more secrets. Only truth. Only love.